RP

Raid on Cochecho

Book Three of The Puritan Chronicles

Victoria—
Happy reading!

PENI JO RENNER

ISBN: 978-1-4834-6317-9 (sc)
ISBN: 978-1-4834-6316-2 (e)

Because of the dynamic nature of the Internet, any web addresses or links contained in
this book may have changed since publication and may no longer be valid. The views
expressed in this work are solely those of the author and do not necessarily reflect the
views of the publisher, and the publisher hereby disclaims any responsibility for them.

Any people depicted in stock imagery provided by Thinkstock are models,
and such images are being used for illustrative purposes only.
Certain stock imagery © Thinkstock.

Lulu Publishing Services rev. date: 12/28/2016

For all the descendants of those whose lives were lost or forever
changed in the aftermath of the 1689 Cochecho Massacre
'O mother, mother make my bed!
O make it saft and narrow!
Since my love died for me to-day,
I'll die for him to-morrow— last verse of *Barbara Allen*

Special thanks to:

Mike Day and Thom Hindle of the Woodman Institute
and Museum of Dover, New Hampshire.
Cathy Beaudoin and Denise LeFrance of the Dover Public Library.
Carol Majahad of the North Andover Historical
Society of North Andover, Mass.
Dana Benner (Penobscot/Piqwacket/Micmac), M.Ed.
Heritage Studies, Prof. History and Social Science
Thanks also to my dependable beta readers,
Sandi, Kelly and Lise! Love you guys!

Part One

"Now I yield up myself to your advice and enter into a new canoe, and do engage to God hereafter."— Pennacook Sachem Wanalancet upon his conversion to Christianity in 1674.

Chapter One

Cochecho, New Hampshire
Early September, 1676

The late summer air wore the perfume of wild honeysuckle and carried the steady, splashing rhythm of nearby Cochecho Falls to Grace Hampton's ears as she sat beneath a locust tree. She was entranced by the mother-of-pearl button suspended on a length of tow linen, a gift from her late father and her most prized possession. She would twirl the button on its tether until it became a hypnotic blur. She carried the toy everywhere, and when she wasn't playing with it she always wound the string securely around her wrist so that the button would easily drop into her palm.

Around her, other children played while the adults conversed about things that didn't interest a nine-year-old girl. Major Richard Waldron, proprietor of the town's mill and trading post, was entertaining two companies from Massachusetts who had come to collect several hundred refugee Wampanoag Indians who had fled the Commonwealth during recent fighting. The townspeople of Cochecho called the Wampanoags "Strange Indians," to distinguish them from the local Pennacook tribe, who had lived peaceably with the whites for many years under the leadership of Wanalancet. The sachem of the Pennacooks had converted to Christianity and was thus called a Praying Indian. Grace knew the adults were concerned about the number of Wampanoags who entered the town, and vaguely assumed that was what Major Waldron and his guests Captains Syl and Hathorne were discussing so intently. Waldron entertained his guests with a feast of roast pig, followed by several games. Finding a shady spot beneath a dying locust tree, Grace unwound her whirligig from her wrist and sent the button twirling.

Whzz whzz whzz

The toy was the last remnant of her former life. Her parents had been killed by Indians three years before, when she was only six and her sister Alice was thirteen. The girls survived the attack because they had been picking ears of corn in the field. They heard the whoops and cries of the Indians and watched in horror as their home was set ablaze. Terrified, they listened to their mother's screams as they huddled among the corn stalks, praying they wouldn't be discovered. They hid for hours until all was quiet and nothing was left of their home but a pile of smoldering ash. Alice wouldn't allow Grace to go near the ruins. Instead, she had seized her little sister's hand and fled to the nearest neighbor's garrison. The neighbors sent word to their next of kin, Captain John Heard, who immediately sent for his cousin's daughters to come live with them in Cochecho. The transition had been difficult, but after three years, Grace was beginning to adjust to her new life. Nightmares in which she heard the Indians' war whoops and her parents' terrified cries, though less frequent, still tormented her from time to time.

She was starting to forget what her parents looked like, and that frightened her. She knew she had her father's coloration: ruddy, with a colony of freckles so plentiful they sometimes blended together. Her hair was as red as an autumn leaf. Errant curls often sprung rebelliously from beneath her coif and she was always being told to tuck them in. Her nose was just a stub. Worse yet were her eyes, which were sky-blue but rimmed with brown. In another face they could be considered alluring, but in Grace's situation they were small and closely-set, which seemed to put people off.

Her sister Alice, however, was budding into feminine loveliness. At sixteen, her heart-shaped face had lost its childish features, and she was often mistaken for being several years older. Alice had her mother's sparkling violet eyes, delicate nose, and mild disposition. She kept her nut-brown hair neatly hidden beneath her coif without any escaping strands to ruin her grown-up appearance. Alice was content to churn butter and spin flax, which endeared her to the Heard household. Grace, on the other hand, was too restless and found herself unable to focus on one tedious chore for very long—another trait she had inherited from her father. The whirligig's soft music always brought her parents to mind, and her throat thickened as she remembered her loss. Whenever she had a spare moment between chores, she would unwind the linen cord and let the opalescent button transport her to a happier place. Overcome with fresh sorrow, she didn't notice another child's approach until he snatched the whirligig from her hands. She looked up into the pimply face of a thirteen-year-old boy.

"Give it back, Johnny Horne!"

Hot tears scalded the backs of Grace's eyeballs as the gangly youth dangled her precious whirligig just above her reach. He was a bully with large front teeth and mocking hazel eyes.

"Crybaby Grace!" the bully jeered as other children nearby observed the exchange. "You want it so badly, see if you can get it now!"

With those words, he flung it up into the lower limbs of the locust tree. There it hung, suspended like a luscious fruit too high for even the tallest child to reach. The commotion drew the attention of other children, including Grace's sister Alice, who ran to the base of the tree, a look of concern on her pretty face.

"That was mean, Johnny!" little Emmie Ham pouted, her arms full of white kitten. She was eight years old and Captain Heard's granddaughter. She was also Grace's best friend. "I'll tell your papa on you."

Grace looked around for any nearby adults. Finding none, she wiped her dripping nose on her sleeve and helplessly looked up at her toy. The branch from which it dangled was leafless and appeared to be dead. Inhaling deeply, she tucked her skirt into her apron before reaching for the lowest limb.

"Give me a leg up, Emmie."

Emmie set down the kitten, which promptly scampered off in

pursuit of a white moth. She stepped forward and formed a stirrup with her hands, into which Grace placed her small foot and hoisted herself onto the lowest limb.

"Oh, Grace!" Alice warned. "Don't! You'll get a beating if you get caught climbing trees again!"

Ignoring her sister's admonishment, Grace flung her stockinged legs around the limb and hung upside-down for a moment. Her untied coif strings dangled from her shoulders. She felt the linen cap slip from her head and tumble to the grass below. A stream of red-gold curls spilled from her bare head as she clambered to straddle the branch. She gave Johnny Horne a defiant look as she perched among the leaves.

"Watch out!" Alice gasped anxiously, pressing her fingertips to her mouth. "The branch is weak. You'll fall!"

The dead limb quivered under her weight, sending the whirligig dancing in midair. She inched closer, and reached out as far as she could. Her prize remained just inches from her grasp. She leaned forward more, until she lay prone against the tree limb.

Cc-ccrrack!

"The branch is going to break!" Alice cried.

Grace felt the limb begin to give way. Instinctively she grasped it with arms and legs as if she were astride a wild horse. Little Emmie Ham's face paled and even Johnny Horne looked worried.

"Yonder comes Old Dick!" the boy warned, pointing at an older man approaching them. 'Old Dick' was what the children called Major Waldron—but never to his face.

"What are you children doing there?" The angry man bellowed. "Get away from my tree!"

Major Richard Waldron strode purposely toward them, his face red with rage. At sixty-seven, he owned most of the land in Cochecho and treated the settlement like it was his kingdom. His dark brows swooped over his face like two blackbirds about to collide above his large nose. In his wake were the two captains from Massachusetts, who looked slightly embarrassed for him.

Determined to retrieve her whirligig, Grace inched farther toward the end, the branch giving way a little more. Her little fingers grasped her prize just as Waldron approached. The other children fled to avoid his wrath, except for Alice and Emmie, who cowered in the angry man's presence.

"Grace Hampton!" he yelled, reaching up and plucking her forcefully from the limb. "Look what you've done! You've broken that branch. Captain Heard will hear about this and I'll see to it I'm compensated for damages. And if he refuses to give you the thrashing you need, I'll beat you myself!"

He set her down firmly on the ground. Placing his hands on her thin shoulders, he shook her for emphasis until her teeth rattled in her skull. The damaged limb slanted downward, partially detached from the trunk.

"Please, sir," Alice entreated. "T'was not my sister's fault. Johnny Horne threw her toy up into the tree. If anyone deserves punishment, 'tis he!"

"Ignore this small matter with the children," Captain Syl suggested with some impatience. "We've business to discuss."

Waldron's eyes still snapped with rage. "Very well," he grumbled. "We'll seek a more private place to converse."

Releasing Grace's shoulders, he said, "Away with all of you!" He lunged towards Alice and little Emmie, who shrieked and ran toward the direction of a group of women. Alice remained, looking chastised, but Grace felt a sob welling inside her. She wanted to call him a name, but when none came to her, she blurted defiantly, "You—you old *thing!*"

Waldron's fury contorted his face into a red scowl as he lunged for her, but Grace dodged his grasp. Snatching her coif from the ground, she ran to the riverbank, the mother-of-pearl button pressed against her palm.

Her mind screamed. *I hate it here!* She plopped heavily onto the riverbank. *I miss Mama and Papa and Salmon Falls.* She had squeezed the button so tightly it left an impression in her palm. Sniffling, Grace jammed her coif on her head. She sat near a smooth sumac bush, still trembling from a mixture of emotions. Determined to forget about the tree incident, she grasped the two ends of the string and prepared to send the pearly button singing.

"*Meow.*"

Emmie's white kitten approached Grace with an upturned tail and pointy pink ears. It eyed her curiously.

"Why, good day to you again, Kitty," Grace said, happy for the unexpected company. "I suspect Emmie is looking for you. Do you want to play?"

She dangled the button in front of the kitten so that the afternoon sun glinted off it. The kitten batted happily at the toy, snagging the string on its sharp claws. Grace giggled until the kitten drew the button to its jaws and clamped down on it. With one swift motion, the little cat had yanked the string from Grace's hand and took off toward the millhouse.

"Stop, Kitty!" Grace gave chase, fearing she would lose her precious toy forever. The cat looked back at her once, but appeared to be spurred on when it realized she was in pursuit. It darted through the grasses with lightning speed and disappeared through a gap in the mill's door.

Grace knelt on the cool flagstones and peered into the hole. She was about to coax the kitten out when she heard men talking in low, hushed tones. Startled, she reared back. She thought everyone was still celebrating at Waldron's garrison. After taking a quick look around to make sure no one saw her, she pressed her face against the hole.

Sunlight illuminated the millhouse through several narrow windows and Grace recognized the men gathered around the giant millstone. The two Massachusetts officers sat on fat sacks of ground meal while Major Waldron stood in their midst. Grace smelled tobacco smoke from their pipes as it wafted out the door. Their grim, somber faces further piqued her curiosity, sending a shiver of foreboding down her spine.

Peering through the hole, Grace saw the white kitten scurry behind one of the sacks. Then she saw her whirligig lying just inches from the door, its linen tail tantalizingly close. She wondered if she could reach the strand and withdraw the whirligig without the men noticing. The thought of doing something so daring thrilled her as she quietly thrust her hand through the hole. Her fingertips pinched the string just as Waldron began speaking.

"I'm in agreement with your proposal, Syl, but I don't want my militia involved," Waldron was saying. "Nay, nor do I want Wanalancet's people to take part. And it goes without saying that all women and children will be confined to their garrisons during the sham fight. We want as few casualties as possible."

Wanalancet was the peaceful sachem of the local Pennacook tribe, and a friend to the English. War games were often played between the whites and peaceful Indians, but nobody got hurt, so Waldron's last statement sounded ominous. It was hard to hear the men speak over the roar of the falls. As each word was spoken, Grace held her breath and slid the mother-of-pearl button slowly across the floor, hoping the men didn't hear the soft scuttle it made across the knotty pine boards. The button disturbed the dust and chaff, tickling her nose so that she struggled to stifle a sneeze.

"Fair enough," Captain Syl agreed. "But those we plan to apprehend might grow suspicious if none of the local savages are invited to the games."

Waldron appeared to consider this. "Then I propose we invite all the savages—Wanalancet's as well as your refugees."

"Some of your local Indians could get caught in the crossfire," Hathorne put in.

"Well, if your men aim their muskets and cannons properly, there ought not be *too* many casualties," Waldron smirked. "Wanalancet's people do business at my trading post and I don't want to lose customers."

Grace pulled the button closer as the men chuckled softly.

"Rum and muskets, Waldron," Syl said, plucking his pipe from his mouth and pointing at Waldron with it. "A bad combination to sell to Indians, friendly or not."

Waldron dismissed this criticism with a wave of his hand. "As long as they bring in the beaver pelts, my purse is fed."

Grace could feel the button now and her hand closed around its cool, familiar smoothness just as Waldron announced, "Gentlemen, I feel we're in agreement. Pray, let's return to the festivities afore we're missed."

Syl and Hathorne rose from their seats as Grace retrieved her toy. *Oh, do go out the back way!* She silently implored the men. She couldn't remove herself from the millhouse without being spotted if they came through the front door, and Waldron would see to it she was whipped if he knew she had been eavesdropping. To her great relief, the men exited through the rear and headed back to join the other guests.

After they vacated the millhouse, Grace released her breath in a *whoosh*. Whatever her nine-year-old mind thought about what she had just overheard, it was readily eclipsed by the return of her whirligig.

Dismissing the men's conversation and immersing herself in the joy of having retrieved her toy, Grace sat cross-legged on the flagstones and sent the mother of pearl button dancing on its string.

Whzzz whzzz whzzz

A curl sprang from her coif and she dropped the whirligig in her lap before tucking it back inside her coif. Then she resumed twirling the button, once again mesmerized by the singing whirligig and oblivious to her surroundings. She wasn't aware someone was behind her until a dark shadow enveloped her where she sat.

After Waldron and the two captains left, Alice stood alone at the base of the locust tree. She felt responsible for her sister, and Grace's constant antics were an embarrassing affliction to her. In one sense, she coveted her sister's impetuous behavior and wished she felt free enough to act out. Too old to climb trees but too young to be considered a grown woman, she was uncertain of her place within her community. With a sigh of resignation, she headed toward the Heard's garrison. She caught the sound of boisterous laughter as two Massachusetts soldiers approached her from the opposite direction.

"Pretty maid!" one of them called, lifting a tankard aloft. "Come drink with us!"

"Watch us during the knife-throwing competition!" the other invited, searing her face with his foul-smelling breath.

Realizing she was alone with the soldiers, Alice's face flushed and a cold sense of dread enveloped her. There was no one else around, and she hid her trembling hands in her skirt as the second reached for her arm.

"Nay, sirs," she said, ashamed at how frightened her voice sounded. "I'm needed at home."

"Don't be a prude!" the first slurred, making a grab for her other arm. He leered at her, displaying a mouthful of rotten teeth. "'Tis a day to frolic, wench!"

"They call me Hiram," the other said. "He's Jackson. Come now. Let us have fun."

"Please," Alice implored, shrinking away from them. "Pray, leave me be!"

Their hands on her arms repulsed her, and a scream formed in her throat as both men began forcibly dragging her away.

"Is there a problem here, gentlemen?" a deep voice inquired from behind Alice.

The two stopped, barely relaxing their grip on Alice as they turned to face the voice addressing them. Alice struggled to free herself from their grasp, turning her head and gazing upward into the somber face of Absalom Hart, a lieutenant in the local militia and a constable in Cochecho. He was an imposing figure, at twenty-four years of age standing head and shoulders above most men.

"Nay," replied Jackson, the dregs in his tankard sloshing. "We only mean to escort this young maid to the knife-throwing competition so she may cheer us on."

Tears welled in Alice's eyes as she looked pleadingly at Hart, too afraid to speak out.

"She's too young," Hart said, drawing closer. "Leave her alone, or I'll have you incarcerated."

Her assailants released her arms, turning their attention now on Hart.

"She looks of age to me!" Jackson argued.

"I'll not warn you again," Hart said, taking another step toward them. "Leave her and be on your way."

While the two soldiers exchanged looks, Alice held her breath, afraid to make a move. Her heart pounded wildly in her chest as she looked into Hart's brown eyes. Despite an air of melancholy, Constable Hart, she realized, was a very handsome man.

"C'mon, Hiram," Jackson said finally. "She's not worth a stay in whatever jail this hamlet has."

Hiram nodded in agreement. After the men retreated, Alice exhaled and released a sob of relief. Absalom Hart stepped closer and with a concerned look on his face, handed her a linen handkerchief.

"Don't cry, Miss Hampton," he said softly. "They've gone now."

Suddenly ashamed of her tears, Alice wiped her eyes and nose. "Thank you, Constable Hart," she managed.

He looked embarrassed for her, and gave her a gentle smile. "'Tis nothing," he said. "Did they hurt you?"

"N-nay," she stammered, her arms still burning from their contact.

Awkwardly, he gave her arm a reassuring pat. But unlike the soldiers' touch, his did not revolt her. His was one of honest respect, and it sent a warm current through her that quieted her pounding heart.

She looked up at him as his dark eyes surveyed their surroundings. Then his eyes met hers again.

"What were you doing out there, unchaperoned? He asked with obvious concern.

"I was trying to keep Grace out of trouble and failed miserably," Alice replied, her cheeks flushing hot again.

"If you allow it, I'll escort you home, Miss Hampton," he said. "These soldiers are getting drunker and rowdier by the minute, and it's not wise for a young maid to wander alone."

Alice smiled and nodded in agreement. As they headed toward

the Heard garrison, she noticed he shortened his pace to match hers, his eyes scanning their surroundings for any potential threats to her.

He's the kindest, most respectful gentleman I've ever known. Why had she not noticed it sooner? *Because he is eight years my senior. To him I am a child. But in two years I'll be eighteen, and mayhap then he'll see me as a peer!*

As they walked on, she grew more and more aware of his presence. A bachelor, he made his dwelling in a small cottage at the base of Little Hill, and was thus the Heard's nearest neighbor.

"Alice! Alice, where have you been?"

Her best friend, Sarah Follett, waved to her from a distance, her pretty face registering surprise when she saw Alice being escorted by the tall man. Sarah was also sixteen and was being courted by Jack Meader. Sarah often shared with Alice delicious tidbits of what it was like to be wooed. Alice longed for a romance of her own, and was surprised to find herself annoyed at her friend's presence as Sarah approached them, giving Absalom Hart a small curtsy.

"Good afternoon, Miss Follett," Absalom Hart said, tipping his hat to her. "If you're heading up Cart Way, please join us."

Alas, Alice thought with sudden despair. *He's respectful to everyone, and doesn't regard me with any special tenderness.*

"Thank you, Goodman Hart," Sarah said, her eyes widening as she gave Alice a curious look. "I was walking up to Heard's to retrieve mother's gravy boat."

As they resumed their trek, Hart walked on ahead of them. Alice's gaze settled momentarily on Hart's broad shoulders and narrow hips. She was lost in her thoughts until Sarah nudged her with an elbow, breaking her reverie.

What's got you so flustered? Alice could almost hear her friend's thoughts. *Tell me!*

Later! Alice mouthed back.

As they passed Elder Wentworth's home, Dog greeted them with ominous growls. The massive dog strained at his rope from the far side of Cart Way, his barks making conversation impossible until they began their ascent up Little Hill. The gate to the Heard's garrison had been flung open, and Absalom Hart paused just outside it.

"Here you are, Miss Hampton, Miss Follett," he announced. "I trust no one will accost you the rest of the way, but I'll keep watch until you're through the gate."

"Thank you, sir," Sarah said, nudging Alice again with her elbow. Sarah's smile told Alice her friend suspected her infatuation with Goodman Hart, and Alice pleaded silently for her friend to say nothing.

"I must get back to my duties," he said with a gentle smile. Did she detect a hint of regret in his voice? "But Captain Heard has enlisted my help in repairing the broken shutter, so I'll be supping with your household tomorrow night."

Oh yes! The broken shutter! She had completely forgotten about that, and her eyes traveled to Captain Heard's workshop, where the damaged shutter hung askew from its hinge. An expensive pane of glass had shattered due to Grace's careless antics, and Captain Heard had ordered Grace to remove the broken shards before sending her out to cut her own willow switch.

"Tomorrow night then," she smiled, ignoring the amused snicker that escaped Sarah's lips.

He tipped his felt hat to both of them once more before descending Little Hill with his slow, easy gait. Alice watched him leave, once again lost in thought until Sarah grasped her shoulder and shook her.

"Have you gone sweet on Goodman Hart?" Sarah asked urgently, her eyes sparkling with mischief.

Alice kneaded her hands restlessly. "Oh, Sarah, don't tease me! He rescued me just as two drunken soldiers were making advances--"

Sarah's eyes widened. "Do tell all! Did he strike them to preserve your honor?"

Alice smiled, letting out a wistful sigh. "He didn't have to," she said. "He diverted any need for violence, and was so--"

"Gallant?" Sarah finished for her. "Chivalrous?"

Alice's heart ached sweetly. He was indeed that, she thought. Like a knight of old.

"Aye, Sarah," she replied, watching Absalom Hart turn onto Cart Way. "Exactly like that."

Dame Elizabeth Heard gathered the dirty wooden trenchers and eating utensils that belonged to her household, glad the celebratory feasting was over but dismayed at the inebriated state of most of the men. At fifty, she was a well-respected lady in the community, renowned for both her piety and compassion. The Massachusetts soldiers were getting particularly rowdy, encouraging similar behavior in Cochecho's own male citizens. Her firm jaw was set in disapproval as her daughter Mary came with her own voiding basket of dirty dishes. Mary's clear blue eyes scanned the surrounding area briefly before asking her mother, "Pray, have you seen Emmie about?"

Dame Heard smiled wryly at the mention of her eight-year-old granddaughter. "Nay, Daughter," she replied. "But wherever she is, Grace Hampton is too. I was just about to search for them both. We've every dish in the household to wash."

Mary nodded. "I've retrieved all my household possessions. I haven't as many dishes to wash as you have, so Emmie is welcome to sleep at your garrison this night."

The older woman acknowledged this with a nod. "That sounds agreeable, daughter. God be with you."

Her granddaughter and Grace Hampton were inseparable, and she often worried that Emmie's docile demeanor was being corrupted by Grace's willfulness. Grace's sister, Alice, on the other hand, was quiet and obedient, as a young girl should be. Someday, Dame Heard hoped for the millionth time, Grace's behavior would emulate that of Alice's, although she had little confidence that that would happen anytime soon.

As if summoned by Dame Heard's thoughts, Alice Hampton approached, accompanied by her friend Sarah Follett. "Dame Heard," she implored, "may I take that voiding basket inside for you?"

"And I've come for Mother's gravy boat," Sarah Follett added, smiling pleasantly.

Elizabeth handed Alice the stack of wooden trenchers she was holding. "Aye, Alice. Take these inside. Your mother's gravy boat is on the side board, Sarah. I've already washed it."

"Thank you, Dame Heard," Sarah said with a curtsy before she and Alice disappeared into the garrison.

She turned to retrieve a ladle that had dropped to the ground when three men passed through the palisade door. "Dame Heard! Whereabouts is your husband?"

Elizabeth stifled a groan as she saw Major Waldron stomping toward her, the two Massachusetts captains trailing behind him. Waldron's hard-set expression was one she had come to know well. *What has Grace done now?*

Before Dame Heard could answer his question, Waldron ranted, "That demon charge of yours damaged my locust tree, and if neither you nor Captain Heard can discipline her, I'll take it upon myself!"

"Major Waldron," she said, standing at her full height, which was as tall as he. "Captain Heard will be home later this afternoon. He's gone to Portsmouth to deliver a cabinet, if it's any business of yours. Pray, how did Grace damage your tree?"

"Climbing on it like a little savage!" he fumed, blasting her face with his foul breath. "Broke a limb. I seek compensation for the damage done."

Elizabeth squared her shoulders. A tall woman, she met Waldron's eyes levelly. "I'll have a word with Grace before we sup, and I'll tell Captain Heard. He'll see to it the girl is rightfully punished and that you are compensated for the damages."

"You do that!" growled Waldron, peering at her beneath the brim of his hat before stomping off like an angry bull.

Elizabeth Heard exhaled, expelling the stench of his breath from her nostrils. *Such unhealthy temperament will be the death of that man.* At that moment she glimpsed her granddaughter Emmie skittishly making her way toward them. Her eyes were downcast and she looked like she herself had recently been chastised.

"Emmie," Dame Heard called. "Emmie, come hither."

The little girl drew closer and stopped in front of her grandmother, fidgeting with her apron.

"Grandmother," the little girl sniffed. "I've lost my kitten! Old Dick scared it away—"

"Never mind that now, Emmie," Dame Heard said. "And don't refer to an elder in such a disrespectful manner. Go find Grace and be quick about it. I'm headed to the garrison now. I wish to speak with her."

"Yes, Grandmother," Emmie croaked. "But please don't be too hard on Grace. That tree limb was dead anyway, and she didn't mean to damage it."

Dame Heard sighed. *Grace never means to cause any sort of trouble. But trouble is that child's constant companion.*

The nine-year-old boy looked on helplessly as his grandmother convulsed with fever. A smallpox epidemic the year before had taken over half of the Pennacook tribe, including the boy's parents. His name was Menane and his grandmother Maliazonis and brother Kancamagus were his only remaining family. The rest of the tribe looked upon him with pity, and that filled him with indignant rage.

"*Nokomis,*" he asked softly, wiping perspiration from her wrinkled brow, "*kagwi lla?* Do you need another *maksa?*"

"*Wlioni, noses,*" the old woman replied weakly. "This is the only maksa I have," she said, pulling the worn woolen blanket up to her trembling chin. "Feed the fire so it doesn't go out."

Menane obeyed, but it was obvious to him that another blanket was needed to warm his shivering nokomis.

"I will get you another one."

"We don't have enough *tmakwaawa* to trade for one," Maliazonis protested.

Menane looked at the three small beaver pelts bundled in the back of the wigwam. He knew it took at least five large tmakwaawa for one woolen blanket. But he was just learning to set traps and hadn't been very successful. He was forbidden to go into the white settlement alone, although he often accompanied his uncle Wanalancet, and he had learned to speak English quite well.

He was aware of a gathering in the town that day, where the soldiers would play games and eat good food. He had often observed such happenings before, and had coveted the white men's weapons and full bellies. He would watch from the forest as the soldiers lounged on blankets and drank from earthen casks until they fell into a stupor. And that gave the boy an idea. "I will get you another one," he said again. "Rest now, Nokomis. I will be back soon."

A handful of Waldron's militiamen assembled near a large oak tree, a target etched onto its broad trunk. Joining them were several of the Massachusetts soldiers. Every man carried a hunting knife, and anticipation was high as they drew lots on who would throw their knife first.

One Massachusetts soldier had offered his hat, and every man etched his initials on a flat stone. The stones now clattered as the soldier jostled the hat. "One of you locals draw," he invited. "You there—big fellow!"

The other men turned to look at Absalom Hart, who had been observing the games with quiet interest, arms folded across his massive chest. He had just returned from escorting the two young women, and the offending soldiers Hiram and Jackson gave him resentful looks. Although his size was intimidating, he emitted an air of gentleness. The crowd parted as he strode toward the stone-filled hat. Averting his eyes, he plunged one hand into the hat and withdrew a single stone, which he passed to the waiting soldier, who read the etched initials.

"S.O," The soldier announced. "Who among us is S.O?"

"Here!" called a voice, and Hart watched a fellow militia member step forward, his own hunting knife poised in his hand. "Stephen Otis, at your service!"

Stephen was solidly built, but shorter than Hart. His blue eyes shone with merriment in deep contrast to the melancholy that emanated from Absalom's brown ones. Despite their differing dispositions, the two men were best friends. They both worked at Major Waldron's mill by day and took turns policing the streets of Cochecho. Stephen slapped his friend jovially on the arm in passing, and took several paces from the target.

Hart watched as Stephen threw his knife. It sailed hilt-over-blade with perfect trajectory before plunging into the tree trunk, almost eight inches from its mark.

The other men chortled as Stephen shrugged sheepishly at Hart. "Never was the marksman you are, my friend!" he laughed good-naturedly.

A bow-legged Massachusetts soldier was next. Rising from the folded woolen blanket upon which he sat, he reeked of rum as he passed by Hart. His blade also missed the target by several inches.

"You fare better drunk than sober, Duncan!" one of his fellow soldiers joked as the inebriated Duncan stumbled back to where he had lain.

When it came to Absalom's turn, five knives protruded from the tree, the nearest being almost two inches from the target.

"Show them how it's done, Hart!" Stephen Otis cheered as the big man stepped up.

Absalom took a deep breath. Aiming carefully, he flung his knife at the tree. It soared in a graceful arc before striking the target dead-center. Behind him, his fellow militiamen cheered and Otis gave him a congratulatory slap on the back.

"None can beat Hart here!" Stephen boasted while the other men shook Absalom's hand. "We ought to have placed some kind of wager."

Absalom's cheeks flushed. He preferred not to be the center of attention, and accepted the compliments with awkward grace.

"My blanket!" Duncan roared, disrupting the celebration. "What the devil? Someone took my—there goes the thief now!"

Absalom looked over the heads of the other men to see where the raging Duncan pointed, only to glimpse a small figure disappearing into the woods.

"After him!" Duncan bellowed, galvanizing his comrades in pursuit.

Chapter Two

Startled, Grace turned to find a half-naked Indian boy standing there, holding a woolen blanket in the crook of one arm. Grace had never been so close to an Indian before, and his scanty attire left her dumbfounded. The boy was nude except for a doeskin breechclout, and his hair fell past his shoulders, as black and sleek as a crow's wing. A small, doeskin pouch dangled against his thin chest. He appeared to be near her age as he regarded her with dark, frightened eyes.

Grace sat with her mouth agape. Was he a friendly Pennacook? Was he a savage? She didn't see a knife, but would he hurt her bare-handed? Before she could react, she heard angry men's voices approaching.

"He went this way!" one of them barked.

Grace glanced in the direction of the voices, and when she looked back at where the boy had been standing, he had disappeared. Confused, she wondered if she had imagined him. She pressed the whirligig into her palm as several Massachusetts soldiers burst into the clearing.

The one in the lead scanned the riverbank before setting his eyes on the frightened little girl. He was short and bow-legged. "Young maid!" he bellowed. "Did you see a little savage run past just now?"

Grace opened her mouth, but no words came. The gleam of blue-black hair caught her eye behind a smooth sumac bush.

"Speak up, girl!" snarled the soldier. "Are you deaf and dumb?"

She returned her gaze to the man and shook her head stupidly.

Her mouth felt dry as she swallowed hard. "I saw no one, sir," she stammered.

"We'll find him yet, Duncan," another man said encouragingly to the first. "Pray, let's return to the games."

Duncan grumbled, giving Grace the impression of an irritated bull. He and the rest of the men dismissed her and headed back to Waldron's picnic, muttering among themselves. Only after she could see or hear them no more did she let out her breath.

She was not accustomed to lying, and Grace felt like a large rock was pressing on her chest. Her eyes immediately went to the sumac bush. She rose on trembling legs.

"They've left," she whispered softly. "You can come out now."

When no Indian boy emerged, she approached the bush cautiously. "They've gone," she repeated, a little louder this time.

Still no response. She walked gingerly around the bush, separating the fronds, but he wasn't there.

"Grace! Oh, Grace! There you are!"

Grace jumped at the sound of Emmie Ham's shrill voice. Her friend ran up to her, breathless. Tears had left trails on her pink cheeks and her eyes were red. "Grandmother sent me to fetch you. Old D--, I mean, Major Waldron told her about the tree limb, and now you are in for a paddling. And—I lost Kitty!"

The very thought of corporal punishment, even if it weren't directed at her, always upset Emmie, and she started to cry again. But Grace wasn't afraid of a paddling from Captain Heard's wife. The stately woman was very reserved, and not prone to spanking children. Instead, Dame Elizabeth Heard would give Grace extra chores, and she groaned at the prospect of being forced to work when she would rather be dangling her bare feet in the Cocheco River, twirling her whirligig.

"Stop crying, Em," Grace said irritably. "'T'will be all right. Dame Heard never gets so mad that she paddles anyone. You know that."

"But Grandfather will have to pay for the damage you did," Emmie sniffed.

Captain Heard, a master carpenter who served under Major

20

Waldron, would be furious with Grace when he heard what she had done. He would most likely be the one to give her a lashing, but such a multitude of emotions were going through her mind she didn't give much thought to future punishment.

"Don't cry," she said a little more gently this time as a current of fresh tears streamed down Emmie's little face. "I can bear Captain Heard's paddling. And look!" She pointed toward the millhouse door, where the kitten emerged. "There's your kitten! And anyway," she added as Emmie gleefully scooped up the little cat, "I've a secret to share, but it must wait until tonight."

Emmie's tear-bright eyes widened at the word "secret," and she snuggled the squirming kitten against her chest. The little girls trudged northward up Cart Way toward the Heard's garrison. It crowned Little Hill like a weathered ship struck aground. Like the other four garrison houses at Cochecho, it was built of solid oak. The thick planks were joined at each corner using the half notch method, where portions of one log were removed to fit snugly into its neighbor. The small windows were constructed of tiny diamond-shaped panes lined with lead and a single chimney poked from the center of the roof. Small embrasures were strategically cut into each wall so musket barrels could protrude from them in case of attack. The heavy oak door was adorned with dozens of iron nails, which served no purpose other than ornamentation. Such a display was one of wealth and status, and the doors of the other garrison houses were decorated in the same manner. The jettied second floor protruded slightly from the first and the floors were made of knotty pine. Each garrison was fortified with a thick blockade of cherry wood, and the gates were locked securely at night. Emmie and her family would sleep in the safety of the Heard garrison, as would many of their neighbors, due to concerns about the strange Indians. The girls would lie on straw pallets under the sloping eaves of the attic, and giggle and gossip until an adult reprimanded them. Grace would have anticipated the upcoming night more if she could have shaken her guilt.

Across from Heard's garrison Elder Wentworth's brindle mastiff Dog raised its head and emitted a low growl when it saw the girls turn off Cart Way and head up to Little Hill. Emmie was afraid of Dog, and her hand trembled in Grace's as they made their way up the footpath. *I wouldn't name a dog "Dog,"* she was thinking, opening the blockade gate. *Elder Wentworth has no imagination. He always names his mastiffs 'Dog'!* Somehow the same logic didn't apply to Emmie calling her cat "Kitty."

Alice was hoeing in the kitchen garden when the girls approached. She stopped and gave them a wary look.

"Dame Heard's at her great wheel, waiting for you."

"Is Grandmother very mad?" Emmie inquired nervously, still holding the squirming kitten.

"Methinks she's madder than she lets on," Alice replied.

Both girls entered the house heavy-footed. Dirty dishes were stacked on the board, the washing bucket turned upside-down next to them. Dame Heard was a very reserved woman who never raised her voice. Rather, she conveyed her displeasure in calm, quiet tones—unless she had reached the point of exasperation.

"Grace Hampton." A woman's voice called from the parlor with a note of urgency. "Pray, come here a moment."

Grace winced at Elizabeth Heard's order. Despite the calmness in Dame Heard's voice, Grace knew she was in trouble. Emmie knew it too, for she looked as though she would burst into tears again at any moment.

"You too, Emmie Ham," Dame Heard said. "And set down that cat."

Emmie's bottom lip trembled and Grace felt badly for her friend, who dutifully set the kitten down on the floor. There was no escaping what was to come, so she took a deep breath, squeezed Emmie's clammy hand and entered the parlor where Dame Heard stood at her great wheel, slowly turning the wheel counterclockwise with her left hand while drafting out a fine thread of cotton yarn. A neat cop formed on the spindle as the wheel creaked merrily.

"Grace, what are we to do with you?" Dame Heard began, her stately face scowling in disapproval. "Last week you broke Varney's fence, and two days ago you got in a fight—*a fight!*—with Johnny Horne. I've never known a little girl to cause so much trouble!"

"Eb Varney dared me to walk the fence," Grace explained. "And Johnny Horne—"

"Don't interrupt!" Dame Heard reprimanded in exasperation. "Trouble follows you everywhere. You simply must stop being so reckless and start acting sensibly!"

There was no sense in trying to explain. She did get into trouble often, but truly, she never meant to. She was rather proud of herself, facing up to Johnny Horne like she did. And anyway, it hadn't *really* been a fight. He had called her freckles *shit stains* once too often, and she had launched into a fury, swinging and kicking. Taller and stronger, Johnny placed his hand on her head and held her off at arm's length, laughing until Major Waldron came from the trading post to see what the fuss was about. Then Johnny let her go and left her to face Waldron's wrath alone.

"No supper for either of you this night," Dame Heard decided. "While everyone else eats, you can sweep the parlor chamber. After that, both of you are going to wash all the supper dishes—*all of them*—alone tonight. Dry them and put them away. When you've finished that, you can empty the chamber pots before bedtime."

Seeing tears slip down Emmie's pale cheeks, Grace insisted, "Emmie didn't do anything. Pray, let her have her supper."

Dame Heard's resolve softened only slightly. "Very well," she relented. "But Emmie will still help with the dishes."

"Thank you, Grandmother," Emmie said meekly as Grace reached for a broom. Properly chastised, she clambered up the narrow staircase to the parlor chamber.

Dust motes danced in the air, agitated by her sweeping. Grace choked as the broom rasped against the pine floor and to her shame hot tears scalded her eyeballs again. *Why am I always in trouble?* she asked herself for the hundredth time. *Am I cursed somehow? I must be, to have been orphaned so early.* But Alice was an orphan too, and she wasn't afflicted with the same bad luck. It didn't seem fair.

Her thoughts returned to the Indian boy as the broom's bristles rasped against the knotty pine floor. If she gazed out the window of the parlor chamber she could see Waldron's mill and the very place along the river bank where she encountered the boy. How old was he? Did he speak English? Why had he stolen the soldier's blanket?

The pleasing aromas of samp and fresh-baked rye bread wafted from the hearth up to her nose, sending her stomach rumbling. She hoped she would fall asleep quickly. The sooner she fell asleep, the sooner it would be morning, and she could eat breakfast.

When Captain Heard arrived home, Grace listened from upstairs while Dame Heard recounted the day's events to him. She heard him mention "that girl" in a tone of sheer exasperation, and after she finished sweeping, she waited for Dame Heard to call her down so she could wash the dishes.

Alice and Emmie gave her pitying looks as Grace rolled up her sleeves and poured a kettle of hot water into the wooden wash basin.

"Grandfather's gone to inspect the damage on Major Waldron's tree," Emmie whispered, handing Grace the pale bar of lye soap. "He's quite angry."

Grace took the soap from Emmie and sighed, resigned to her role of unwitting troublemaker. Dishwashing was a least favorite chore. The hot water and slimy lye soap made her hands and arms red and itchy.

"Mayhap I'll finish my chores afore he returns," Grace said without much hope.

After finishing the dishes, both girls retrieved the chamber pots, an even worse chore than dishwashing. The nasty buckets were emptied into the woods, then rinsed out with more lye soap, but the stench of human waste still clung to them. Grace saw Captain Heard trudging up Little Hill, his stony face set in grim lines. She returned the wooden chamber pots to their proper places, hoping she looked properly chastised when inside she was seething with indignation at once again being misunderstood. He entered the house with a grave look on his sunburnt face. Placing his felt hat on its peg, he turned to Grace, who stood with her hands clasped in front of her, the whirligig pressed into one palm.

"Grace Hampton," Captain Heard said her name with such severity it chilled her blood. "I've inspected the damage you inflicted on Major Waldron's tree. I first considered thirty lashes, but I'm taking into account the limb was dead. So although you'll receive but twenty, that doesn't lessen the fact that such ungodly behavior is not to be tolerated in any child, much less a girl."

"Yes, sir," she replied, stifling the urge to explain her actions.

He handed her his sheathed knife. No words were necessary as she accepted it. The routine had become familiar. A clump of willows grew just outside the palisade, and she struggled to fight back tears as she selected a single branch and cut it loose with the knife.

Menane returned to his ailing grandmother, breathing hard as adrenaline surged through his veins. He had evaded the soldiers, but their angry voices still rang in his ears.

"Here, Nokomis," he said, removing the sweat-dampened blanket and replacing it with the new one.

She tried to lift her head, but fell back as he smoothed the new blanket over her thin form.

"Where did you get that, noses?" she demanded feebly. "Did you steal it?"

Menane had been taught to be honest, and he was not a good liar. *The blanket was lying there, unattended,* he told himself. *That's not the same as if I stole it from the trading post.*

"I found it on the ground," he replied.

The old woman seemed too weary to pursue the matter further, and Menane exhaled with relief. He stoked the fire and offered his grandmother sips of water until she fell into another fitful sleep. While she snored softly, he sat outside the wigwam and ground *skamon* in a stone mortar and pestle. It shamed him to have to do women's work, but it was either that or starve. Between being trampled by the white's cattle and being torched by marauding Mohawks, the Pennacook's corn fields were nearly obliterated.

Thinking of women's work made him think of women, which brought to mind the white girl who didn't betray him to the soldiers.

He had gotten a good look at her, and if he hadn't been running from the soldiers, he would have laughed at her outright. He had never seen anyone with so many pronounced freckles, and her ruddy complexion reminded him of the speckled shell of a wild turkey egg. He had also caught a glimpse of her red curls before she covered them with her little white cap. Her eyes were a surprising blue, like a cloudless sky.

In his mind, he dubbed her "Turkey Egg Girl," and wondered if she were a friend. He had never spoken to a white child and she had piqued his curiosity.

A pair of mocassined feet came into view and Menane looked up into the face of his older brother, Kancamagus.

"*Nijia*," Kancamagus said, scowling. "put away that women's work. Uncle wants all the men at council."

Their uncle was Wanalancet, the Pennacook sachem. Boys his age were never invited to men's council, and for a moment Menane wondered at the invitation. *It shames Kancamagus to see me grinding corn*, he realized, his cheeks growing hot. But the prospect of being included with the grown men was exciting, and he quickly abandoned the mortar and pestle to join the circle of men outside Wanalancet's wigwam.

A man's place in the hierarchy was determined by status, with Wanalancet and his fellow sachems clustered together, lesser warriors fanning out across the circle. Menane sat a respectful distance from the inner circle, but close enough to feel included.

Two years before, Wanalancet had converted to the white man's religion, and a silver cross hung from his tattooed neck. He regarded his council members with patience and waited until everyone was seated and quiet before he began.

"We have been invited by Brother Waldron to join the whites in a sham battle," Wanalancet announced. "The Wampanoags are invited also."

"What is the point of a sham battle?" Kancamagus demanded. "It's never a good idea to keep company with whites. They can't be trusted."

Other men muttered similar feelings as Menane sat behind

the grown men, wondering the same thing, although he had never spent enough time around whites to determine whether they were trustworthy or not. For that matter, could Turkey Egg Girl be trusted not to tell the soldiers she saw him? He pondered this while the grown men debated the wisdom of participating in the proposed sham battle.

"I don't like the idea either," a warrior named Bomazeen stated. "How many times have the whites ignored our pleas for help against the Mohawks?"

"Brother Waldron is our friend," Wanalancet insisted.

While the council continued to argue, Menane etched a crude face in the dirt with a stick while his mind wandered. He considered ways to improve his beaver traps and hoped he could catch enough beavers to trade for food and blankets for Nokomis. His stomach growled and he wondered how much dried venison was left in his grandmother's wigwam. Mindlessly he jabbed a series of holes all over the face he had drawn.

"Then it's decided," Wanalancet declared. "We will inform the Wampanoags and visit the white settlement in two days' time."

Voices were raised in excitement, shaking Menane from his musings. As the men dispersed, Menane scrambled to his feet. As Kancamagus and his friend Wahowah passed by him, Menane asked, "Am I allowed to come too, *Nidokan?*"

Kancagmas was nineteen, lean and sullen. He had fought against the Mohawks many times, and his young face was already displaying the battle-hardened acerbity of a warrior. Putting a hand on Menane's small shoulder, he replied, "You can watch with the women, but I don't want you involved in the sham battle, in case things go bad."

"Even a sham battle is no place for a skamon-grinding girl," Wahowah smirked. Despite being Kancamagus's friend, he often abused Menane with such insults, and Menane despised Wahowah.

As Menane was about to protest in indignation, Kancamagus noticed the face Menane had drawn in the dirt. "Who is that supposed to be? It looks like a victim of the white man's pox."

Embarrassment heated Menane's face as he looked down at the image. Staring up at him was a decidedly feminine caricature with long hair spilling beneath a cap. The dots on the face represented freckles, he realized with horror. Turkey Egg Girl! He didn't know why he had drawn her, and a sensation other than hunger made his stomach feel odd.

"It's nothing," Menane insisted, rubbing out the sketch with his bare feet.

"Why do you do things you know you'll get a lashing for?" Emmie whispered in the semi-darkness as the two little girls lay on their pallets, Kitty purring between them.

"'Tis my lot in life," Grace replied, trying unsuccessfully to find a comfortable position. It was bad enough her arms were chafed and itchy to the elbows from the lye soap, but she doubted she would get any sleep with her bottom throbbing from the twenty lashes. "I never mean to get myself in trouble."

"Quiet, both of you," Alice hissed from her pallet. "Afore we all get a beating!"

Grace and Emmie waited until Alice's breathing became rhythmic and they detected Captain Heard snoring in his string bed downstairs. Then Emmie poked Grace's arm impatiently.

"What is your secret? You promised you'd tell me!"

Grace's mind was so filled with anguish over the whipping she had forgotten about the Indian boy and the lie she told. The guilt of lying to the soldier spread like a stain on her heart as she whispered to Emmie what she had seen and done. She couldn't make out Emmie's features in the dark but she could envision her friend's eyes widen and her little mouth hang open in sheer astonishment.

"Oh, Grace," Emmie breathed, "'tis a grievous sin to lie. What if someone finds out?"

The likelihood of her deceit being discovered seemed minimal, yet it gnawed on her conscience like a mouse nibbling an ear of corn. "I know not," she admitted.

"Did you pray about it?" Emmie asked, stroking the sleeping kitten. "If you pray for forgiveness, mayhap all will be well."

Grace didn't want to confess that she had lost faith in prayers and forgiveness. She prayed her parents would be returned to her, but they never were. She prayed to be made more obedient, yet she often found herself at the wrong end of Captain Heard's switch. She prayed that Johnny Horne would leave her alone, but he remained the bane of her existence. In answer to Emmie's question, she rubbed her sore bottom and muttered, "I doubt that." Turning her head in Emmie's direction, she hissed, "Don't you breathe one word of this, Emmie Ham!"

"I promise!" Emmie replied.

"Swear it, Emmie! Swear on…swear on Kitty's head!"

She heard the little girl gasp. After a moment, she felt Emmie place her hand protectively over the little white cat, who *ttrrrpppped* at Emmie's touch.

"I—I swear," Emmie whispered gravely.

"Good," Grace said with satisfaction, knowing Emmie was sincere. "Now good night to you."

She felt Emmie take her hand and give it a gentle squeeze before the younger girl turned over to face away from her. Grace stared into the gloom until she fell asleep with her whirligig clasped in her hand.

Chapter Three

race stumbled and fell amidst green cornstalks taller than she, choking on smoke that rose from her parents' burning farmhouse. She was alone, and she didn't know which way Alice had run. War whoops rang in her ears, chilling the blood in her veins.

"Run, Grace!" someone—Alice? cried. "This way!"

Suddenly the cornstalks grew hands that grabbed at her arms, holding her fast. As she struggled to free herself, the cornstalks turned into marauding Indians, their painted faces glowering down at her. One of them, wielding a tomahawk, raised it above his head—

As she released a throat-grating scream, the Indians turned into ravens. They flew off into the cloudless sky with a flurry of flapping wings. One of them clutched two flaming arrows in its talons.

"Grace, wake up!"

Grace awoke in the dark loft, two shadowy figures looming over her. She cried out in alarm.

"Grace, you're having another nightmare," Alice whispered, her hands on Grace's shoulders.

"What brings on all this wailing?" Captain Heard demanded from the bottom of the stairs.

"'Tis Grace having another bad dream, sir," Alice replied.

"Well, if she doesn't quieten, I'll give her another lashing!"

"Yes, sir."

Grace's throat still ached from screaming, and she sat up, trembling. Tears dampened her cheeks and she swiped at them with the sleeve of her shift. She wanted to explain to Captain Heard she couldn't help what she did when the nightmares came upon her, but she knew no explanation would be accepted. She pressed the whirligig to her chest and rocked back and forth, the essence of the dream lingering like a stench.

"Do try to get some sleep," Alice implored, rubbing Grace's back. "The last thing you need is another beating. 'T'will be sunup soon, and we've plenty of chores ahead of us."

As the terror of the nightmare evaporated, Grace inhaled shakily. "I won't cry out again," she said more as an order to herself than a promise to Alice and Emmie.

"See that you don't," Alice whispered back.

As Alice made her way to her own bed, Grace sunk back onto her pallet, the Indians' war whoops still echoing in her ears.

Grace awoke stiff and sore just as the rooster crowed at daybreak. Even her tear-streaked cheeks felt stiff until she splashed her face with water from a bucket, hoping to wash off any remaining bad luck from the day before. Alice and Emmie dressed silently, offering her empathetic glances.

The girls descended the narrow stairs and began their morning routines. While Alice stoked the fire, Grace and Emmie retrieved baskets from the board and headed toward the hen house to gather eggs.

Their footsteps left trails in the glistening, dew-dampened grass just as the orange sun emerged above the trees. Birds greeted the morning with song and Grace inhaled deeply the clover-scented air. *This day will go well*, she told herself. *I'll finish all my chores and be as respectful and well-behaved as Alice.*

The broken shutter on Captain Heard's workshop creaked on its rusted hinge as the girls walked past, grating on Grace's nerves. She glared at the cockeyed shutter in irritation. The additional damage to the window had been her fault too: a month before, Johnny Horne had told her that girls couldn't play ball because they couldn't throw.

To prove him wrong, she pitched a rock, intending to hit a target Johnny had drawn in chalk on the workshop's clapboard side. Her pitch went far to the right, shattering the single pane of glass. Glass was a rare and expensive commodity, and she had received thirty lashings for that infraction.

Grace's mind wrestled with the events of the day before, and she was sure the consequences of her actions had not yet fully come to fruition. Although she had received her punishment for damaging the tree, there was still the matter of lying to the soldier, and now Emmie knew about that too. Emmie would never intentionally tell on her, but her skittish disposition did not lend itself well to keeping secrets. She was as transparent as a raindrop, and if she were asked outright, she would tell all she knew. This intensified Grace's anguish. She shouldn't have told Emmie, she realized as she slipped her hand beneath a fat hen. It was too late now, and all she could do was hope nobody asked Emmie directly about the incident.

"Are you mad at me?" Emmie inquired anxiously.

Grace shook her head. "Nay, Emmie," she replied. "I just don't feel good about...what happened."

"I won't tell on you, I promise," Emmie insisted, tears already shimmering in her eyes.

Grace exhaled so forcefully her breath fanned a hen's feathers. The bird clucked in protest and pecked at Grace before rearranging her plumage.

"Pray, let's forget it ever happened," Grace suggested after counting the eggs nestled in her basket.

Emmie nodded solemnly and opened her little mouth to speak, but before any words formed, they heard Elder Wentworth's bull mastiff barking in alarm. Grace grabbed Emmie's hand just as the color drained from the younger girl's face.

"Come, let's see what Dog is barking about!" Grace cried, glad for the distraction.

Abandoning their egg baskets in the hen house, they ran toward the dooryard of the Heard garrison. Both Alice and Dame Heard stood in the kitchen garden, looking anxiously down Cart Way. All

Grace could discern was a large group of men, mostly Massachusetts soldiers, crowding together and yelling. Across the road, Dog strained at his rope, barking until Elder William Wentworth appeared on his own stoop, leaning on his cane.

"Dog!" he ordered. "Be quiet!"

After the dog obeyed, the duck-footed old man ambled toward them and peered down the road.

"What's going on?" he demanded. "Dame Heard, can you make out what this commotion is about?"

Dame Heard's stern face was shaded by her own straw hat. "Nay, Elder Wentworth," she replied, hiking up her skirts. "But I'll soon discover the reason. You there, Jack Meader--"

Grace looked to see Jack Meader running past Little Hill on his way to the pandemonium down the road. He was accompanied by Johnny Horne, and Grace made a face at her constant tormentor.

"What's the commotion all about, lad?" Dame Heard demanded.

"Some soldier's whipping a savage!" Jack Meader said, barely breaking stride.

Grace exchanged a glance with Emmie as excitement grew. "Dame Heard, may we go see?" Grace begged. "Half the settlement's already assembled there!"

Dame Heard wiped garden dirt onto her apron as she considered this. "Very well," she acquiesced. "Alice, stay here and mind the hearth. We'll be back presently."

"Aye, ma'am," Alice replied with a hint of disappointment.

Dame Heard led the procession down Little Hill, followed by Grace and Emmie.

"Wait for me," Wentworth demanded, hobbling after them, muttering about painful bunions.

The old man waddled behind them, his cane tapping excitedly upon the packed dirt road. Grace followed in Dame Heard's wake, clutching Emmie's hand. Men shouted and cheered, apparently encouraging the beating of some unfortunate soul in their midst. Jack Meader and Johnny Horne had joined the men's enthusiasm, punctuating their cheers with fists thrust into the air.

Amid the confusion, she glimpsed the center of the commotion. She recognized the soldier from the day before, a horse whip in his raised hand. The whip bit the air with a *crack* to the delight of his fellow soldiers. Beside her, she heard Emmie start to cry. Emmie couldn't bear to witness such cruel behavior and hid her face in her apron. Jostled by adults standing around her, Grace's jaw dropped when she saw the victim. Cowering in the dust, bleeding from multiple lacerations, was the Indian boy. Blood ran from a diagonal gash across his small face.

"Sergeant Duncan!" Captain Syl bellowed, followed by Hathorne and Major Waldron. "Cease this immediately! Why are you whipping this boy?"

The enraged Duncan coiled his whip and pointed it at the defenseless child. "'Tis the little heathen that stole my blanket!" Duncan explained. "Caught him this morning trying to steal my knapsack."

Syl ordered Duncan to put away his whip, but his words sounded garbled to Grace, whose ears rang while her face flushed hotly. Before she could avert her eyes from him, the Indian boy met her gaze. His dark eyes flashed in recognition, surmounting their look of pain and anguish. Blood ran down his face and arms, matting his sleek black hair.

"Is that the one you saw?" Emmie whispered. "It is, isn't it?"

Grace shot Emmie an intense look and put her finger to her mouth. "Hush, Emmie!"

"I say we hang the little thief where he lies!" Duncan bellowed, swaying on his bowed legs. Though it was early morning, it was clear Duncan was drunk.

"Duncan!" Syl ordered. "Return to your quarters or I'll have you demoted. Major," he said, turning to Waldron, "have you somewhere we can put this man until he sobers up?"

"Damnable Waldron," Grace heard Elder Wentworth mutter bitterly. It was common knowledge the two wealthiest men in the settlement despised each other. Grace didn't know the reason for their mutual animosity, but if she had to choose between one and the other, she would choose Wentworth, despite the fact his snores disturbed everyone when he spent his nights in the Heard garrison.

Major Waldron's black brows met over his nose in a scowl. "I do, Captain. Hart! Escort this man to the jail."

"I'm not going anywhere 'till I teach this savage a lesson!" slurred Duncan, reeling back with his whip. But before he could strike the child again, a large hand seized his wrist. An irritated Duncan glowered up into the dark, solemn face of Absalom Hart.

"Come with me, sergeant," Absalom said in his low, even voice.

Duncan took a swing at Hart with his free arm, but missed and was easily flung over Hart's shoulder. The crowd parted, allowing Hart to carry the drunken soldier away.

"I'll see to Duncan," Syl said to Waldron, rubbing his bearded chin. "As for the boy, I'll leave him to you."

In the excitement, no one had been watching the Indian boy, and when Grace looked in his former direction, she gasped along with the others. The child had disappeared.

"Was no one watching the boy?" Syl demanded.

The crowd murmured, glancing around, but the Indian boy had indeed vanished. Grace clutched the whirligig in her palm anxiously as Waldron gestured broadly, begging the crowd to relax and disperse.

"If we find the boy, he'll be dealt with accordingly," Waldron pledged. "Pray, go on to your homes and tend to your own affairs."

"They'll not find that little savage, I daresay," muttered Elder Wentworth, who stood behind Grace. "Stealthy as a catamount, and quiet as smoke they are."

Grace felt Dame Heard's hands on her shoulders. "Come along, girls," she urged firmly. "We can stop at Otis's shop and pick up the new hinges for the shutter."

Grace and Emmie shared a look before falling into step behind Dame Heard. They would pass the blacksmith's garrison on their return to Little Hill. Elder Wentworth lingered to speak to some of the men, and Grace could tell Emmie was bursting with questions. She prayed her friend would wait until they could speak privately. The two young girls lagged several feet behind. When a good distance separated them from Dame Heard, Emmie turned to Grace, her eyes glittering with excitement.

"Where do you think he disappeared to?" Emmie whispered.

"I know not," Grace hissed back, pressing the mother-of-pearl button into her palm.

"Do you think he might return?"

"Nay," Grace replied.

"He looked right at you," Emmie continued, worrying the hem of her apron. "Surely he recognized--"

"Hush now, Emmie!"

Richard Otis's blockade door stood open, and Grace heard the blacksmith pounding away at his anvil within. He was a jolly man whose sky-blue eyes sparkled merrily in his soot-darkened face. Broad-shouldered and stoutly built, Grace often likened the middle-aged blacksmith to a gentle ox. His apprentice, sixteen-year-old Eb Varney, worked the bellows as Dame Heard and her charges approached. Eb, a Quaker boy who lived on the outskirts of Cochecho, had a nose too large for his long face and drooping gray eyes. He wore his wide-brimmed hat indoors, as Quakers did, even in the hot forge. A shy boy, he kept to himself, practicing his violin when he wasn't at the forge learning his trade. It was also clear he had an interest in Alice, which unfortunately for him was not reciprocated.

"Goodman Otis," Dame Heard called over the sound of the bellows as she and the girls entered the hot forge. "Are my hinges ready?"

Otis set down his hammer and tongs, sweat running in dark rivulets down his blackened face. He smiled, wiping his brow with a rag. "Good day, Dame Heard!" he greeted. "Eb, that fire's hot enough now," he instructed as he retrieved a pair of shiny new hinges from a workbench. "Eb here finished them just yesterday."

"I can wrap them in bunting if thee prefers," Eb Varney offered.

"That would suit us fine, Ebenezer," Dame Heard replied.

While Eb hastened to wrap the hinges in a square of burlap, Otis said, "I can have Eb here help with the installation if you like."

Hopefulness flickered over the boy's face, but was quickly

extinguished when Dame Heard replied, "Thank you for the offer, Goodman Otis, but my husband's already enlisted the help of Goodman Hart."

This clearly extinguished the glimmer of hope in Eb Varney's eyes, and Grace would have been inclined to tease Alice about him if she weren't so shocked at seeing the Indian boy again.

The blacksmith's usually jolly face contorted in a frustrated scowl. "Curse it," he mumbled, looking among his tools. Suddenly he seemed to remember ladies were present, and he looked abashed. "My apologies, ma'am. I've misplaced my heaviest sledge and it's nowhere to be found."

Dame Heard appeared unoffended and brushed his apology aside with a graceful hand. "Think nothing of it, Goodman Otis."

"Oh, and do stop at Stephen's," Richard Otis said as though he suddenly remembered something. "Margaret has that linen dyed for you."

Stephen was Richard Otis's son, and his wife Margaret was renowned for her lovely dyed fabrics. The length of linen Dame Heard had given Margaret was to be dyed with mulberries, which rendered a lovely, royal purple hue. Stephen and Margaret's home would be the next house they passed by on their way home, and Grace looked forward to seeing their year-old daughter, Maggie, who was just beginning to toddle and talk.

"Then we'll collect that on our way home, also," Dame Heard smiled. "Thank you. Good day to you, Goodman Otis." Taking the hinges from Eb Varney, she nodded her thanks and headed out the door with the two girls in her wake.

Grace unwound the whirligig from her wrist and spun it on its cord as she walked. As the button *whzzzed* into a blur, she could still see the Indian boy's slashed face in her mind's eye.

The moment the crowd's attention was diverted, Menane slipped silently away, looking for a place to hide. Blood dripped into his eyes and it hurt to take a deep breath. He saw several dwellings, but he would likely be found if he hid in one of them. Then he saw the small outbuilding with the broken window. *I'll hide in there*, he thought, scrambling up the hill.

The window was just low enough that he could reach it. The wooden shutters were at odd angles and they creaked on rusted hinges as he pushed them aside. Gripping the sill with his fingertips, he hoisted himself up and over, landing with a soft thud onto the sawdust-covered floor.

A white man's tools hung on pegs on the far wall. An unlit hearth dominated one end of the rectangular structure. Barrels and sacks rested under a work bench that ran the length of the building. His empty stomach growled loudly, and he lifted a lid of one of the barrels, only to find it contained wood shavings. Disappointed, he looked around for something he could eat. Finding nothing, he touched his bruised ribs gingerly and considered what to do.

He heard girls' high-pitched voices approaching. Alarmed, Menane looked for a hiding place. Some large object sat covered with burlap, and planks of timber were stacked beside it. Wincing with pain, he darted beneath the burlap and held his breath as he heard the door open. Footsteps grew closer, and he hugged his knees to his chest, praying to Kitchi Manitou he wouldn't be discovered.

The home of Margaret and Stephen Otis was just next door to Richard Otis's garrison, and the pleasant scent of mulberries made a shocking contrast to the forge's sooty heat. The length of freshly-dyed linen lay neatly folded on the board, and Grace resisted the urge to bury her nose in the fragrant cloth. Grace liked the Otis family, and she was especially fond of baby Maggie. Setting the wrapped hinges on the board next to the fabric, Grace knelt by Maggie, who had been placed in her standing stool well away from the hearth. The one-year-old squealed with delight when she recognized Grace and Emmie, and the three youngsters played quietly together while Dame Heard and Margaret Otis talked.

"Stephen told me the menfolk are planning some war games come the Sabbath," Margaret Otis said, handing Dame Heard the length of dyed linen. She was a slight, pretty woman with soft features. "Do you reckon you'll watch?"

"Indeed we will not," Dame Heard answered primly. "I object to such frivolity on the Sabbath. The girls and I will spend the day as intended, in prayer. Captain Heard is obliged to take part, being a militia member. But I and the girls will have no part of it."

Grace was suddenly reminded of the conversation she overhead at the mill, and she was awash with a fresh wave of guilt. She fingered her whirligig nervously as she and Emmie exchanged a secret look.

"Well, I daresay you'll hear the ruckus, clear to Little Hill," Margaret went on, stooping to pick up Maggie. "The sham battles will take place right near the mill. Mother Otis has worked herself into a tizzy worrying about Stephen and his father."

Rose Otis's inclination toward worry was common knowledge in Cochecho. Tormented by frequent headaches, she spent much of her time lying in bed, leaving daily chores undone unless Margaret did them for her.

"In any case, I'll surely see you at the meetinghouse," Margaret added.

"You shall," Dame Heard confirmed, disapproval over the men's war games lingering on her stern face. "Emmie, take the linen. Grace, carry the hinges. Good day to you, Goody Otis."

"And to you, Dame Heard."

For a moment Grace was pricked with envy when she saw Emmie burrow her face in the sweet-smelling linen, but then Emmie held the bundle out to her. "Here, Grace!" She offered. "Smell!"

"Stop wrinkling that fabric, Emmie. Come along now, both of you," Dame Heard scolded before Grace could catch a satisfying whiff. Obediently, both girls bade Margaret and Maggie goodbye and followed Dame Heard out the door.

"Elizabeth Heard! Elizabeth Heard, may I speak with thee?"

Dame Heard and her charges turned to see Eb Varney emerge from the forge in his shuffling gait. He had taken the time to remove his leather apron and wipe the soot from his face, but black traces had etched deeply into his young visage, making him appear much older. Dame Heard acknowledged him with a slight nod. "Certainly, Ebenezer," she said.

The young Quaker shifted awkwardly from foot to foot before peering up from his hat's wide brim. "I'm sure thee has heard of the sham battle proposed this First Day," he began hesitantly.

"Aye, Ebenezer."

Eb swallowed audibly, and Grace resisted a sudden urge to snicker.

"As thee are aware, the Friends will be holding a social at that very same time—"

"Aye, Ebenezer," Dame Heard replied with a trace of impatience.

"And I'd like to ask permission of thee to invite Alice to it after services."

He's so sweet on Alice! Every time Grace thought of how smitten Eb was, she giggled. This time a bemused snort erupted from Grace's lips, and Dame Heard slapped her arm smartly as the awkward young man waited for a response.

"You may ask," Dame Heard said curtly, "but nay, she won't be joining you. Immediately after services we are going home to observe the Sabbath in prayer."

The young Quaker looked crestfallen, but just as he was about to turn away, Dame Heard said in a lighter voice, "But you're welcome to sup with us this night. Mayhap Captain Heard could use your help with the hinges as well."

Like the sun bursting through a cloud, Ebenezer's long face lit up and he smiled with gratitude. "Thank thee, Elizabeth Heard. I would be honored to help!"

"Eb!" Richard Otis bellowed from the forge, "Find me that twelve-pound sledge!"

He put a hand to his hat's brim before darting back to the forge, his mood clearly brightened.

"Now come along, girls," Dame Heard prompted, putting a hand on each girl's back. "We've wasted far too much time."

Grace's arm still stung from Dame Heard's slap, and she rubbed it absently as she and Emmie fell into step behind their benefactress. Only the prospect of teasing Alice about Eb Varney offered her a measure of anticipatory delight.

Grace clutched the bundled hinges to her chest as she put her hand on the workshop's latch.

"Pick up my basket too, Emmie," she instructed her friend, "and I'll carry both the rest of the way to the house."

As Emmie skipped off in the direction of the hen house, Grace opened the heavy oak door of the workshop. Morning light spilled through the broken window, illuminating the workbench along one side. Hammers, axes and saws hung from pegs on the walls while the carpet of sawdust and wood shavings on the floorboards emitted the scent of cedar. A stack of pine boards ran the length of one wall. Buckets held various sizes of treenails and a large barrel in the corner contained gathered sawdust. A treadle lathe, draped with an old burlap feed sack to keep off the dust, rested in one corner.

Grace crossed the room, avoiding the sight of the broken window. She set the bundle on the work bench next to Captain Heard's vise and unwrapped the burlap bunting. Fingering the smooth black hinges, she sighed and turned to leave when a slight motion caught her eye.

The feed sack covering the lathe twitched.

Likely a kitten is hiding there, Grace thought, her spirits lifting at the thought of playing with a kitten again. She approached the lathe, unwinding the whirligig from her wrist. This time she would be sure to grip it more tightly lest this kitten try to steal it like the one at the riverbank.

"Here, kitty," she called softly, crouching next to the lathe, prepared to dangle the whirligig in front of it.

When no kitten emerged, she lifted the feed sack.

"Here kitty—oh!"

Instead of a playful kitten hiding beneath the feed sack, Grace found herself eye-to-eye with the Indian boy.

Both children regarded each other wide-eyed, mouths agape. The boy was covered in dried blood and his ribs protruded from his bare chest. His dark eyes returned her gaze with a mix of surprise, fear and defiance.

"Why—why are you hiding here?" Grace asked, for lack of anything better to say.

"Had to get away before bad soldiers find me again," he explained in a harsh whisper.

Grace glanced quickly over her shoulder. The door was ajar, and anyone walking past would easily see him.

"This isn't a good place to hide," she said. "Captain Heard will find you here."

"I will be gone before anyone finds me."

"I found you."

His only response was to grimace as he inhaled sharply.

"Are you bad hurt?" Grace asked.

"*Nda*," he insisted, thrusting his bloodied chin forward. "Leave me alone, girl!"

"Grace, I have your basket," Emmie called from the open door before her eyes fell on the young boy. She dropped both egg baskets as her hands flew to her mouth to stifle a scream.

"Emmie, come in and close the door!" Grace hissed.

Emmie obeyed, retrieving the dropped baskets as egg innards began to seep through the weave and drip onto the workshop floor. Her eyes were as big as full moons as she approached them, her mouth hanging open stupidly.

"Emmie, don't start crying. We need your help."

"But Grace--" Emmie stammered. "Oh, Grace, we will be in so much trouble! Grandmother and Grandfather will surely see him!"

Grace considered this. Captain Heard would be in need of his lathe soon, so the boy definitely needed a better hiding place. She looked at the pine boards thoughtfully, wondering if she and Emmie could rearrange them in such a way that the boy could hide beneath them, when all three children froze at the sound of footsteps.

"Grace, Emmie," Dame Heard called, her voice growing closer. "Where are those eggs? 'Tis not the time for you to be playing."

The door opened with a screech, and Dame Heard stood framed in the doorway, a rectangle of morning light behind her. Her eyebrows rose at the sight of the children and her face set in grim lines.

"Dame Heard, 'tis not my fault," Grace began as Emmie prepared to burst into tears beside her. "He's hurt."

To Grace's surprise, Dame Heard glanced around quickly before shutting the door behind her. Then the woman stepped purposefully toward the cowering boy, her face softening more than Grace ever imagined it could.

"What's your name, lad?"

"I am called Menane," he replied after a moment of hesitation.

"Well my boy," Dame Heard said, "would you like some breakfast and have those wounds tended to?" Dame Heard eyed the baskets filled with shattered eggs. "I fear we won't have many eggs this morn, but there's pottage on the hearth. That will have to do."

"What shall we do, Grandmother?" Emmie whispered anxiously.

Grace watched Dame Heard contemplate this question. "Grace, get the wheelbarrow from the barn. He can lie inside it as we take him to the house. We'll bring him in through the lean-to, lest any neighbors see him. Alice has gone to the orchard and Captain Heard will be back soon with a fresh load of lumber, so we must make haste."

Grace ran to do her mistress's bidding, feeling oddly excited. Dame Heard was involving them all in a secret! This lightened the burden of her old secret considerably, replacing it with a thrill of shared conspiracy.

Menane clambered into the wheel barrow, holding his thin arms over his chest. Grace saw Dame Heard frown with concern and mutter something about cracked ribs before throwing a coarse scrap of burlap over him and taking up the wheel barrow. Grace and Emmie followed behind, holding the egg baskets out at arm's length so the dripping eggs wouldn't soil their skirts. Making sure no one was watching, Dame Heard hustled the boy into the lean-to and sat him on a salt barrel. His bony shoulders drooped and he winced as she dabbed at his wounds with a damp rag.

"Fetch him a bowl of pottage, Emmie," Dame Heard instructed. "Grace, salvage the unbroken eggs and get me the pot of plantain ointment."

As the girls went about doing her bidding, Alice entered from the front door with a basket of apples. She eyed Grace and Emmie quizzically as they bustled to and fro. "Pray, what are you up to?" Noticing the ruined eggs in the basket, she frowned. "Oh, you girls are so careless!"

Emmie's hands shook so that Grace took the bowl of pottage from her lest she drop it. Surely Alice would soon discover the boy in the lean-to.

"Alice, pare those apples on the stoop. Emmie will help you," Dame Heard called from the lean-to. "Then take the cores to the hen house."

Grace's shoulders sagged with relief as Alice replied without question, "Aye, Dame Heard." Retrieving two paring knives from a drawer, Emmie left with Alice eagerly, throwing a surreptitious glance over her shoulder at Grace before disappearing outside. It was only then that Grace returned with both the pottage and ointment.

Dame Heard had washed off most of the blood, but some was still caked in the boy's long black hair. A white swath of plantain ointment covered the gash across his face; blood seeped around the edges, tinting the ointment pink. Dame Heard had also wrapped his scrawny chest in clean linen strips. He took the bowl and spoon from Grace without a word of thanks and devoured the pottage like a starved dog while Dame Heard applied healing ointment to the worst of his wounds.

"There," Dame Heard declared softly, recapping the crock of ointment. "Take shallow breaths, my boy. Grace, sit with him until he finishes eating. While he eats, wrap that heel of rye bread and the remnants of ham in some bunting for him to take. Then, take him in the wheelbarrow back to the barn. He can leave through the woods from there."

Grace nodded in affirmation, freeing the wayward curl. After Dame Heard left them, she retrieved the bread and ham from the buttery and wrapped them in a scrap of linen while Menane consumed the pottage with relish. She wondered if he were truly a savage or perhaps one of the Praying Indians who had converted to Christianity. Setting the ham and bread next to him on the salt barrel, she blurted, "Are you a savage or a Praying Indian?"

His dark eyes glared at her and he reached out to touch her freckled cheek. Then with the same hand he pulled on the curl that had escaped her coif and watched it spring back into shape. "Are you a turkey egg or an autumn leaf?"

Grace didn't know if she should be insulted or not. Nonetheless, she felt her cheeks flush hot. The place his fingers touched her tingled oddly and she put her hand to it.

"You ought to be thankful for our help," she muttered.

His dark eyes regarded her coldly. "I did not ask for your help."

The boy's ungrateful attitude suddenly made her angry and she balled up her apron in her fists. "Well, next time don't go hiding in Captain Heard's workshop if you don't want our help!"

He set the emptied bowl down on the barrel, and the two children glared at each other in silence. Finally, Grace's curiosity got the best of her once again.

"Why did you take that soldier's blanket?" Grace asked calmly, fidgeting with the whirligig on her wrist.

"For my grandmother," he replied around a mouthful of pottage. "She has a fever and she shakes."

Grace absorbed this information thoughtfully. "Can't you buy a blanket at the trading post?"

Menane shook his head. "He cheats."

This wasn't news to Grace. Major Waldron was known to put his thumb on the scale when dealing with Indians. She regarded him silently while he ate, eyeing him with blatant curiosity. She reached a hand out to grasp the bag around his neck, and was startled by his quick and negative reaction.

"Nda!" he snarled, concealing it protectively in one fist.

Taken aback by his offense, she dropped her hand. "What is it?"

"It is mine," he grumbled into the pottage bowl. "Leave it alone." His eyes then went to the button dangling from her wrist. Grace unwound it.

"'Tis a whirligig," she explained, demonstrating how the button danced on the string until it was blur.

"Is it good medicine for you?"

Medicine? What was he talking about? "Don't be silly," she replied. "'T'is a toy."

"Well, I would not just reach out and grab it without permission, because it is yours," he said.

Grace understood that, and appreciated that he respected her property. Suddenly feeling ashamed for her unintentional rudeness, she said, "My father made it for me before--" *Before he and Mother were killed by savages like you.*

"Is your father dead?" he asked bluntly.

A heavy sadness settled in her stomach as she returned the whirligig to her wrist. "Aye," she managed to say, holding back tears. "My mother also."

"Mine are dead too," he said flatly, sorrow flashing in his eyes for a moment. "Your white pox killed them."

Was he blaming *her* for his parents' death? Incensed, she balled up her fists. "Well, 'twas your people who killed *my* folk!"

He threw the empty bowl against the wall. It clattered to the floor along with the spoon. Then he hopped off the salt barrel and faced her, his face just inches from hers. "I am Pennacook! We did no slaying of whites!"

"Nay, but you're a savage all the same!"

The boy stared her down, his eyes boring so intently into hers she felt as if he looked directly into her soul. "I cannot stay here," he said at last.

Their argument sent Grace's heart beating wildly, and she

marveled at how Menane's temper could go from hot to sullen within minutes when her own blood hadn't stopped boiling from his insults. Without another word, the two children crept out of the lean-to and once again Menane climbed into the wheelbarrow, throwing the old burlap over himself while cradling the bundle of food to his chest. Grace heard the voice of Alice's friend Sarah Follett and wanted to hurry, but if any eyes were watching, she wanted to appear to be returning an empty barrow to the barn.

Does he go to school? she wondered, her eyes on the burlap-covered form in the wheel barrow. *Good riddance to him, in any case! Nasty savage boy!*

Once she unlatched the barn door and stepped inside, Menane clambered gingerly from the wooden conveyance, holding his bandaged torso. His dark eyes regarded the sickle and scythe resting on pegs on the far wall briefly before looking for an escape.

"That door yonder opens out into the woods," Grace said, pointing to the back door. "Begone with you!"

He regarded her silently before grasping her wrist where the whirligig hung. His hand was firm and hot on her wrist, and her jaw dropped. Raising her forearm, he said, "You are wrong. That toy is good medicine for you."

Why does he think a toy can be medicine? Before she could ask, he released her arm and opened the barn's back door. She could still feel his fingers around her wrist, and she glanced briefly at the dangling button. When she looked up again, Menane had gone.

"Alice! Alice, oh did you hear?"

Alice looked up from the apple she was paring to see her friend Sarah Follett running excitedly through the garrison's open gate. She and Emmie both sat on the stoop, a bowl of apples resting at their feet.

"What's happened that's got you in such a state?" Alice asked anxiously. Winded, Sarah put her hand on her chest to catch her breath. "Jack just told me about this morning's commotion. One of those horrid, drunken Massachusetts soldiers was whipping this little savage boy," Sarah explained between pants.

Emmie let out a faint gasp, but Alice's focus was on her friend as Sarah went on.

"Old Dick put a stop to it, and called Goodman Hart to arrest the soldier."

Alice's heart softened as she mouthed the name, Absalom! She looked at Emmie, whose little mouth was agape. She wanted to hear more, but in private.

"Walk with me to the chicken house while I dump these apple parings, Sarah." She rose with the bowl of parings and gave Sarah an intent look as both girls walked toward the chicken house.

Sarah looked pleased at Alice's response, and continued breathlessly. "Jack said the soldier took a swing at Goodman Hart, and Goodman Hart flung him over his shoulder like a sack of corn!"

Oh, why couldn't Dame Heard have ordered Grace to tend the hearth? Alice thought as bitter resentment rose in her heart. She would have swooned if she could have witnessed Absalom in such a deliciously commanding scene! Chickens clustered around their feet as they approached the coop, and she treaded carefully so as not to trip over them.

Sarah's eyes glittered brightly with even more information. "And I overheard Mama tell Margaret Otis why Goodman Hart's never married."

Alice stopped and put a hand on Sarah's forearm. "Tell me!"

"He courted a woman in Boston—that's where he's from, you know—"

Nay, I didn't know that, she thought as she gestured impatiently for Sarah to go on.

"—and the woman spurned his advances and broke his heart! And that's why he came to Cochecho so many years ago, to start afresh!"

Alice digested this new information while Sarah regarded her with gleeful satisfaction.

"Mama also said she heard he's started courting some young miss from Portsmouth last month."

Alice's heart dropped.

"But Mama doesn't think anything will come of it," Sarah amended, patting Alice's shoulder comfortingly. "Old Dick keeps him too busy to make the trek to Portsmouth very often."

Tears welled in Alice's eyes. "Oh, Sarah, then do you think—do you think there's a chance he might—?"

Sarah smiled encouragingly. "I do, Alice."

The chickens pecked impatiently at Alice's hem, and she promptly emptied the bowl of parings onto the ground. They clucked excitedly, seizing apple cores in their beaks as Alice glanced at the workshop's broken window.

"He's promised to aid Captain Heard in repairing that shutter," she said, hope swelling in her chest. "Methinks he'll be by this afternoon."

The sparkle in Sarah's eyes dimmed. "You won't like what else Jack told me."

A vague sense of dread squelched Alice's joy. "What, pray?"

Sarah exhaled, giving her friend a pitying look. "You know the Quakers won't take part in the sham battle, so they're having a picnic social of their own this Sabbath—"

"What of it?" Alice asked, afraid she knew what Sarah was going to tell her.

"—and Jack said Eb Varney asked Dame Heard for permission to ask you to the picnic after services," Sarah finished.

Alice groaned and resisted the urge to kick at a hen who pecked too closely to her feet. She knew Eb Varney admired her, but she never felt anything but mild indifference toward the awkward young Quaker. He often offered to help carry her purchases from the trading post or help weed the garden when he wasn't busy at Otis's forge.

"Oh, what am I to say to him, Sarah?" she asked. "Eb is a nice enough boy, but I've no interest in him."

Sarah patted Alice's arm in an impotent attempt to comfort her friend. "Well, Dame Heard wouldn't give her consent, but did invite

Eb to help install the new hinges. I'm sorry to have to spoil everything for you, Alice, but I thought you ought to know."

Alice's head began to throb. The very thought of Absalom Hart made her heart flutter like a hummingbird in her chest, while the thought of Eb Varney annoyed her like a gnat buzzing in her face. But was it true Absalom was courting a woman from Portsmouth?

Sarah clasped her hands as she often did when an idea came to her. "I know! You and Goodman Hart have the same initials! Surely that's a good omen. So when you put the bottom crust in the pie pan, be sure to score two A's and two H's into it before you pour the filling in."

Alice gasped. "That's witchcraft!"

Sarah smiled. "But suppose it makes Goodman Hart forget about the dame in Portsmouth?"

Alice bit her lip. Who would know if she enchanted the pie in secret? What if it worked? A wonderful shiver of anticipation passed through her.

"I'll do it," she said at last, envisioning their initials etched in the raw crust, secretly entwined.

"Nijia!" Kancamagus exclaimed when Menane returned, his ribs bandaged and greasy ointment smeared on his face. "What happened to you?"

"I got in a fight," Menane responded weakly as his brother scrutinized his injuries with scorn.

"Who bandaged you?" he demanded. "Who tended to your wounds?"

It was obvious a white hand had beaten him, and even more obvious a white hand had treated his wounds. He had tried to concoct a good explanation for his appearance, and now he faced his brother's wrath with shame.

"Tell me what happened, Nijia."

It was against his nature to lie, so Menane recounted the morning's events, watching Kancamagus's broad face darken with rage.

"Do not go to the white settlement alone again," Kancamagus ordered. "Now, go rub ashes on your face and sit with Nokomis. You can stay with her tomorrow when we go to the settlement."

Menane's shoulders drooped. To sit in front of the wigwam with ashes on his face was a common punishment for children. They sat in front of their wigwams, the ashes announcing their disgrace in front of the entire tribe. It was a punishment inflicted upon him at least twice a month.

"Please, Nidokan," Menane implored, hating the whine in his voice. "Don't make me stay back with the old women! Please let me go with you. I'll behave."

Kancagmagus had a soft spot in his heart for his little brother, and Menane knew it. He also knew Kancamagus wanted him to be exposed to as much battle as he could—even if it were only a sham battle. Menane waited anxiously until Kancagmagus let out an exasperated sigh.

"If you can stay out of trouble the rest of today, you may come with us. I'll tell Aunt Toloti to sit with Nokomis."

"Wlioni, Nidokan," Menane said.

Glad to have received his brother's permission, Menane returned to the wigwam where Nokomis lay, her thin gray hair clinging to her sweat-dampened brow. An earthen bowl containing cool river water and a soft cloth had been placed beneath her bed frame beside her sewing basket and supply of dried herbs. She appeared to be sleeping fitfully. When Menane wrung out the cloth and dabbed her wrinkled brow, her eyelids fluttered open.

"Noses," she mumbled. "Where have you been? Your face is cut."

"It's nothing, Nokomis," he said in what he hoped was a soothing tone.

She raised her head up, her febrile eyes taking in the linen bandages that girded his thin torso. No Pennacook in the village possessed white linen, so it would be just as obvious to his grandmother as it was to his brother that he had been both abused and assisted by a white hand.

"Stay away from the whites, Noses," the old woman said, echoing Kancamagus's earlier admonition.

"I will," he promised, returning the cloth to the water bowl. "After the sham battle."

His grandmother's eyes widened and for a moment a fearful clarity flashed in them. She seized his arm with talon-like fingers. "No! Promise me you will not go. Just now I had a dream. I saw you at the white settlement and a big red hawk swooped down and tore out your heart. Stay with me!"

Menane wanted to pry the bony fingers from his arm. He didn't like defying her wishes, but Kancamagus had already given his approval, and he was determined to be present at the sham battle. "I was granted permission, and Aunt Toloti will sit with you," he said.

Apparently too sick to argue further, his grandmother's face crumpled and her hand fell away from his arm. She sobbed weakly, which made him feel even worse. An old woman couldn't be expected to understand the importance of being involved in such an event, and he was sorry to cause her distress.

He rose and pulled the blankets up to her chin, then dipped his hands in the fire pit ashes. As Kancamagus instructed, he smeared his face with the soot, then seated himself outside the wigwam, his shameful disobedience displayed for all to see.

"Where are you off to in such a hurry, pray tell?" Richard Otis inquired of his young apprentice.

Eb Varney smiled into the wash bucket as he again washed soot from his face and hands. He knew the old blacksmith was aware of his feelings toward Alice Hampton. His cheeks flushed hotly beneath the damp rag when Otis flashed him a conspiratorial wink.

"Dame Heard said I could be of assistance after all," he explained, neatly folding the rag and returning it to its place by the bucket. "She invited me to sup with them."

"I see," Otis smiled, raising his bushy brows. "Then be off with you. Don't keep Captain Heard's shutters waiting!"

"Thank thee, Richard Otis."

With his master's blessing, Eb Varney placed his hat on his sweat-dampened head and exited the sooty forge. His lungs craved the fresh outdoor air, and he inhaled deeply, giving due thanks for the late afternoon sun. Glancing down Cart Way, he recognized Absalom Hart and Stephen Otis just leaving Waldron's mill. On most days, the men and boy bade each other good afternoon and parted ways, since Eb's home was to the west of town. But today, Eb hailed them and ran up to join them.

"Good afternoon, gentlemen," he greeted them politely. "May I walk with thee? Dame Heard invited me to help with the hinges."

Absalom Hart smiled at the teenager. "Another pair of hands is always helpful, Eb."

Eb flashed them both a grateful smile as he joined them in the center of Cart Way. Stephen Otis's home was next to his father's, so before departing he shook both their hands and said, "Good day to you both. Mayhap in the coming week Margaret and I will have you both over to sup."

"Looking forward to it," Absalom replied, and Eb mumbled his own reply, then fell into step with Absalom as they ambled toward Little Hill. Their shadows lilted to the left, mingling, then separating again on the dusty road. As they passed the Quaker meeting house, Eb glanced at a cluster of wild violets growing in the small cemetery. The violets reminded him of Alice's eyes, and he was considering stopping and picking a handful of them for her when he became aware Hart was asking him a question.

"Where did you go just now, Eb?" Absalom asked.

"Pardon?"

"I was asking, how many more years of apprenticeship have you yet with Old Man Otis?"

"Two," Eb replied. "Then I become a journeyman if the guild

accepts my work," he added, gazing longingly at the violets as he and Absalom passed them.

"'Tis another five-year commitment, that." Hart commented. "Good future for you."

Eb smiled thoughtfully. If he could get Alice alone for a quiet moment, he was going to ask her—ask her what? Would thee marry me when I've returned from my journeymanship in seven years' time? No, he couldn't ask that. He had never even made a real attempt to court her.

The two continued on in companionable silence until they reached Little Hill. Past the palisade gate they found Captain Heard outside his workshop, a pair of saw horses and his tool box set out in preparation for the repairs. He raised a hand in greeting, and Eb's glance strayed toward the house. *Therein lies Alice Hampton*, he thought, enjoying a pleasant quiver of anticipation as he imagined her at the hearth, gently stirring a pot of stew or sitting demurely at her spinning wheel.

"Ebenezer!" Captain Heard greeted warmly, extending his hand to the young Quaker. "Elizabeth told me you'd be lending your services as well. Good to see you both. Won't take long to get this shutter fixed, with three pairs of hands. Then we can enjoy Elizabeth's stew and Alice's apple pie."

The last three words were spoken directly to Eb in a tone that brought another embarrassing flush to his long face. *Is there no one in this town unaware of my feelings for Alice Hampton?* Then, glancing at the house again, he saw Alice herself standing on the stoop, water bucket and ladle in hand.

Chapter Four

*A*lice Hampton met Ebenezer Varney's gaze across the yard and groaned inwardly. He looked so obviously cow-eyed at her she wanted to turn back in the house and shut the door, but Dame Heard had asked her to take water to the men. "Why couldn't she have sent Grace or Emmie?" Alice grumbled to herself. Next to the thin, gawky Quaker boy stood Absalom Hart, broad shoulders flaring out over narrow hips. *It would take three, maybe four Ebenezer Varneys to equal one Absalom Hart in stature alone.*

With an exaggerated sigh, she arranged her face in more pleasant lines and approached the men, her gaze fixed on Absalom like a horse wearing blinders.

"Good afternoon," she said, smiling prettily at Absalom. "'Tis hot, and 'twill be awhile before supper's ready. I'll leave this water with you."

"Thank you, Miss Hampton."

"Thank thee, Alice Hampton."

Although both Absalom and Eb spoke at once, Alice continued to ignore the latter. She handed Absalom the bucket, and when his warm fingers touched hers, she almost swooned as a pleasurable wave of excitement shot up her arm. With his other hand, Absalom tipped his hat graciously at her, then dipped the gourd ladle into the bucket. She watched entranced as he brought the vessel to his lips, his Adam's apple bobbing with each swallow. Water trickled from the corner of his mouth, cutting a damp path through a forest of black stubble, and she wondered what it would be like to be kissed by a man with stubble.

Finished, Absalom passed the ladle and bucket to Eb. Her mind searched frantically for an intelligent way to excuse herself when Dame Heard called from the stoop.

"Alice, bring in some more wood on your way back in."

"Aye, ma'am," she replied too softly for Dame Heard to hear as her eyes strayed to the several cords of wood stacked neatly against the palisade. She smiled at Absalom and with palpable reluctance crossed the yard to the wood pile. She heard the men return to their work, engaging in easy conversation.

"The pane of glass should be in by now," Captain Heard was saying. "Would you be heading to Portsmouth within the week?"

"I will," Absalom confirmed. "'Tis been over a month since I've seen Cassandra and she'd appreciate a visit."

Cassandra! Alice stopped in her tracks as her heart stilled. *So that's the name of the woman Absalom is wooing.* Carefully she removed a piece of wood from the pile, her ears tuned to the men's conversation.

"Have you still not convinced her to move to Cochecho?" Captain Heard punctuated his inquiry with several hammer raps.

Alice heard Absalom chuckle softly. "Nay, she's more stubborn than I. After the nuptials she'd like to see me move to Portsmouth."

A cold, sick lump formed in her stomach. *Absalom is betrothed!* She reached for another piece of wood, her vision so blurred with jealousy she didn't see the protruding sliver until it had lodged itself painfully beneath her thumbnail. In pain and frustration, she dropped the wood in her arms and cried out. The piece of wood landed on her right foot, sending fresh pain coursing up her leg.

"Ouch!"

The hammering and conversation ceased abruptly. "Alice?" Captain Heard asked. "Are you hurt?"

Her eyes smarted with hot tears as she thrust the injured thumb into her mouth. Before she could reply, Eb Varney was beside her, retrieving the dropped wood.

"Allow me to get that for thee," he said, his gray eyes wide with concern.

She avoided Eb's gaze as he gathered an armful of wood. She dared not speak lest she burst into tears, which the men would probably attribute to her injuries. Miserable, she walked back to the garrison with Eb beside her.

"After we've supped, mayhap we could sit out and watch the sunset together," Eb Varney blurted.

His chatter was giving her a headache. What was he blathering about? She thought of the apple pie she had so lovingly prepared with the hidden A's and H's scored on the bottom crust. Oh, what did it matter now? Absalom was affianced to the mysterious Cassandra, lost to Alice forever. She felt sick and the scent of beef stew mingled with cooling apple pie made her stomach roil. She had no appetite. Indeed, she felt like she would never eat again.

"I think not, Eb," she heard herself say. "I've too many chores after supper."

"I'd be happy to assist thee with thine chores."

"Nay, not this night."

He looked crestfallen. "Another time, then?" he asked, opening the door for her while awkwardly balancing the armload of wood.

He was a nice boy and she didn't want to hurt his feelings, but he was becoming as irritating as the sliver beneath her nail. "I'll think on it," she muttered.

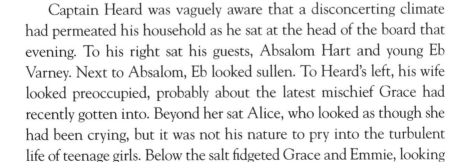

Captain Heard was vaguely aware that a disconcerting climate had permeated his household as he sat at the head of the board that evening. To his right sat his guests, Absalom Hart and young Eb Varney. Next to Absalom, Eb looked sullen. To Heard's left, his wife looked preoccupied, probably about the latest mischief Grace had recently gotten into. Beyond her sat Alice, who looked as though she had been crying, but it was not his nature to pry into the turbulent life of teenage girls. Below the salt fidgeted Grace and Emmie, looking suspiciously guilty of some devilment.

"I hear you had to arrest some drunken soldier, Ab," Heard said conversationally.

"Aye," the big man replied, tearing a hunk of bread in half and dipping it into his stew. "He was beating a defenseless young native. That's three arrests since they've arrived. I'll be relieved when the lot of them return to whence they came."

At the foot of the table Grace spilled the tankard of ale she shared with Emmie, and a pale stain bloomed on the board cloth.

"Watch what you're doing, clumsy girl!" Heard bellowed, embarrassed in front of his guests. "Clean that up then leave the board. No pie for you, either."

His wife's face seemed to pale slightly, which provoked him to ask, "Has the girl spawned any other catastrophes this day?"

Elizabeth Heard met her husband's angry face evenly and said, "Nay, husband. She has not."

"Well that's a blessing," he grumbled. Then seeing his guests had finished eating, he said, "'Tis a fine evening. Let's have a smoke, Ab. Alice, cut us each a slice of that pie and bring it out to us, will you?"

The girl's muttered "Aye, sir" was drowned out by Heard's chair legs grating against the floor boards as he rose from the table. As Absalom and the young Quaker followed suit, Heard asked, "Will you join us, Ebenezer?"

Eb peered at him from beneath the brim of his hat. Quakers didn't remove their hats indoors, which mildly irritated Heard, but he allowed Eb this one indulgence because he liked the boy.

"Nay, John Heard," the teenager replied, looking more downtrodden than usual. "I must get home before sundown. Thank thee for such a fine repast."

Eb tipped his hat graciously to Dame Heard and Alice and left quietly. Heard and Absalom lit their pipes and sat on barrels to enjoy the evening. Eb Varney's thin figure grew smaller as he descended Little Hill, his shoulders drooping as if great weights were bearing down on them. From his perch, Captain Heard eyed Absalom's modest cabin at the base of the hill.

"That dwelling of yours is fine for a bachelor," Heard said, gesturing with his pipe. "But surely not room enough for a family. Have you given any thought to expanding?"

Absalom laughed easily. "Haven't had time. It all depends on what Cassandra decides, first and foremost."

A soft gasp from behind them made the men turn to see Alice bearing two slices of pie in her hands. She looked oddly pained as she handed a plate and fork to Captain Heard, but he was not inclined to ask what pained her. She turned to hand Absalom his pie, but released the plate too soon and it clattered to the ground. To Heard's dismay, Alice burst into tears and fled to the wood pile against the palisade. Heard shook his head in bewilderment and was going to apologize to his guest when Absalom got to his feet.

"Excuse me a moment, sir," Absalom said, before ambling toward the girl who stood weeping amongst the corded wood.

No matter what their ages, Captain Heard thought as he drew deeply on his pipe, *women will forever confound me.*

"Miss Hampton?"

Ashamed, Alice raised her head from her arm. Her sleeve was damp with tears when she turned to face him. His gentle look of concern rent her heart.

"Miss Hampton, is something wrong?" he asked, handing her a handkerchief.

Could she even speak over the painful lump in her throat? She accepted the handkerchief and swiped at the tears that sat on her cheeks. "I—please forgive my clumsiness," she managed. "I'll cut you another slice."

She took a step toward the garrison, but he clasped her upper arm gently to stop her. Her heart leaped. Even after he released her arm she could still feel the warmth of his touch.

"Forget about the pie," Absalom said. "Have I done something to offend you?"

Offend her? *Only planning to marry another!* she wanted to say, suddenly angry. But she was so confused. Why should she be angry at him? He had every right to marry whomever he wished, and how could he know her feelings? She looked up into his handsome face and mustered as much dignity as she could.

"Nay, Goodman Hart," she managed.

"'Tis not my place, but you and Eb seemed to be at odds this evening. I know he cares deeply for you—"

What? Eb? Why was he talking about Eb?

"I haven't any feelings for Eb," she blurted, her cheeks growing hot.

His expression went from concern to confusion, and she suddenly couldn't bear being so near him.

"I do pray for your happiness when you and Cassandra are wed," she almost spat, trying again to move past him. Her mouth tasted foul after uttering the woman's name, and she resisted the compulsion to spit. Then she realized Absalom was smiling down at her with a look of bemusement.

"I'm not marrying Cassandra! What gave you that idea?"

Now she was completely confused. Wringing the handkerchief in her hands, she explained, "I heard you and Captain Heard talking about meeting her in Portsmouth, and Sarah Follett said—"

He put a hand on her shoulder and again her heart jumped. "Cassandra is my sister. She and her betrothed are considering moving to Cochecho, but are still debating it."

Had she heard him right? Her jaw sagged in astonished relief. A tiny flutter of hope tickled her soul.

"Do you ever think of marriage?" she heard herself say.

If he continued to look at her like that, she would swoon for certain. "May I speak honestly, Miss Hampton?"

"Of course," she croaked, suddenly afraid of what he might tell her.

"Only recently have I encountered a matrimonial prospect, but I'm inclined to wait two years."

Her heart plummeted again. So he *did* have someone in mind.

"What, pray tell, happens in two years?"

He took both her limp hands in his and her heart felt as though it would burst free from her ribcage.

"In two years, this prospect comes of age, and I'll formally ask her benefactor if I might court her."

Her ears were ringing. What was he saying? She looked stupidly at her own hands encased in his. Then she looked up into his face again, and realized what he had just said.

"That is, if the prospect is interested."

Angels in heaven couldn't have been happier than she was at the moment. She wanted to leap into his arms, but they were still within Captain Heard's view, so she contained her joy as well as she could. Speechless, all she could do was nod.

"Now I believe I'm ready for that pie," Absalom said, releasing her hands with a smile.

Alice's heart sang as she walked back to the garrison with him. Absalom Hart was interested in her! And she discovered this before he had eaten even a crumb of the enchanted apple pie!

Chapter Five

Johnny Horne and Jack Meader got their heads whacked by the tithingman's staff that Sabbath Day for fidgeting and whispering during the service. Teenaged boys were seated in the back, where the tithingman could keep a close eye on them.

Grace heard them but dared not turn around in her seat to look at them for fear her own head would get a knocking. She couldn't blame them for being restless. They, like everyone else, were excited about the upcoming festivities, especially the sham battle, which Grace and other ladies wouldn't be allowed to witness. Not that she wanted to witness it necessarily, but it seemed far more interesting than spending the afternoon praying and memorizing Bible passages. Wanalancet and his warriors were expected to arrive shortly after the service and everyone anticipated the continuing festivities. The men's side of the meetinghouse was especially crowded, because Captains Syl and Hathorne and some of their men had come to attend the service also.

Gunfire and cannon blasts would be heard all the way to Little Hill, and Grace intended to peer out the small window in the parlor chamber. *'T'would be worth a whipping to watch even a little of the excitement,* she thought, fidgeting with the whirligig wrapped around her wrist as she sat between Dame Heard and Emmie. The more she thought about it, the more restless she became. Her feet dangled off the floor and kicked the pew in front of her until Dame Heard laid a firm hand over her knees and stilled her with a chastising glare. With effort, Grace relaxed her restless legs.

As Reverend Pike droned on about the book of Daniel, Grace's thoughts returned to the secret meeting she had overheard in the mill. Everyone knew about the upcoming sham battle, so why were Major Waldron and those Massachusetts officers being so secretive? With one hand she tucked a stubborn curl beneath her coif while with the other she slid the mother-of-pearl button between her fingers, caressing its familiar smoothness.

Thwack!

The knob of the tithingman's staff struck Grace's coifed head so soundly her eyes teared. She peered up sheepishly into the stern face of the tithingman. Scowling, he held out his free hand expectantly.

"Give him your whirligig," Dame Heard hissed, clearly embarrassed.

Grace gripped the toy in her palm, rubbing her sore head with the other. "Nay!"

"You'll get it back if you behave yourself," the tithingman whispered, waggling his fingers.

For three years the whirligig had never left her. To be without it would be like going without one of her limbs. Other people in the meetinghouse were throwing disapproving glances her way, and when she still refused to comply, Dame Heard seized Grace's wrist and unwound the toy from it.

"Please don't!" Grace begged. "I won't fidget with it anymore! I promise!"

Grace watched in disbelief as Dame Heard dropped her precious toy into the man's waiting hand. She wanted to cry—her heart felt as if part of it had been torn away. Struggling to control her sobs, she watched as the tithingman strode purposefully to a series of pegs on the back wall. There among men's hats and women's cloaks he hung her whirligig.

She rubbed her wrist. It felt bare without the familiar cord and button. Sniffing, she turned forward. She wanted to drop her head in her hands, but feared she would receive another sharp blow. The unfairness fed her resentment until she was so angry her vision blurred. She clenched her fists in her lap until her hands ached. The sand in the hourglass seemed to cease flowing, and the benediction took a long time in coming.

She was so completely immersed in self-pity she barely noticed Reverend Pike's sermon being drowned out by barking dogs. Then, from the back pew, Johnny Horne, who had apparently been peering out one of the windows, stood up and cried, "Indians!"

Pennacook sachem Wanalancet, accompanied by his people and two hundred Wampanoags, walked proudly toward the white settlement. Two years before, he had converted to Christianity and remained neutral when it came to disputes between other tribes and the whites. He preferred peaceful neutrality like his father, Passaconaway, but his nephew Kancamagus was another matter.

"How can you let these English tell you where you can and cannot hunt?" Kancamagus grumbled, kicking a stone in his path. At nineteen, Kancamagus had already established a reputation among the whites, who addressed him as John Hawkins.

"Warring with the whites is a bad idea," Wanalancet explained. "More of them are coming, and it's best to extend peace, lest we live in a constant state of war."

Old fool! Kancamagus thought, his mood darkening as the white settlement came into view. *These English bring disease. They take our land. They treat us like dogs.* With these thoughts, his gaze fell on his younger brother, Menane, whose thin chest was wrapped in white men's linen. A diagonal welt slashed across the nine-year-old's face where some soldier's whip had landed. Until that recent abuse, Menane had always been a miniature version of Kancamagus. The brothers shared the same prominent nose and sharp jawline, although Menane's still retained the softness of childhood. Now his little brother walked beside him, his miniature bow in his hand and his little knife and tomahawk strapped to his waist.

"Keep an eye on your brother," Wanalancet said as they strode down Cart Way into the heart of Cochecho. "I don't want him getting any more hurt."

Kancamagus huffed in exasperation. He didn't want to be among the whites in the first place, and now he was expected to look after his little brother!

Dogs barked in alarm as the party of Indians ambled towards the meetinghouse. Major Waldron had arranged for them to meet there first, just as services were being let out. Kacamagus saw many white faces peering at the approaching Indians through the small diamond-shaped panes of glass. Most of them looked distrustful and concerned, and Kancamagus grinned in satisfaction. *Yes, be concerned,* the young Pennacook thought, resting a hand on his sheathed knife. *Better yet, be fearful!*

The entire congregation rose as one and pressed themselves against the leaded panes. Grace struggled to see, but was too small to look past the adults.

"Our guests have arrived!" Major Waldron boomed. "Reverend Pike, bid us a hasty benediction so we might welcome Wanalancet and his men!"

"Be seated, all!" Commanded Reverend Pike. Everyone dutifully returned to their assigned seats, but as soon as the benediction was over, men snatched their hats and women retrieved their cloaks from the hooks and streamed out of the meetinghouse. They assembled on the uneven flagstones with wary excitement.

Wanalancet halted and offered his hand to Waldron, then to Captains Syl and Hathorne. Grace had never seen the sachem up close before, and she gaped in awe at his proud stature. Adorned with feathers and wampum beads, he held his shaved head high. Behind him stood a scowling young Indian with piercing black eyes. Next to him stood Menane, still wrapped in Dame Heard's bandages. The gash along his face looked red and irritated. Involuntarily her right hand rose in greeting and he acknowledged her briefly before looking away.

The four men talked for a moment before Waldron gestured for Wanalancet to join him at his garrison. As the men departed, the women collected their children and headed to their various homes.

"Come along home now, girls," Dame Heard said, shoving Grace and Emmie along.

Watching the Indians depart, Grace instinctively felt for her whirligig to comfort herself. When she remembered it had been removed, she stopped, still on the flagstones of the meetinghouse. "Dame Heard! We can't forget my whirligig."

Dame Heard sighed. "Then go fetch it."

Grace almost tripped on an uneven flagstone as she ran back into the empty meeting house. Anxious to be reunited with her toy, she looked up at the empty row of pegs. Each one was bare.

A flicker of panic lapped at her. She looked on the floor, under the pews. No whirligig. The panic grew. *It's gone!* Her mind screamed. *My whirligig is gone!*

"Grace, come along now!" Dame Heard called.

"I can't find it!" she cried, her eyes welling up with fresh grief as she emerged from the meeting house. "Dame Heard, my whirligig is gone!"

Emmie offered her a sympathetic look but Dame Heard's hard features didn't soften. "Well, we've no time to look for it now. It may show up." She took Grace by the shoulders and steered her in the direction of home. "If it doesn't, you can make another one."

Grace found it hard to breathe and her stomach knotted. She covered her face with her hands and wept.

I don't want another one! She cried silently. *Father made that for me, and now it's lost forever!*

Steeped in misery, she collapsed on the hardwood bench just outside the meetinghouse. She felt as lost as she did after her parents had been killed.

"Compose yourself, Grace Hampton!" Dame Heard scolded. "Come along home now—"

"Grandmother, look!" Emmie interrupted, pointing to a group of young boys.

Somehow the clamor of young boys' shouts permeated Grace's cocoon of grief and she looked to where Emmie was pointing. Echoing the crowd of adults from the day before, she saw several young boys encircling a pair of combatants, excitedly cheering them on. She recognized Johnny Horne's lanky form wrestling with a smaller boy whose shirtless torso was wrapped in white linen. A small broken bow and quiver of arrows lay within the circle of boys.

"It's Menane," Grace breathed, her whirligig momentarily forgotten.

"Who?" Alice inquired, looking confused as Dame Heard marched toward the group of boys with Grace, Emmie and Alice in her wake.

The lacerations Menane had received the day before were bleeding and the linen strips were torn. Nevertheless, he fought the older boy with the ferociousness of a young bear cub. Menane unsheathed his knife and pointed the blade at Johnny's chest.

"Stop it this instant!" Dame Heard demanded, breaking through the circle of onlookers. Grace pressed close behind her, her vision scoured by sorrowful tears. She heard Emmie burst into frightened sobs as the woman approached the quarreling boys and seized Menane's arm before he could stab his opponent. "Stop it, I say!"

Alarmed by the commotion, Major Waldron traversed the distance from the mill to the meetinghouse with angry steps. Wanalancet and Kancamagus joined him, their faces stern. The audience groaned in disappointment when Major Waldron stepped forward and seized Johnny Horne by the shoulders. Likewise, Kancamagus retrieved his little brother.

"What's the meaning of this?" Waldron demanded, shaking the teenager by his nape. "Johnny Horne, how dare you cause such an embarrassing spectacle in front of our guests! I'll have you flogged and in the stocks for this outrage!" Turning to a crowd of militiamen, Waldron bellowed, "William Horne! Attend to your son! He's in need of discipline!"

With musket in hand, William Horne trotted up beside Waldron.

He regarded his son with a disconcerted scowl. "What's the boy done now, Major?"

"That little heathen threatened to stab me!" Johnny Horne spat, thrusting an accusing finger at Menane. Grace saw Johnny's nose was bleeding and his left eye was beginning to swell.

"He took it, Nidokan!" Menane countered, turning to Kancamagus. "He took it and he broke it!"

The look of hatred Kancamgus gave the white onlookers froze Grace's blood, and she shivered. She tried to catch Menane's eye, but he only looked from his brother to Wanalancet. For his part, Wanalancet looked woefully disappointed in the whole affair.

William Horne shook his head in tired disgust. "Johnny, can't you go one afternoon without causing mischief?" He came forward and grabbed his son by the ear. To Waldron and Wanalancet, he said, "My apologies, gentlemen. With your permission, Major, I'll escort him home and see that he stands in the corner for the rest of the afternoon."

"Pa!" Johnny whined.

Waldron looked satisfied with this outcome. "Very well, Horne. See to it."

Grace struggled to stifle a snicker as the elder Horne led his son away. She hoped a more severe punishment would follow, and was quietly relishing her nemesis's fate when Wanalancet spoke up.

"Take up your bow and quiver, nephew," Wanalancet instructed Menane. His low, even voice was in stark contrast to Waldron's angry bellowing. "Go back home and have your wounds tended to."

"Nda!" the boy cried. "I want to stay!"

"Major Waldron," Dame Heard said, raising her chin. "The youngster's wounds need attention. I insist on tending to them."

Kancamagus turned a fearsome look on Dame Heard and Grace saw the woman recoil.

"You whites have done enough," he snarled with such venom Grace shivered again.

"Then may the child join us?" Dame Heard implored, a slight quaver in her voice. "We'll be going the same direction, after all."

Grace regarded Menane while Wanalancet and Kancamagus consulted with each other in their own tongue. The little boy looked embarrassed and angry, and still refused to meet her eye. After much gesticulating, the two Indians arrived at an agreement, and Wanalancet said to Waldron, "We will allow him to walk with the women."

Menane scowled up into his uncle's face. "Nda!"

Before Wanalancet could say more, Menane broke away from the circle of onlookers. Kancamagus made a move to pursue his little brother, but Wanalancet stopped him.

"Let him go, Kancamagus," he said quietly.

"Now that that disruption has been dealt with," Waldron said, "Let's get on with the festivities!"

While the group of men and boys dispersed, Grace looked back to see Menane's small figure retreating down Cart Way. She felt Dame Heard's hands on her shoulders.

"Homeward, girls," Dame Heard said firmly.

With great reluctance Grace fell into step behind Dame Heard and Alice, with Emmie walking abreast of her. Menane disappeared into the woods, and she wondered what he would do. *He really ought to have let Dame Heard treat his wounds again*, she thought, remembering how the scab across his face had ruptured. She had completely forgotten about the whirligig until her fingers instinctively searched for the familiar smoothness of the button. Reminded of her loss, a fresh cloud of sadness settled over her. She stopped near a sweet fern shrub and removed a leafy frond. Crushing the green leaves between her fingers released a pleasant, sweet odor, and she raised the bruised leaves to her nose, inhaling deeply.

"I'll help you look for your whirligig on the morrow," Emmie offered softly. "It can't have gone far."

Grace clamped her lips against a sob. Looking into Emmie's earnest face, she attempted a grateful smile. "Thank you, Em," she managed.

"Grace, Emmie, I'll not summon you again," Dame Heard called over her shoulder.

"Catch up with Dame Heard, Emmie," Grace said. "I need to think."

"You'll be scolded if you don't go on home with us," Emmie reminded her.

"I care not," Grace said. "Pray, go on with Dame Heard and Alice."

Emmie hesitated long enough to give Grace's hand a supportive squeeze before she ran off to catch up with the others. Tossing the fern frond aside, she looked at her left wrist. It felt bare without the whirligig wrapped around it and she caressed the empty spot with fern-scented fingers.

Whack! Whack! Whack!

Sniffling, she raised her eyes and gasped in surprise.

Several feet from her sat Menane, hacking viciously at a maple sapling with his small tomahawk. Sapling limbs littered the ground around him, and when he looked up he scowled. Intrigued, Grace drew nearer.

"Leave me alone, girl!" he snarled, the sapling lying across his lap.

"Pray, what are you doing?" she asked, ignoring his rudeness.

"I am making a new bow," he explained tightly. "That boy broke my old one."

Although he appeared to dismiss her, Grace came closer and sat cross-legged on the ground. The determined curl again sprang free and she mindlessly tucked it back in. She watched him carefully remove more leafy limbs, exposing the pale wood beneath. He looked up from his work and scowled deeper, the laceration across his face oozing slightly.

"I said, leave me alone!"

"You needn't be so nasty to me!" she retorted. "I've been nothing but kind to you! I could have told that soldier where to find you, you know!"

"I do not need your kindness!"

The two children glared at each other, and instinctively Grace placed her right hand over her left wrist. Remembering her whirligig was lost, she looked away forlornly and swallowed against a sob.

"Do not cry in front of me," he said, going back to his work.

"I lost my whirligig," she blurted before she could stop herself.

He glanced at her with a look of confusion. "Your toy?"

"Aye."

"That is bad," he agreed, resuming his work on the sapling. "So go look for it and leave me alone."

He doesn't even pretend to care, she thought, at the same time wondering why it bothered her so much. She tried to think of an insulting retort when distant musket fire startled both children.

Bang! Bang!

The sham battle has begun! Grace thought excitedly as she and Menane scrambled to their feet. The boy secured his tomahawk and together they ran to look down Cart Way, in the direction of Waldron's mill.

"Grace Hampton!" Dame Heard demanded from several yards away. "Where are you?"

Ignoring the woman's anxious call, Grace stood shoulder-to-shoulder with Menane, her mouth agape at the scene by Waldron's mill. A thick cloud of smoke concealed the crowd of men, but Grace heard both English curses and Indian whoops.

BOOM!

"Grace!" Dame Heard's voice sounded closer and more frantic.

The cannon blast shook the ground and Grace clapped her hands over her ears. She watched in fearful confusion as Indians fell to the ground, their cries more painful to hear than the cannon blasts. As she turned to gauge Menane's reaction, he took off like a rabbit toward the ensuing chaos. Instinctively, she took a step to follow him when from behind her a hand seized her arm.

"Grace Hampton, come home with me now!"

Straining to pull away, Grace looked up into Dame Heard's scowl.

"Menane ran off!" she cried, pointing to the little figure disappearing down the lane. "He'll get killed!"

The woman's face blanched, her expression now more that of fear than anger as she watched the horrifying scene before her.

"What's happening?" Grace cried, tears blurring her vision.

"Methinks the Massachusetts soldiers are seizing their quarry,"

Dame Heard explained tightly, turning Grace forcefully homeward by the shoulders.

"What will happen to Menane?"

Dame Heard glanced back quickly, and Grace thought she detected a flash of regret in the woman's eyes.

"I know not," the woman said.

Captains Syl and Hathorne had each brought with them two cannons, which were now positioned like four grazing horses along the banks of the river near Waldron's mill. Absalom Hart stood near his friend Stephen Otis, his musket at the ready. An incessant premonition of impending disaster clung to him like a stench, and he drummed his fingers against his musket barrel nervously. Captain Heard stood nearby, as did Stephen Otis, built as solidly as his father with the same merry blue eyes.

"Why so glum, Hart?" Stephen asked, turning toward Absalom.

Absalom chewed his bottom lip thoughtfully. His eyes scanned the assembled Massachusetts soldiers, their bodies crisscrossed with bandoliers and powder horns. He recognized Duncan, who was handling his musket carelessly. Some of the Massachusetts soldiers had stationed themselves beside the four cannons.

"I've a bad feeling about this whole affair," he muttered.

Stephen slapped Absalom on the back. "That accursed sight of yours prevents you from enjoying a game of sport! Cheer up, my friend. All is well!"

It was agreed the Wampanoags would give first volley, and they did so good-naturedly, aiming their arrows and muskets harmlessly into the air.

Bang! Bang!

Captain Syl then gave the command for both Massachusetts companies to take their positions. The soldiers formed a horseshoe around the Wampanoags, leaving the open end blocked by the four cannons.

"Make ready!" Syl ordered.

Nay, this is all folly, Absalom told himself as his sense of disaster grew.

"Present upon your piece!" came the command.

Stephen Otis gripped his friend's arm. "By God, Hart! You're right! Methinks they mean to—"

"Open your pan…Give fire!"

Bang!

Multiple muskets fired, filling the warm air with acrid smoke. The unsuspecting Wampanoags'screams turned into whoops of outrage, and those not hit by musket blast prepared to defend themselves.

BOOM!

The first cannon blast knocked several Indians off their feet, shattering the bodies of three. Absalom looked to Major Waldron for direction, but Waldron only quietly observed the siege while Wanalancet stood next to him, wearing a mask of sheer disbelief.

Menane's sore ribs hindered his breathing as he raced toward the chaotic scene. Grace's freckled face formed in his mind. *Stupid Turkey Egg Girl! If not for her, I'd be there in the fight right now!* He also harbored wrath toward Tall Kind Woman and Little Weeper. He hated having to explain the salved wounds and bandaged ribs to Kancamagus, who berated him for going to the white settlement alone. Seeing the white woman and girls sent an embarrassing flush to his cheeks, and he hated them for that. But he was also grateful for their kindness, and that left him confused.

And then that tall white boy had begun taunting him, grabbing for his bow. In the tussle, the bow had broken, renewing Menane's dislike for whites. He would have relished plunging his knife into his enemy's chest if Major Waldron and Kancamagus hadn't separated the two.

"Kancamagus, get Menane out of here!" Wanalancet bellowed when Menane ran up to his uncle. "This is a trap!"

The scene grew more chaotic by the moment, and Menane's ears rang from the musket blasts. Kancamagus grabbed Menane's arm. "Run to the woods and wait for us!"

"But I want to—"

BOOM!

"Menane, *go!*"

The unexpected cannon blast galvanized the terrified little boy more than his brother's orders. He fled, blinded by tears of fear and anguish. His bound ribcage prevented him from taking full breaths, and he tore at the white linen bandages frantically.

Ashamed of his cowardice, he was even more appalled to discover he was crying. *This has turned into a real battle, and here I am, running away like a child!* He rounded the corner of the white men's meetinghouse. A toe caught on one of the protruding flagstones and he fell, skinning both knees.

BOOM!

A second cannon blast rocked the ground and he sat there, wiping his eyes and nose on his hands. He was glad nobody saw him. He could collect himself, and maybe summon the courage to return to the fight like a man.

And then, something between the flagstones glistened white in the afternoon sun.

Curious, Menane picked it up. It was a polished mother-of-pearl button, pierced twice with a thin linen cord threaded through both holes. It felt warm and smooth in his fingers, and its iridescent beauty brought him a sense of comfort. Maybe it would provide some protection for him in battle. He held it for a moment, trying to recall where he had seen it before. Then he remembered.

This belongs to Turkey Egg Girl. The beautiful button winked at him as if to say, "But now I belong to you."

Hastily he tied the linen cord around his neck, the sounds of battle still raging behind him. The large button rested on his small chest like a medallion. It was a sign. It was a sign that today he would prove he was ready to be a warrior.

It took less than a second for Absalom and Stephen to react. Their muskets were primed and ready, but it would take too long to reload, so they resorted to their bayonets and swords after firing their first shots.

Choking on musket smoke, Absalom listened for Waldron's orders. In the chaos, it appeared to be Indian on white, meaning the peaceful Pennacooks were fighting both the Massachusetts soldiers and the Cochecho militiamen. Nothing could be heard over the outraged war whoops of the Indians and the cries of the whites. Absalom aimed his musket carefully at an approaching Wampanoag who brandished a tomahawk, his face ablaze with rage. He squeezed the trigger, dropping the warrior where he stood. The Indian's blood splattered onto Absalom's face.

"Behind you!" Stephen cried next to him. Absalom spun around to face another Indian—Wampanoag or Pennacook? He couldn't tell—wielding a large knife. Absalom jabbed this assailant with his bayonet, and the Indian went down. Absalom withdrew the bayonet from the man's chest and retrieved the dropped knife.

Thwttt!

Stephen screamed, and Absalom saw an arrow protruding from his friend's right arm. When Stephen dropped his musket, another Indian lunged at him, tomahawk in hand.

"Get down, Otis!" Absalom ordered, and Stephen obeyed, just as the warrior leaped in the air with a blood-curdling war cry. With the first Indian's knife in his hand, Absalom threw it. The blade sank into the warrior's throat, silencing his war whoop forever. Running to Stephen's aid, Absalom grabbed his friend by his good arm and dragged him behind the millhouse. Stephen's face was pale and his right arm hung limply, gushing blood.

"By God, Hart!" Stephen Otis breathed. "How did you know?"

Absalom tore off Stephen's sleeve and examined the wound. The arrow had penetrated deeply, but not clear through. While the pandemonium continued on the other side of the mill, Absalom unfastened an empty powder cartridge from his bandolier and handed it to Otis.

"Bite," he instructed.

Stephen took the cartridge between his teeth, blue eyes brilliant with pain. Absalom seized the arrow's shaft and with as much force as he could muster, drove it clear through Stephen's arm. Stephen, for his part, screamed behind the cartridge and promptly passed out.

Breaking off the arrowhead, Absalom then pulled the shaft out. Blood flowed freely, and he wrapped the torn sleeve around it as tightly as he could.

The chaos had somewhat subsided, and Absalom got to his feet. With his sword in hand, he peered around the millhouse. The Massachusetts soldiers had subdued and disarmed the surviving Wampanoags and were tying their hands together. Wanalancet had gained control of his Pennacooks, and Major Waldron stood with his hand on his own sword. Absalom went back to Stephen and hefted the unconscious man over his shoulders. Then he joined the rest of his militia as they milled about, awaiting their next orders.

What just happened? Absalom wondered, his face still stained with the first Indian's blood. His mind was clouded again, but his confusion was quickly replaced with a cold sense of dread.

Empowered by his new-found talisman, Menane raced back to the fight. He wished he had his bow. Defenseless, he watched, unsure what to do.

"Thieving little bastard!" a white man bellowed.

From the mass of fighting men, Menane recognized Duncan as he lumbered toward him, sword raised high. His face wore the same ugly grimace of rage as before, and he charged at the boy, releasing his own enraged battle cry. Menane froze in terror.

Thwtt!

Duncan's expression went from rage to surprise to pain as he stopped just a few feet from where Menane stood. Dropping his sword, he plunged face-down before Menane's bare feet. Behind him, Kancamagus stood, his face registering hateful satisfaction. Disregarding the fallen man's body, Kancamagus ran to his little brother and shook him by the shoulders.

"I told you to leave!"

"I wanted to help!"

Kancamagus shook his head in disapproval, then pointed at the mother-of-pearl button that hung from his brother's neck. "What's that?"

"It's mine," Menane said, putting a hand protectively over it. "I found it."

Kancamagus looked back at the battle, which seemed to be reaching an anticlimactic conclusion. "Let's get out of here."

Before Menane could protest, his brother had grabbed his arm and dragged him into the woods. Fingering the button, Menane was certain it had protected him from Duncan's sword. He would wear it forever, and it would keep him safe.

Chapter Six

ichard Otis's wife Rose and daughter-in-law Margaret observed the sham battle just outside the palisade of Richard's garrison. Like Dame Heard, they had intended to spend the Sabbath in prayer, but neither could resist watching the spectacle. Both women perched on a bench they had placed where they could see everything without having their eardrums shattered by musket blasts.

Rose had married Richard twenty-five years before, when he was thirty-six and she was twenty-two. Her anxious, fearful demeanor contrasted sharply to her husband's jolly disposition, and she was often tormented with sick headaches. In an attempt to relieve the headaches, the surgeon had performed bloodletting on each hand, piercing the vein between the thumb and forefinger. Despite his efforts, Rose continued to suffer grievously. As the various troops and Indians assembled, she alternated between picking at the scabs on her hands and rubbing her temples.

"I don't like this one bit," she complained to Margaret, who jostled baby Maggie on her knee.

"'Tis too many savages to keep in line. Why, they could turn on our men like mad dogs and slay them all without an ounce of remorse."

"Now, Mother Otis," Margaret chided softly, "the men look to be enjoying themselves."

She felt rather than saw Margaret's placating smile, but she knew Margaret worried about Stephen. The sun on her back suddenly felt too warm, and she dabbed perspiration from her brow with her apron. "In any case, Richard is getting too old for this nonsense. Just yesterday I told him—"

Bang! Bang!

Despite the distance, both women jumped and baby Maggie shrieked. Margaret shushed the baby, rocking her gently on the bench. Rose clapped her hands over her own ears and closed her eyes as a sharp pain bore into her head.

Bang!

Maggie was bawling now, but over the baby's wails Rose heard men shouting and what sounded to her like war whoops. She opened her eyes just when the first cannon fired.

BOOM!

What is happening? Where are Richard and Stephen? She couldn't locate them in the crowd of men as the fray escalated into a scene of sheer madness. Through the haze of musket and cannon smoke she saw several bodies fall and remain motionless. She and Margaret rose in unison from the bench.

"Look, Mother Otis!" Margaret cried, pointing toward the mill. "Yonder is Stephen! Goodman Hart's leading him toward Waldron's mill!"

At last Rose discerned Absalom Hart's hulking figure dragging her son away from the melee. She cried out when she saw the arrow protruding from Stephen's bloody arm. She was only slightly relieved when Stephen disappeared behind the mill. Absalom Hart was her son's best friend and known for his level-headedness in times of crises. Absalom would tend to Stephen.

But where is Richard?! She searched in vain for her husband's stocky figure, but to no avail. More gunfire from the Massachusetts soldiers exacerbated her headache and she sank back down on the bench wearily, massaging her temples with trembling fingertips.

"I see them!" Margaret cried excitedly, pointing with her free hand while Maggie squirmed against her other shoulder.

Rose looked up. The haze of smoke was beginning to thin, and the Massachusetts soldiers appeared to be securing the fugitive

Indians who had been living among the local Pennacook. Cochecho's militiamen slowly separated themselves from the soldiers, and she cried out in relief when she detected Richard's stocky form limping toward the mill, accompanied by John Heard. They were soon joined by Absalom Hart, who had an unconscious Stephen thrown over his massive shoulders. Both Otis women ran to meet their men.

"Da!" Little Maggie cried, seeing her father and grandfather.

"Richard! Richard, are you injured?" Rose demanded, looking from one man to the other with palpable concern.

"I'm all right, Rose," the blacksmith insisted, laying a hand on his wife's thin shoulder. "Just twisted my ankle is all."

Rose looked frantically at her son's pale face. Blood seeped through the tourniquet on his arm, emitting the unmistakable coppery odor. The scent brought on a wave of nausea, intensifying her headache further.

"He's lost a good deal of blood, Goodwife Otis, but he'll recover," Absalom Hart assured her in his deep, soothing tone.

Thank the Lord Stephen has such a brave and true friend, Rose thought. *And thanks also Richard's suffered nothing more than a twisted ankle!*

As they made their way back to the Otis garrison, Rose eyed the feverfew growing just outside the front door. Feverfew tea sometimes helped alleviate her headaches and she made a mental note to steep herself a pot as soon as she could.

Absalom gently deposited Stephen on his parents' board. Rose sank onto the hearth, still dazed and nauseated. Margaret placed Maggie in her arms, and she accepted her granddaughter indifferently while Maggie tended to Stephen's shattered arm.

The door burst open, startling Maggie and causing her to bawl again. Her husband's apprentice, Ebenezer Varney, rushed in.

"Pray, what happened?" Ebenezer demanded over Maggie's wails, his gray eyes wide beneath his wide-brimmed hat. "We heard the commotion, and it sounded not like innocent war games."

"Methinks Waldron was in league with Syl and Hawthorne," Richard Otis offered as Margaret applied pressure to Stephen's wound.

"He seemed surprised not at all," Captain Heard agreed, speaking for the first time.

"But why for?" Eb asked, looking stunned.

Before anyone could offer a reply, Stephen's eyes fluttered open and he moaned. Captain Heard gave a meaningful look to Absalom Hart, then turned to Richard.

"If our presence is no longer needed, Otis, Ab and I will go on to Little Hill."

"Aye, go on to your household," Richard said, assisting his daughter-in-law with cleaning Stephen's wound.

"Shall I accompany thee, John Heard?" Eb volunteered, his voice cracking on a hopeful note.

Captain Heard regarded Ebenezer, then Absalom, in a peculiar way that would have intrigued Rose were she not so foggy-minded. Mercifully, Maggie's wails had subsided and the child had fallen asleep.

"Nay, stay with us, Eb," Richard Otis said from where his son lay. "We need you to help set this shattered bone."

Disappointment settled over the young Quaker's long face, and Rose felt a pang of pity for him. Everyone knew how sweet he was on Alice Hampton, and everyone but Eb himself understood the feelings were not mutual. As Captain Heard and Absalom Hart departed and Eb took his place at the board near Stephen's head, Rose got up from her seat and carefully placed Maggie in her cradle near the hearth.

"Mother Otis, could you tear us some more bandages?" Margaret asked.

"Aye."

Rose took a step toward the trunk where scraps of linen were stored for just such a purpose, but when she passed by the board where her son lay prone, she detected a fresh whiff of blood, and barely made it out the garrison door before vomiting onto the feverfew bush.

Alice jumped at the sound of the first musket reports. When the barrage of cannon fire began, she feared for Absalom, and bit her knuckles until they bled.

"Oh, Dame Heard," Alice exclaimed when Dame Heard returned, dragging a weeping Grace into the house, "Do you think anyone is getting—hurt?"

"Return to your seat, Alice," Dame Heard ordered firmly, but Alice saw concern lining the woman's own face. "Emmie, hand me the Bible and open it to—"

BOOM!

Alice wrung her hands and peered out the window. She took no notice of Grace and Emmie, who fidgeted on the hearth like a pair of fledglings on a tree branch. As Dame Heard began reading from Ephesians, disturbing images of Absalom lying with his chest blown open taunted Alice, and she wanted to run screaming from the garrison to make sure he was unharmed.

Only when Dog announced someone's approach did Dame Heard set aside her Bible and open the door. The palisade gate was opened, and Captain Heard, Absalom and Elder Wentworth entered the yard, barring the gate behind them. Alice gasped in horror when she saw Absalom covered in blood. Wild with concern, she ran toward the men, stopping just short of throwing her arms around Absalom's neck.

"What's happened?" Dame Heard demanded, running out the door with Grace and Emmie in her wake.

"Near as we can figure," Captain Heard said, wiping his sweaty brow, "Waldron was in league with Syl and Hawthorne to apprehend those fugitive Wampanogs."

"Connivin' whoreson," Elder Wentworth muttered. "He could have let the militia know of such plans, and not surprise us all."

"Are any of you hurt?" Dame Heard inquired, shooting Elder Wentworth a scathing look.

Aye, are you hurt, Absalom?! Alice ached to ask.

"'Tis not my blood," Absalom answered Dame Heard, but his reassuring look was directed at Alice. "Some's from an Indian, some's from Stephen Otis. He took an arrow in the arm. Shattered the bone."

'Tis not my blood. 'Tis not my blood. The words echoed in Alice's head, and she sighed with relief.

"We saw no other injuries to the militiamen," Captain Heard continued as they approached the garrison. "I daresay we were as surprised as those unsuspecting Indians."

"Alice, fetch a clean shirt from the trunk for Absalom," Dame Heard ordered, reverting back to her authoritarian manner. "Grace, draw a bucket of well water. I want to get that shirt soaking afore the stains set."

As Alice headed for the trunk in the hall, the others assembled around the board. Kneeling before the large wooden chest, she gave a silent prayer of thanks that Absalom had not been harmed. Nonetheless, her hands trembled as she worked the latch and lifted the lid. Selecting a white linen shirt, she returned to the parlor just as Captain Heard said, "Once the soldiers fired those first muskets, we realized this was no game. Madness ensued, and Waldron just stood there—"

"I'd trust ten of those savages afore that deceitful bastard," Wentworth interjected.

"Elder Wentworth," Dame Heard said, turning on the old man as they entered the parlor. "Speak one more vulgarity on the Sabbath and I will insist you leave this house immediately."

Wentworth glared at her with his rheumy eyes before grudgingly looking away. Grumbling, he took the only chair in the house, at the head of the board, leaving the others to sit on benches or barrels.

Grace returned, well water sloshing onto the floor, a curly lock falling over her eyes. With evident exasperation, Dame Heard snatched the bucket from Grace's hand, splashing even more water onto the floor herself.

"Grace, mop up that spill afore someone slips, careless girl! Goodman Hart, go wash yourself in the hall." Handing a fat tallow candle to Grace, Dame Heard ordered, "Light this candle—no, better to have Alice do it. You're likely to burn yourself. Alice," Dame Heard said as Absalom passed into the adjoining room with the water

86

bucket, "light this and take it to Goodman Hart. The hall gets dark this time of day."

It was indeed becoming evening, and with the shirt pressed against her chest, Alice carefully lit the tallow candle and placed it in its holder. Captain Heard continued to tell about the day's events, and Alice was only half-listening when she walked into the hall where Absalom waited for his clean shirt.

He was bent over the water pail, his hands concealing his face as he rubbed away the blood. He had removed his hat, and water glistened on his brown curls. His bloodied shirt was untucked from his breeches, the gaping front lacing exposing a mass of dark chest hair. Her mouth suddenly went dry and when she cleared her throat, he looked up, his handsome face freshly scrubbed.

"I thought—Dame Heard said it was growing dark and you might need a candle," she stammered, setting it next to him as her cheeks flushed hotly.

"Thank you, Miss Hampton," he said, giving her a smile that made her feel like a pat of butter in hot sunlight. He wiped his face and hands with the soiled shirt, then crossed his arms to remove the garment, hesitating as he gave her an expectant look.

"Miss Hampton," he said pointedly.

She was so flustered she didn't know what he meant, and suddenly she realized he desired her to leave, or look away, or something.

"Oh! Of course!"

Feeling stupid, she turned her back, facing the wall where the candlelight had thrown his silhouette. She watched in silent admiration as his shadow image removed the soiled shirt. Her eyes devoured the V of his bare torso, and she was so lost in private thoughts she didn't hear him at first when he addressed her.

"Miss Hampton, may I have that clean shirt?"

Keeping her eyes on his silhouette, she held the shirt out behind her, and when his fingers brushed hers she bit her lips against a shriek of joy. They were cool and damp from the well water, and she shivered deliciously. Releasing the shirt, she listened and watched the silhouette put on the shirt. Oh, why couldn't they begin courting *now?* Better yet, why couldn't they elope, and exchange vows of everlasting love to each other.

She heard his footfalls behind her, and watched his shadow merge with hers. She was wishing shadows had substance and the sense of touch when Dame Heard summoned her from the parlor.

"Alice! Leave that shirt to soak and come watch the hearth for me."

"Aye, ma'am," she replied faintly. She turned to face him, and her heart swelled like rising bread dough.

"Thank you, Miss Hampton."

She accepted the bucket with the bloodied shirt in it. "Will you call me Alice?" she asked in a quavering whisper.

His smile warmed her even more, and then he placed a knuckle under her chin and tilted her face up slightly. She was dissolving into nothingness under his solicitous gaze, happier than she could ever remember being.

"Alice! What's taking so long? Don't leave that candle burning in there."

And then he said her name.

"Thank you, Alice."

She had never heard anything sweeter.

The Wampanoags who weren't killed outright were bound by ropes at the wrists. More rope encircled their necks, and they were lashed together in a queue like a team of oxen, in preparation for their forced march back to Massachusetts.

Like the rest of the Pennacook, Menane was confused and outraged at the unexpected turn of events. Kancagmagus argued with Wanalancet the entire trek home, inciting the others to swear revenge. Unlike most of the younger Pennacook, Menane tagged along with his brother and uncle, listening with interest as they disputed how best to deal with the situation. He knew the whites could not be trusted— the soldiers' actions confirmed that—but then he remembered Tall Kind Woman, and how she tended to him after the soldier beat him. She seemed genuinely concerned for his welfare. And although he found her irritating, Turkey Egg Girl had somehow burrowed into his conscience, and he often saw her freckled face in his mind. Could it be that only white men were dishonest, but the women could be trusted?

"We will destroy the whites for what they did!" Kancamagus insisted, encouraged by his friend Wahowah as they approached their camp.

"Nephew, we need to discuss this in council," Wanalancet chided. "It's never wise to act with a hot head."

Menane's Aunt Toloti stepped out of the wigwam where his ailing grandmother lie. Her broad face wore an expression of fresh sorrow, and the sickening stench of death wafted from her graying hair. "I just heard what happened," Toloti said. She was Wanalancet's sister, and they shared identical profiles. "Will this bring on new war with the whites?"

"I'm afraid it will come to that," Wanalancet said. "How is our mother?"

Toloti's countenance grew sadder as she looked from Wanalancet to Menane, and Menane felt a cold sense of dread settle over him. "The fever took her while you were away, nephew. We were washing her just as you returned."

Menane tried to digest this news, but he felt strangely numb. Wanalancet put a hand on his shoulder, but he derived no comfort from his uncle's touch. He looked up into Kancamagus's face, but his brother took the news stoically, the rage toward the whites still evident in his face.

"We have to act now against the whites!" Kancamagus reminded his uncle impatiently.

Wanalancet's usual calm demeanor deteriorated, startling Menane out of his numbness. The old sachem turned to Kancamagus, matching the young warrior's vitriol. "We will discuss that in council, but only after we've laid our sister to rest."

Clearly dissatisfied with this, Kancamagus glared at his uncle before stomping off. Still feeling detached from his surroundings, Menane watched his brother join his peers, and then his gaze fell on the wigwam where his grandmother's body remained.

His uncle's hand on his back gently urged him forward, and as they entered the wigwam, the stench of death became stronger. The body would be buried in a seated position, with her head facing southwest. Her finest jewelry and baskets would be buried with her, and Menane would undergo a period of mourning. A deep regret stabbed Menane's heart when he saw her lying on her bedframe.

Toloti had washed his grandmother and smoothed the long gray hair, but Toloti had not been able to remove the sorrowful expression from the old woman's face.

Part Two

Thirteen years later
June 1689

> *"Why, I could raise one hundred men as easily as raising a finger."*—Major Richard Waldron's reply when Pennacook leader Masandowit asked him, "Brother Wadron, what would you do should strange Indians come?"

Chapter Seven

Tuesday, June 18

*A*s time passed, the growing hostilities between the whites and the Pennacooks caused Major Waldron to designate specific times of day during which Pennacooks could enter the settlement, and only for purposes of trade. Despite this daily reminder, the disastrous sham battle faded into an unpleasant memory the whites chose to forget.

Having been widowed the year before, Dame Heard spent most of her time either at her wheel or her loom. Now sixty-three, the skin at her throat had become thin and crepey, but her jawline still retained its notable prominence. She had nearly become a recluse, were it not for Grace remaining at the Heard garrison. And so it was a great shock to many when the Widow Heard announced that she desired to visit relatives in Portsmouth.

Widow Heard sat at the head of the board, regarding her guests thoughtfully. Her daughter Mary and son-in-law John Ham sat to her left. Across from them sat Emmie, twenty-one and newly married to Johnny Horne, whose evolution from a contentious bully to a mature young man surprised everyone. Widow Heard smiled at her granddaughter, and strongly suspected it was Emmie's gentle demeanor that brought him to the right path. Next to Emmie, Grace idly stirred her venison stew, unruly curls spilling from beneath her coif. Her freckled face looked pensive as she stared into the gourd bowl.

Ah, Grace. Such an unpredictable girl, that one. Unlike her happily married sister, Grace had assumed the persona of an industrious single woman. When it became apparent that no matrimonial prospects were likely, Captain Heard built her a cheese press, and with her own egg money she purchased a fawn-colored Guernsey heifer she named Queenie, due to the crown-shaped blaze between the cow's gentle eyes. Grace had since become a renowned cheesemonger all over Stratford County. As Captain Heard's health declined, his carpenter's workshop was slowly converted to a cheese house. Where his workbench and tools were once housed, Grace's cheese ladders, press, and kettle now took prominence. After the transformation from workshop to cheese house was complete, Captain Heard's carpentry tools found a new home in Absalom Hart's shed. Sometimes the scent of sawdust lingered, conjuring up images of Captain Heard. Although he had been a strict benefactor, his recent passing left a painful void in the Heard household, and Widow Heard knew that even Grace missed him.

"I've spoken to Goodman Hart," Widow Heard said suddenly, bringing everyone's eyes up from their bowls. "He's agreed to take me to Portsmouth in two days' time."

Mary's eyes widened. "Why, Mother?"

"Because, dear heart," Widow Heard explained, "if I stay in this garrison much longer, I'll go mad. We can visit the cousins for a week."

"We?" everyone chorused.

Widow Heard reached for the bread and cut herself a slice. "Aye. I want us all to leave this sorrowful place. Elder Wentworth has agreed to keep watch on the garrison and Alice will keep up the garden." When John Ham and Johnny Horne, both farmers, looked prepared to protest, she added, "Your crops will manage fine on their own for a week, and Absalom will tend to your livestock."

Their faces still registered uncertainty until she added, "Goodman Hart will borrow Goodman Meader's cart and Jericho to transport us."

Utilizing Jack Meader's trusty ox and cart apparently convinced them. The two men shared a satisfied look across the board, then John Ham smiled at his mother-in-law.

"I could use the distraction myself. What say you, Horne?"

"Aye," Johnny Horne agreed around a mouthful of stew.

Amid murmurs of happy surprise, Widow Heard surveyed the table, and saw one face lacking in celebratory good cheer. Grace's eyes had returned to her bowl, and she looked somewhat forlorn.

"Grace?" Widow Heard said, "I'm including you on this journey."

"Thank you, ma'am," Grace said, shoving a curl under her coif before propping her head on one elbow. "But if you don't mind, I'd rather not. Queenie's due to calve any day, and I want to be here."

Emmie's lower lip protruded, and Widow Heard felt a pang of disappointment herself. Over the years, she had grown fond of Grace, despite the accident-prone girl's penchant for getting into trouble.

"Oh, do go with us!" Emmie pleaded, placing a hand on her friend's arm. From her seat at the head of the board, Widow Heard suspected more was troubling Grace than an enceinte cow.

"Absalom can check on Queenie," Widow Heard said. "Pray give it some consideration at least."

Grace's despondent look pierced Widow Heard's heart. She detected the glimmer of tears in her blue eyes when the girl finally looked up at her.

"I think not, ma'am." Pushing her bowl aside, Grace rose from the table. "Excuse me. I want to get the evening's milking done afore it grows too dark."

What's got that girl in such a doleful state? She watched Grace pluck her cloak from its nail and head to the barn. After the door closed softly behind Grace, Widow Heard turned to her family, who regarded her expectantly.

"Grandmother," Emmie said, worry creasing her brow, "may I see to Grace?"

Widow Heard smiled at her gentle-hearted granddaughter. Emmie and Grace had been best friends for sixteen years, and if anyone could discover the source of Grace's melancholy, Emmie could.

"Aye, you may."

Rising to her feet, Emmie came to the head of the board and planted a loving kiss on her grandmother's cheek before leaving for the barn.

Widow Heard forced a smile said to Mary, "Pray, let's clear the table while the men have their evening smokes. When Grace and Emmie return, we'll have prayers."

Clouds painted a deep blue swelled against the sky, and Grace smelled approaching rain as she headed toward the barn. She opened the door with a *creak*, and her mood lifted when Queenie looked up from her trough and greeted her with a mellow *moo*. The scent of hay and cow brought a smile to her face as she placed the bucket beneath Queenie's engorged udder and seated herself on a milk stool.

"Won't be long now for you, girl," she cooed, pressing her cheek against the cow's turgid abdomen. She felt the calf stir within as she grasped two fleshy teats in each hand and sent four streams of milk hissing rhythmically into the bucket below. Blue veins branched out beneath the udder's pale skin. Nothing gave Grace more pleasure than tending to her dairy business, and she indulged in the peaceful solitude until she heard the door creak once more. She turned around on her stool.

"I do wish you'd reconsider and come with us to Portsmouth," Emmie remarked from the doorway. "'T'will be such fun to see our cousins again!"

In truth, the cousins to whom Emmie referred were not kin to Grace, but she didn't bother to remind Emmie of that fact. Instead, she waited until Emmie came to stand near Queenie's head before she replied, "I want to be here when the calf arrives."

Emmie scratched Queenie's ears and pouted. "Can't Elder Wentworth keep an eye on her for you? He could also watch the cheese house—"

Grace released a derisive snort, imagining Elder Wentworth posting Dog the Fourth—or was it Fifth now?—outside the cheese house. "You and your family go and tell me all about it when you return."

Emmie looked for a moment as though she might pursue the

argument further, but an instant later relented, exhaling in defeat. A slight smile curled her lips and her face flushed pink. "Then if you won't come for when I make the announcement to the rest of the family, I'll tell you now...."

Grace shot a look of surprise at her friend. "Emmie! Truly?"

Emmie blushed deeper and nodded. "Mother says I'm a good three months along now."

"Have you told Johnny?"

"He suspected weeks ago."

"Oh, Emmie! I'm so happy for you!" Grace smiled, still maintaining the rhythm of her milking. "You're as far along as Alice is! I'm glad it didn't take as long for you as it did her and Absalom. Married eleven years and finally she's with child! How are you feeling?"

Emmie suddenly looked tired—Grace recognized the aura of expectant motherhood. How could she have missed it?

"I'm grateful I'm not as sick as poor Alice, although I do get queasy now and then."

Grace smiled sympathetically. "The very smell of my cheeses sickens Alice. Mayhap you don't feel up to going to Old Dick's with me on the morrow?"

"Nay, but Johnny will escort you if I ask him."

Grace missed the days when women could walk freely into town without an armed male escort. But recent tensions between the whites and the Indians had grown volatile.

"I have six cheeses to deliver, and I'm perfectly capable of delivering them myself," Grace said stubbornly. "'T'isn't that far to the trading post."

"But Grace—"

"I'll be fine," Grace assured her. "Hardly an Indian comes into town early, and if they do it's usually women with children, and they pose no threat."

Emmie's expression grew more anxious. "But that nasty savage Wahowah's been seen in town twice this week. He's frightfully dangerous, Grace. I really wish you'd wait, at least until Absalom comes home from the mill."

After Captain Heard's death, Absalom Hart had somewhat assumed the role of head of the household for the Widow Heard and Grace. He and Alice lived in his cabin at the base of Little Hill, but much of their time was spent behind the garrison's palisade.

"Ab doesn't finish work at the mill until evening," Grace reminded her. "And Old Dick wants these cheeses before noon."

The milk bucket was filling up fast, and Emmie handed Grace a second one. As Grace exchanged the full one for the empty, Emmie asked, "But what's got you in such a dark mood? You looked as though you were about to cry earlier."

Grace stared thoughtfully into milk bucket. She had a good, productive life, so what *was* causing her dark mood?

"I know not," she admitted.

Emmie offered an encouraging smile. "You'll find a husband one day. I just know it."

Grace resisted the urge to roll her eyes. She was happy for Emmie and Alice, and glad that they were content in their marriages. But she rather liked being an independent single woman, and the drudgery of being someone's wife held little appeal for her. But she couldn't deny she felt a lack of...something...in her soul.

"I don't want a husband," she confessed as Queenie's ropey tail swished against her back.

Emmie looked stunned. "Every woman wants a husband."

"Not I."

Emmie looked befuddled. "Then what *do* you want, Grace Hampton?"

Grace considered the question. Sometimes on quiet summer evenings, she would creep out of the garrison, lean a ladder up against the cheese house and sit on the roof, alone. The lull of cows in the common pasture and the far-off cries of forest creatures provided a meditative backdrop while she gazed at the star-peppered sky and pondered her desires. "I know not, Em," she finally admitted. "But one day I hope I do."

Richard Otis sat on the stoop of his garrison, puffing clouds of blue smoke into the late summer air. He was seventy-four, widowed twice. After Rose succumbed to one of her sick headaches shortly after the sham battle, he married Anne Starbuck, whom he had also survived. Now married to twenty-seven-year-old Grizel Warren, the old blacksmith was the proud father of two-year-old Hannah. The child was the joy of his life, but also his greatest regret. It tore at his heart whenever she sat on his lap or grasped one of his fingers with her tiny hand, for he could only imagine the beauty of her sweet face. He delighted in having her sit on his lap, where he could revel in the sweet scent of youth that emanated from her covered head. For years his field of vision had grown smaller and smaller until he was now completely blind. Richard heard the squeak of the palisade gate and cocked his head. He recognized Ebenezer Varney's shuffling footfalls. His former apprentice, now master blacksmith, took over Otis's forge after he returned from his three years as a journeyman. Eb had left with a heavy heart shortly after Absalom Hart and Alice Hampton announced their intentions to marry, but later returned having reconciled his fate. Eb delved into his blacksmithing, and became one of the best apprentices Richard had ever had.

"Good evening to thee, Richard Otis," Eb said as he drew near. "I've brought an old friend of thine."

Interest flickered in Richard's once-merry blue eyes. "What's that you say, Varney?" he asked around his pipe.

He felt Eb grasp his forearm, then place something in his hand. His fingers wrapped around the familiar smoothness of a wooden handle, and the heft of the object alone told him it was a twelve-pound sledgehammer. He caressed the trusty old tool and smiled.

"After all these years, I found it buried in the charcoal heap. I since have acquired another, and need not two."

The old blacksmith's fingers fondled the implement lovingly. Although he would never wield it again, it comforted him to have it back in his hand. Tears welled in his eyes and he found himself speechless.

"Thank you, Eb," he finally managed.

"Thou art welcome," Eb replied.

A tear traveled down the old man's creased cheek as he remembered all the times Eb wielded the sledge, hitting the mark every time. "You were the best striker I ever worked with, Eb."

"I thank thee, Richard Otis," Eb replied.

"I trust you brought your violin, also," Richard said around his pipe. "You know my granddaughter especially looks forward to singing along with that fiddle of yours."

He could sense the young Quaker's smile in his voice. "That I did, Richard Otis."

They sat together on the stoop in companionable silence, listening to Grizel wash the supper dishes, occasionally admonishing little Hannah for some slight transgression. As twilight bathed the settlement, he expected Stephen, Margaret and Maggie to arrive soon. They, along with Ebenzer, had lately been spending their nights within the Otis garrison as tensions between the settlers and Pennacooks grew more uncertain.

"You missed supper," Richard said, setting the sledge down reverently beside him.

"I've eaten, thank thee. But I assure thee, I'll have room for popcorn."

Richard smiled. Once everyone who intended to spend the night in the garrison had arrived, it was customary at the Otis garrison to serve popcorn. Drizzled in butter and sprinkled with salt, it would be served in an earthen bowl and passed around while stories were told and games were played.

"Papa!"

Little arms went around Richard's neck from behind, and he clasped the pudgy hands with one of his own.

"There's my good girl," he said, his heart swelling with love. "Did I hear your mother scolding you just now?"

"Nay, Papa," the child denied in her sweet lisp. "Blow me rings, Papa!"

Richard obliged, taking a long drag on his pipe, filling his lungs with smoke. To his little daughter's delight, he emitted three perfect rings of blue smoke that quickly vanished into the summer air.

The palisade door creaked open once again, and Hannah squealed, "Maggie!"

Richard chuckled as Hannah released her grip on his neck and pushed past him and Ebenezer. He envisioned the child running across the yard toward Stephen's fourteen-year-old daughter Maggie, to whom she had become intensely attached.

"Good evening, Pa!" Stephen Otis called. "Yo there, Eb!"

"Good evening, son," Richard replied, his ear still ringing from Hannah's shrill outburst. "Help me up, my knees have gone stiff. Now that we're all here, let's have a game of noddy afore we pop the corn."

"A better idea I never heard," Stephen remarked agreeably, taking his father's arm and helping him to his feet.

"Father Otis," Margaret said, "Is Grizel about? I have that dyed wool for her and Stephen finished repairing your boots."

After his arm was injured by an Indian's arrow thirteen years before, Stephen could no longer work at Waldron's mill and had since took up cobbling.

"She is, Daughter," Richard confirmed. "Go on in. I smell rain on the way."

Margaret glided past him, followed by Maggie, who gave her grandfather an affectionate kiss on the cheek. With his family near, Richard smiled contentedly. Even without sight, he was grateful for all he had.

Chapter Eight

*R*ainfall had puddled overnight, causing Grace to step carefully as she made her way to Waldron's. Water seeped through the sole of one of her shoes, dampening her woolen sock and souring her mood.

I'll have to pay Stephen Otis a visit, she thought grudgingly as she parked the creaking wheel barrow outside Waldron's trading post. Brushing an escaped curl from her face, she lifted three cheeses out of the barrow, nearly dropping them when an angry voice bellowed from inside.

"You lie!"

As she pushed open the door she saw a tall Indian pound his fist on Waldron's counter, the force of which sent the brass scales swaying.

"Nay, it's all here in the ledger, Wahowah," eighty-year-old Richard Waldron insisted, pointing at scribbled figures in his account book. "Last week you brought in forty beaver pelts, and that wasn't enough for a keg of powder."

"I brought you fifty pelts!" the Indian insisted, a scowl darkening his broad, hairless face. "Your scale is broken."

"Nay," Waldron contradicted. "My fist weighs exactly one pound on the scale, and 'tis an accurate counterweight. Bring in sixty this week to make up for last week's shortage and you can have your powder."

Grace watched this exchange from the threshold. She had

enjoyed strolling unescorted into town, despite the disapproving looks from men and her foot growing cold and wet. But now, seeing the unexpected Indian confronting Waldron, she hesitated, and ducked behind a bale of pelts to avoid being noticed. Wahowah was known for his nasty disposition, and the townspeople avoided him whenever possible. Peering over the musty-smelling furs, she saw Wahowah lean over the counter, his nose just inches from Waldron's.

"You will not live to cheat me again!"

Grace felt her spine go cold. She heard a gasp from the storage room and looked in that direction. Elsie Winston, Waldron's slow-witted servant girl, was cowering behind a hogshead of Jamaican rum. Waldron, however, seemed more annoyed than afraid as he met the Indian with an equally hostile glare.

"Threaten me again and I'll have you hanged. Now get out of my trading post and don't return until you have sixty beaver pelts."

Wahowah stood erect, his bare, tattooed back facing Grace. Then he turned on his mocassins and stalked towards the door, deliberately sending a bushel of apples tumbling in his wake. Before the last one stopped rolling across the knotty pine floor, the Indian was gone. Then from outside came a sickening *crash!*

Stepping over the spilled apples, Grace emerged from behind the pelts and gasped in exasperation. The Indian had upset her wheel barrow, and the three remaining cheeses sat like smooth white stones in the mud.

"How dare you!" Grace yelled from the doorway. The Indian kept his back to her and stomped out of town, the sun glinting off his shaved head. Infuriated, Grace ran back inside and placed the three cheeses down on Waldron's counter; then she returned to set the wheel barrow aright and retrieve the other three cheeses, wiping off as much mud as she could from each one before bringing them inside.

"Those three are ruined," Waldron commented, pointing at the soiled ones on the counter. "I saw them hit the ground."

Grace was in no mood for this. She glared into his hard face as she tried to control her temper. "The cheeses are fine. I wiped them off."

"I don't want those now," Waldron complained, his dark brows knitting above his nose. "I'll take the clean ones. Bring me back three fresh ones before noon today."

"There isn't any aged enough to sell but these six."

"Then you're not fulfilling your contract," Waldron replied. "Six cheeses every two months. That's the deal we struck."

For a moment, Grace wanted to grab the brass scales and send them crashing to the floor. But Waldron seemed to have dismissed her already as he dipped his quill in the ink pot and scribbled in his ledger. "I've noted that you owe me three cheeses by the end of this month."

The old man's insouciance infuriated her even more, and her nostrils flared. *I'll just bring these three back in two days and you'll be none the wiser, you old cheat!* She inhaled the combined scents of gunpowder, tobacco and cured beaver pelts, and struggled to arrange her face in more composed lines.

"Very well," she acquiesced, gathering the soiled cheeses in her arms. "Methinks I do have some at home that are properly aged."

"Then gather up those spilled apples on your way out and be gone with you," Waldron muttered, resuming his record keeping.

"Indeed I will not," Grace retorted as she collected the cheeses from the counter. "'T'was not I who spilled them!"

"Elsie! Come retrieve these spilled apples!"

The meek servant girl emerged from the storage room and scurried like a frightened mouse to do her master's bidding. She was nineteen, and had been bonded out to Waldron after his wife Ann passed away four years before. She met Grace's eyes briefly before kneeling to gather the spilled fruits.

Thank the Lord I'm not a timid mouse like poor Elsie. She pitied the young woman, and for a moment considered helping her, but decided against it. Standing as tall as her armload would allow, she turned on her heel and left, avoiding the apples that lay bruised on the pine floor.

As the proud buck dipped its antlered head into a patch of moist

105

grass, Menane raised his bow, aiming for the animal's tawny neck. Now twenty-two, he had established his reputation as a fearless warrior and a proficient hunter.

The scar on his face had faded with time and now resembled a white snake.Thus, when Menane reached adulthood, his childhood name was discarded and he was now called Wôbi Skog Wsizokw, or "White Snake Face."

He held his breath, his muscles as taught as the bow string, and was about to release the arrow when the buck raised its elegant head and looked eastward toward the white man's trail. Wôbi Skog Wsizokw heard the creak of wooden wheels. *Splash!*

"Hellfire and damnation!" a white woman's voice cursed.

The buck bolted, leaving Wôbi Skog Wsizokw with no choice but to lower his bow. Angered at the interference, he returned his arrow to its quiver and stalked in the direction of the disturbance. Ready to confront the intruder, he discovered it was indeed a white woman.

She was on her hands and knees in a large mud puddle, an upset wheel barrow and three round cheeses lying in the mire with her. Her linen cap had slid off her head and a mass of red curls spilled down her back. Her piteous state amused him and he began to laugh aloud, forgetting his lost quarry. The white woman looked up at him with a scowl framed by a constellation of freckles and mud spatter. *Turkey Egg Girl!* She knelt before him, covered in mud like a pig. "How dare you laugh at me!" she admonished as she struggled to her feet. She plucked the soiled cap from the puddle, wrung it out, and slapped it on her head. She faced him directly and her eyes grew wide. "*Menane?*"

He shook his head. "I am called Wôbi Skog Wsizokw now," he corrected her, stepping closer as she righted the wheelbarrow and plucked the cheeses from the muck. At her look of confusion, he indicated his prominent facial scar. "White Snake Face."

"Do you remember me?" she asked, her soiled fingers swiping a strand of mud-caked hair from her face. "I'm Grace."

The young Indian paused. He had never heard her name used. Or if he had, he had forgotten.

"Whites are not supposed to be trading now."

"I care not," she retorted, wiping mud from each cheese with her soiled apron. The futility of her efforts brought on a dejected pout and Wôbi Skog Wsizokw laughed again.

"Stop laughing at me!"

"If something is funny, I laugh," he said, grinning. She was amusing, that was for certain.

"Well, they weren't ruined before but they are now," she muttered, trying to clean her hands on her filthy apron. "Waldron will never buy them now." He watched her eyes travel up and down his body, and her face reddened beneath the mud before she averted her eyes. "Would you trade something for these cheeses? Mayhap you Indians won't mind a little mud."

"We do not eat your cheese," he said, offended that she would want to trade him a ruined product. "Nor your milk or butter. Hurts our guts." Was the girl not aware that Indians did not consume cow's milk in any form?

She sighed, apparently even more discouraged than before.

"Go home now," he said. "It is not safe for you to be out alone. Go home. I will watch."

She looked up at him in surprise, and he thought he detected gratitude in those peculiar blue eyes. Her mud-saturated bodice clung to her breasts which swelled above her stays.

"Thank you, Men— Wôbi Skog Wsizokw," she corrected herself, looking somewhat perplexed. "Will I—will I see you again?"

The request surprised him. "Do you want to?"

She looked even more flustered and her face reddened again.

"Go home," he said again in a firm but gentle tone.

He watched her turn, grasp the handles of the wheel barrow and resume her path homeward, her shoes squishing with each step.

"I appreciate your help so much, Sarah," Alice Hampton Hart said, rinsing the turnips and parsnips in a bucket of water as she sat on the stoop. The rain-softened earth had made it easy to pluck the root vegetables, and while Alice washed them, Sarah sliced them in preparation for the midday meal they would share at Widow Heard's. Meals were being eaten behind garrison palisades more often due to increasing tensions with the Pennacooks, and they were often a compilation of neighbors' bounty.

Sarah smiled over the cutting board placed over the ash barrel. They had become fast friends, ever since Alice and Grace came to live with the Heards sixteen years before. "I'm happy to see you finally with child," Sarah remarked. "Jack tells me Absalom finds it hard to contain his joy, which amuses Jack because, you know, Absalom is usually so somber."

Alice sighed contentedly as her husband's face formed in her mind. His brooding, solemn demeanor appealed to her since the day he rescued her from a soldier's unwanted advances thirteen years before. They were all married now, except Grace. "What news have you to share?" Alice prompted, handing Sarah a parsnip.

Sarah's shapely brows met over her nose. "Jack's heard rumors the Indians are up to mischief. He shared this with Old Dick, and do you know what Waldron said?"

Alice shook her head.

"'Go plant your pumpkins! *I'll* tell you when the Indians are up to mischief!'" Sarah mimicked Waldron's deep baritone, bringing an amused smile to Alice's lips. "That's what he said. Just as dismissive as you please."

"I'm not surprised," Alice commented. "Absalom says he never initiates conversation with Major Waldron, because the old man won't listen to anyone." She cocked her ear toward Cart Way. "I hear Grace's wheel barrow. I do hope this morning's transaction went well—she and Old Dick clash so!"

Sarah nodded in agreement. "That sister of yours is the most headstrong woman I've ever met, next to Widow Heard. I'm surprised Waldron doesn't put her in the stocks for insubordination."

Both women laughed softly as the wheel barrow came into view. When they saw Grace, covered in mud from head to toe, they gasped.

"Good heavens, Grace!" Alice exclaimed as the girl approached with the wobbling wheel barrow. "What happened to you?"

"Old Dick can go to the devil!" Grace cursed, eyes flashing above her spattered cheeks. "He wouldn't accept half my cheeses because they'd fallen on the ground. They're perfectly good! Just a smudge of mud on them which came right off—"

"Well, to be honest, Grace, 'tis a tad more than a smudge on those cheeses," Sarah pointed out.

Catching a whiff of cheese, Alice felt a fresh wave of queasiness. Nonetheless, she smiled affectionately at her sister's frustration. "How did they get soiled?"

"Oh, that hateful Wahowah was arguing with Waldron and on his way out he kicked over my wheel barrow," Grace explained, thrusting a muddy curl beneath her coif. "The wheel's been knocked askew and I had a devil of a time pushing it home. Then I slipped and fell in a puddle."

Alice gasped. "You went to the trading post *alone* when *Wahowah* was inside? Grace, I wish you'd be more careful!"

Grace seated herself next to her sister and plunged a turnip into the water bucket. "Oh, I'm so furious I could spit fire!" She accepted the damp rag Alice handed her and scrubbed the turnip fervently. "If that Indian had even attempted to assault me, I'd have kneed him in the—"

"Grace!" Alice admonished, feeling a chuckle rise to her lips. She and Sarah exchanged looks and both women burst into raucous laughter. The image of diminutive Grace standing her ground against any man, much less a feared warrior, was comical.

"So what, pray, will you do with the remaining cheeses?" Alice inquired when she could speak again.

Grace relaxed her scowl and replied, "I'm bringing those same cheeses back in two days. He won't recognize them from today."

Alice smiled lovingly. With no man to fight her battles for her, Grace seemed to handle confrontations well on her own. "Well, do promise me you won't go into town alone again—it worries me. And you know worry isn't good for the baby."

Her words had the desired effect, and Grace's eyes softened. "Very well, Sister. Absalom can escort me this Friday." Turning to Sarah, Grace asked, "Where's Beth? I could use her help in the barn this afternoon if you haven't need for her."

"She's with Mother. We'll be at the garrison by midday," Sarah replied. Beth was Sarah's five-year-old daughter who had taken a particular liking to Grace. Alice wondered if it was due to Grace's status of being the only adult woman in Cochecho with no children of her own. Grace enjoyed the child's company and thought of Beth as a beloved niece. In any case, little Beth could always be found at Grace's side when her whereabouts were in question.

"Allow me to rinse off these three cheeses, then I'm off to return them to their ladders," Grace said, indicating the water bucket.

"Certainly," Alice consented, sensing something else besides soiled cheeses was bothering her sister. She had never seen her face so flushed. "Grace, is everything else all right? You look feverish."

"I'm fine," Grace insisted, immersing the rag in the water.

Grace swiped at her face and throat until they were free of mud. The cool water chased the redness from her face and Grace released a long sigh. Then she got to her feet and handed Alice the wet rag.

"Thank you, Sister. I'm off to check on Queenie now."

Alice and Sarah exchanged a puzzled look.

"I thought you wanted to rinse off your cheeses," Sarah said.

Grace looked confused for a moment, and Alice was alarmed that her sister had suddenly become addle-brained. "My what? Oh, of course."

"And do change out of those muddy things afore the stains set!"

Grace muttered an inaudible reply over her shoulder.

What on earth is the matter with her? Alice wondered as Grace selected a cheese from the wheel barrow.

Wôbi Skog Wsizokw watched Grace's progress until she passed safely through the Heard's palisade gate.

Grace. He repeated her name silently to himself. To him, she would always be "Turkey Egg Girl."

The irritating white girl from his childhood had established herself firmly in his conscience, and over the years he kept an eye on her as she went about her daily routine.

He fingered his medicine bag anxiously. Inside the doeskin pouch he felt the familiar textures of two firm objects. One was a pale, egg-shaped rock speckled with brown spots. It came into his possession on his first vision quest when he was twelve years old. Alone in the wilderness, he had fasted and meditated, holding the found object in his hands. On the third day, his grandmother came to him in a vision, repeating the admonition she gave him before she died.

I saw you at the white settlement and a big red hawk swooped down and tore out your heart.

Then Nokomis vanished, and a red hawk soared into a starry sky, a flaming arrow clutched in each talon. Its screeching cry echoed against the night as a single tail feather fell to the ground.

When he awoke from the meditation, a red hawk's tail feather lay within arm's reach of where he sat. That too now dwelled in his medicine bag. The feather matched her fiery hair. Likewise, the rock brought to mind her freckled face. For whatever reason, she was important to him— his twin flame.

Maggie Otis's days were filled with stirring fabric in her mother's dye pot with a wide wooden peel. She didn't mind the monotony usually, but today she felt bored and out of sorts. The teenager's most enjoyable moments were in the evenings when her grandfather's former apprentice, Eb Varney, spent the nights at her grandfather's garrison. Eb Varney played the violin and Maggie was always coaxed into singing along. Her gentle alto harmonized seamlessly with the violin's sweet whine, and could bring even some of her male listeners to tears. Many Puritans maligned the violin, calling it the "Devil's fiddle," but those who spent their evenings in the Otis garrison enjoyed the instrument's sweet cry. During uncertain times, Eb's violin soothed his neighbors' anxieties.

The dye pot was suspended on a tripod over a fire pit a safe distance from the Otis's clapboard house. While Maggie stirred, her father straddled his cobbler's bench, burnishing the sole of a boot.

"Good day to you, Otis family," a familiar voice said.

"Good day, Eb," her mother called from the front door, her hands and apron covered in cornmeal.

"Eb!" Maggie heard the smile in her father's greeting as she looked up to see the young blacksmith shuffling toward them. He was accompanied by William Adams, an elderly Quaker sheepherder whose posture resembled that of the shepherd's hook he carried. A timid, reclusive little man, he acknowledged the Otis family with a gentle nod when Margaret wished him good day.

Eb carried a pair of boots in one hand while wearing an older pair. The latter were beyond repair, but she could see where the uppers of the ones he carried needed to be reattached to the soles. "Finally remembered to bring those boots in, I see," Stephen Otis said from his cobbler's bench. "Set them beside me here. I've just finished patching this sole for Elder Wentworth."

Eb complied, tipping his hat to Maggie. He was eleven years older than she, and not a particularly handsome man, with his long nose and drooping eyes, but he was the kindest, most respectful bachelor in Cochecho, and her secret wish was that he would remain a bachelor until she came of courting age. She knew her family liked Eb, and would agree to the match, if the Quaker was ever so inclined.

"We look forward to listening to your violin this evening," Margaret said.

"I assure thee, I'll bring it," Eb said, "if thine daughter will accompany me."

"Indeed I will!" Maggie responded agreeably. "Oh, Goodman Varney, let's do *Barbara Allen!*"

"As thee wishes, Maggie Otis," Eb replied with a tip of his hat. He placed an affectionate hand on William Adams's bony shoulder.

"Mayhap thee will take up thine own fiddle this night. You were my teacher, after all."

Maggie smiled as the shy old Quaker's sunburned face blushed redder. "Nay," replied Adams. "My hands are too gnarled to hold the bow."

The tender look Eb gave his old mentor touched Maggie's heart. She knew that what Richard Otis was to Eb in blacksmithing, William was to him in music.

"Where are you off to, Goodman Adams?" asked Margaret gently in what Maggie knew was an attempt to bring the old man further into the conversation.

"A lamb has escaped its pen," Adams explained, establishing eye contact with Margaret for the briefest moment before lowering his gaze to the ground again. "Ebenezer Varney hath forged me a lock for it."

The Otis family nodded in united understanding.

"May you find your lost lamb, Adams," Stephen offered from his bench.

"Thank thee, Stephen Otis."

Removing his hand from his friend's shoulder, Eb turned back to the Otis family.

"We're off to the forge. God be with thee."

"And to you," the three chorused.

Watching the pair leave, Maggie sighed in the wistful way of teenage girls. "Goodman Varney's so nice, Mama."

"Aye, he is, Daughter," Margaret replied, drawing closer to the dye pot to inspect her daughter's work. "Don't stop stirring, Maggie."

"Why hasn't he ever married?"

Her mother's sad look intrigued her. "I fear his heart was broke beyond repair when Alice Hampton was betrothed to Goodman Hart."

Maggie's young heart felt a sorrowful ache. "How sad." Resuming the stirring, she asked, "Do you think he prefers being a bachelor, as Goodman Adams does?"

"Methinks there's a Jack for every Jill," Margaret replied. "Lift that wool out now, Maggie. 'Tis taken on a strong enough hue."

The saturated wool draped heavily on the wooden peel. Marigolds had lent their warm golden color and Margaret gave her daughter a satisfied look.

Maggie smiled at her mother's assurance as she wrung out the sodden wool and smoothed it on the grass to dry. When she looked up her mother was gazing off in the distance. Maggie's grandfather's wife, Grizel, was heading their way from her garrison. In one hand she grasped the leading strings of two-year-old Hannah's smock and in the other she carried a basket of brown eggs. The toddler's padded pudding cap was tied tightly under her chin, forcing the child's honey-colored curls to spring from her cap like tendrils on a grapevine. At the sight of Maggie, she quickened her steps and held her arms out, but was detained by her mother's hold on the strings. Hannah was her grandfather's child, thus Maggie's aunt, but she couldn't bring herself to call the child Aunt Hannah. Once the little girl had drawn close enough, Maggie picked her up and gave her an affectionate hug.

"Your hands are wet and cold!" Hannah complained as she squirmed against Maggie.

"You gave me no time to dry them off, silly girl!" Maggie replied, nuzzling Hannah's neck until the child giggled and shrieked with delight.

"Good day, Margaret, Maggie," Grizel greeted them.

"Good day, Grizel," Margaret replied, brushing away a strand of hair that clung to her damp forehead. "How fares Richard?"

Grizel was a short, pretty woman with sloping shoulders and soft features. "He's spinning that tow flax left from last season," Grizel replied. Despite having lost his sight, the old blacksmith had learned to use Grizel's flax wheel, and spent much of his time treadling, allowing the fibers to glide through his dampened fingers. "I came to ask if Stephen could escort me to Waldron's on the morrow." She held up her egg basket. "Pray, inspect these for me, will you? I fear they're a bit on the small side."

Maggie peered over Hannah's head as her mother inspected the clutch of brown eggs with an expert eye.

"Oh, Grizel," Margaret said, shaking her head, "Barred Rocks are not the best layers. I do wish you'd get some Dominicker chicks. The eggs will still likely be brown but they'll be a mite bigger."

Grizel sighed and Maggie saw her shoulders droop even more. The darker the shell, the less Waldron paid for them. "I'm afraid you're right."

"Mama is sad her eggs are so small," Hannah observed somberly, still in Maggie's arms.

Margaret shook out her apron as if to dismiss the matter. "Well, naught's to be done about it now. Richard's out back on his cobbler's bench. He has an order of shoe leather to pick up, so he'll be happy to escort you in the morning. Maggie, go tell your father Grizel's request."

"Aye, Mama."

She set Hannah down, and the child immediately grasped her thumb with her dimpled hand. "I'll come too!"

Maggie smiled at the little girl, the pair of leading strings dangling down her back like twin tails. Someday she would find love and marry and have a passel of children just like Hannah.

There's a Jack for every Jill.

Chapter Nine

Elsie Winston emerged from the storage room and groaned. A simple-minded girl with dull brown eyes, she lived a life of endless servitude. She prepared Waldron's meals, cleaned his home and stocked the trading post shelves. And now, kneeling to collect the spilled apples, she realized she would have to mop up the mud tracked in by both the Indian and Grace Hampton.

"Wash those apples off first," Waldron barked from the counter. "Don't you see how grimy they've gotten?"

"Aye, sir."

Kneeling, she polished each apple with her apron while he grumbled over his ledger. Her life was a series of miserable disappointments, and she was awash with self-pity. After she placed the last apple in the basket, she sighed in dismay at her filthy apron.

"Go to the garrison and get a clean apron, you fool! I don't want you looking like a tatterdemalion. What will my customers think?"

"Aye, sir."

Elsie got her to feet stiffly. Although she was only nineteen, her knees ached like that of an old woman's and she groaned aloud. She was close to tears as she headed for the door, only to crash face-first into Absalom Hart's massive chest. He carried a fifty-pound sack of cornmeal on one shoulder, and the impact knocked his hat over his eyes.

"Pardon me, Miss Winston," he said, gently grasping her forearm before adjusting his hat.

When she looked up into Absalom's handsome face, a pang of

jealousy flared in her heart. *Oh, why couldn't I have met this man first? Oh, how dreadful I must look!* In another second, shame overtook her. It was a damnable sin to covet another woman's husband.

"Elsie! Watch where you're going!" Waldron bellowed. "Sorry, Hart. That girl hasn't enough brains to pour piss out of a boot. Set that bag right over there."

"My apologies," she stammered before tearing past him, trailing an anguished sob behind her like a wisp of tobacco smoke.

That afternoon, Queenie delivered a bull calf, fawn-colored like his mother with a white blaze between his brown eyes. As evening grew near, Sarah Meader brought her five-year-old daughter Beth to see the newborn, taking care to keep a safe distance.

"Has he got a name, Miss Grace?" Little Beth asked, peering at the nursing calf from the safety of the barn's threshold.

"Not yet," Grace admitted. She still hadn't changed into clean clothes and the mud stains had dried. "Why don't you think of one for me?"

Beth scrunched her little face into a thoughtful scowl and Grace smiled at how the child was taking this matter so seriously.

"Methinks you could consider his blaze," Sarah said helpfully. "It brings to mind a lightning bolt. Mayhap you could call him Bolt?"

"Oh, Mama, I like that!" the child squealed, which caused Queenie to raise her head from the mound of hay. The cow cocked her ears and regarded Beth with languid eyes while her son suckled hungrily, his wobbly legs braced beneath him. "Miss Grace, will you name him Bolt?"

Grace felt an odd flutter in her heart. When she first saw the calf's marking, it reminded her of the scar on Menane's—no, Wôbi Skog Wsizokw's—face. Ever since their encounter that morning, she couldn't get him out of her thoughts. The last time she saw him, he was a scowling, rude boy with a thin chest who was no taller than she. Now, his voice had deepened and his chest, still hairless, was filled out with sinewy muscle. She had seen plenty of other Indians in town, but none had left such an impression on her. She was thinking about the sound of his laughter and how even and white his teeth were when she realized Beth was tugging at her skirt.

"Miss Grace!" Beth said impatiently. "Do you like that name?"

"What, Beth?"

"Bolt!"

"Oh. Aye. That's a very good name."

She met Sarah's eyes and flushed red when she saw the quizzical look on her friend's face.

"Beth, why don't you go pick some sweet timothy for Queenie?" Sarah suggested.

"Aye, Mama."

After the little girl had left to grab handfuls of the sweet herb from the nearby garden, Sarah stepped closer to Grace and put a hand on her arm.

"What's got you so flustered, pray?" Sarah asked. Then, her face was aglow with revelation. "Why, Grace Hampton! Could it be you've become smitten by some man?"

Grace gave Sarah a hard look. "Don't talk nonsense, Sarah. I'm just overwhelmed by—by all the work ahead of me."

Sarah smiled knowingly. "Well, Alice thinks you've a sweetheart, and I daresay I'm inclined to agree with her. She's seen you sitting on the cheese house roof staring up at the heavens, as if you're pining for someone."

Grace's cheeks grew hot again, and she yanked her arm away.

"That's silly," she insisted, striding across the barn to stroke Queenie's large head. "I simply enjoy looking at the stars on nights sleep eludes me. And I'd appreciate it if you and Alice wouldn't speculate about my affairs."

Sarah was still chuckling when Beth returned with her dimpled hands full of sweet-smelling timothy. The child was oblivious to the change of mood between the two women, and smiled broadly. "Here I am!"

Grace stifled a groan of disappointment when she saw Beth had pulled the plants up by the roots and beckoned the child to approach. "Good girl," Grace said with a hint of irritation still in her voice. "Now, come slowly and hold it right out under Queenie's muzzle."

The child complied, walking gingerly toward the docile cow. Little Bolt never paused in his nursing as Beth held out the offering to Queenie.

"Look, Mama!" The child breathed excitedly. "She's eating right out of my hand!"

"I see," Sarah confirmed from the threshold. "'Tis near supper time. Let's head on to the garrison."

"Aye, Mama."

Grace watched the little girl wipe her grass-stained hands on her apron and give Queenie a pat on the nose before rejoining her mother. Sarah glanced at Grace expectantly.

"Coming, Grace?"

"I'll be along."

After mother and daughter left, Grace turned her attention back to Queenie. Evidently sated, Bolt detached himself from his mother's teat. Only three hours old, he wobbled over to Grace, and she traced the jagged blaze between his eyes with her finger.

"Oh, Queenie," she muttered, stroking both animals' heads simultaneously. "Of all the markings for your calf to have! Is it your intention to torment me also?"

Queenie replied with an ambiguous moo.

Thursday, June 20

"Masandowit! Come in," Waldron greeted the sachem warmly. "What brings you to my fine establishment this morning?"

"Brother Waldron," Masandowit addressed the old man cordially as he and Wahowah entered the trading post. "We come with sixty pelts for a full keg of gunpowder, as you requested."

"Excellent!" Waldron exclaimed as the younger Indian deposited the pelts on the floor in front of the counter. The warrior regarded the old man coldly as if he still bore contempt for yesterday's encounter. The glowering Indian's scalp lock trailed down his back like a snake. *A ridiculous custom, that!* Waldron thought with distaste. *I've got to establish a dress code for those heathens posthaste.*

"I hope you haven't forgotten my invitation to sup next week. I'll have Elsie here roast a duck, then we'll have a game of noddy."

The sachem smiled. "I look forward to it."

Wahowah hefted the wooden keg onto one shoulder and followed Masandowit out the door.

Waldron followed them with his eyes. *If I didn't know better, I'd say Wahowah is up to mischief.* The old man considered reducing Absalom's hours at the mill and posting him as a guard at the trading post. "Elsie! Stop cowering in the storeroom and put these pelts where they belong."

"Aye, sir."

Worthless girl! Waldron shook his head as Stephen Otis walked in, escorting his father's young wife Grizel and her little daughter Hannah. Stephen and Grizel looked about searchingly as they approached the counter.

"Did we confuse the hours?" Stephen asked as Grizel set a basket of brown eggs on the counter.

"Nay, Otis," Waldron replied. "Sometimes those heathens disregard the schedule. Have you come for shoe leather?"

"That I have, Waldron."

"—And my eggs," Grizel said. "I've two dozen here."

"—And candy!" Little Hannah piped up, peering up at Waldron, her cherubic face framed in her pudding cap.

Waldron raised his bushy brows. "Candy? Why, young Otis, all I have is what's in this box here."

The toddler's eyes widened as Waldron produced a small lidded box and held it out before her. He was not normally fond of children, but Hannah Otis was a well-behaved child, and her father was a good friend and neighbor. With a great flourish, he opened the box, revealing a variety of suckets. The assortment of candied fruits emitted a sweet, tannic scent, and the adults smiled at the child's anticipation.

"Just one piece, Hannah," Grizel cautioned.

The little girl's tiny hand hovered over her choices —lemon or orange? But there was also candied gingerroot, sugared marigolds and violets. As his patience wore thin, Hannah's chubby fingers selected a yellow slice of candied lemon. Just as her dimpled hand cleared the lid, he slammed it down. She jumped, then smiled up at him before she crammed the treat into her bow-shaped mouth. It was a game they played every week.

"Say 'thank you, Sir,'" Grizel reminded her daughter.

"Thank you, Sir," Hannah parroted, her pink lips coated with sugar.

Returning the box of candy to its rightful place, Waldron's shoulder hit the oak plank that served as his counter, knocking it askew. It was supported by two wooden barrels, with wooden crates for storage beneath. The brass scales swung, and he grumbled as he adjusted the plank.

"Blast it!" he cursed, disregarding Grizel and Hannah. "I keep forgetting to have Absalom fix that."

"He just left this very morn to take Widow Heard and her family to the ferry, I believe," Stephen said conversationally.

Waldron had forgotten about that. Begrudgingly, he had given Absalom Hart permission to take time off from the mill to drive the Heard family to their ferry. Absalom was a very productive worker at the mill.

"Well, Ab better make haste his return," Waldron complained, opening his ledger to Stephen's account page. The sixty pelts still sat where Wahowah had set them. "Elsie! Get Otis's shoe leather from the storeroom, and come get these pelts!"

"Aye, sir."

Worthless girl, he thought again, adjusting Stephen Otis's account in the ledger. Elsie scampered in, making no eye contact as she handed Stephen his leather. Waldron watched her scornfully as she hoisted the heavy bale of pelts onto her back then lumbered away like a packhorse.

"—and three pence for the eggs, Goody Otis," he noted. Darker eggs sold at half the price of lighter ones, and even though Richard Otis was a friend, Waldron wasn't inclined to cut Goody Otis a break.

"We square now, Waldron?" Stephen asked good-naturedly, tucking the bundle of leather under his damaged arm.

"We are, Otis."

"Thank you again for treating our Hannah," Grizel said. "Your generosity is appreciated."

"My pleasure, Goody Otis."

"Say 'God be with you,'" Hannah," Grizel prompted, steering her daughter out the door.

"God be with you," the child repeated, waving a sticky hand as the family prepared their exit.

Waldron returned her wave with one of his own, and when they had left, he dipped the quill in the ink bottle again and added a fresh hash mark under the column, *H.O.* Unbeknownst to the Otis family, they were charged half a penny each week for their daughter's indulgence.

Little Bolt frolicked in the common pasture, never straying more than a yard away from Queenie. For her part, Queenie wouldn't permit any other cows to come near her calf, and they respectfully kept their distance as Bolt explored his new surroundings.

The rising sun colored the sky in orange and yellow light. Dew had seeped into Grace's punctured shoe, reminding her that she needed to pay Stephen Otis a visit. Her wet woolen sock did nothing for her mood as she headed for the pasture gate. She had not milked Queenie since the morning before Bolt's birth, and now it was time to resume her routine. As she pushed open the heavy wooden gate, she spotted the hayward, Tristan Coffin.

"How now, Milk Maid?" he called as Grace entered the pasture.

"'T'is unwise for you to be walking unescorted." Appointed to check the pasture's fences, he patrolled the perimeter, checking for any areas that needed repairs. A pleasant young man who hid a mop of golden curls under his hat, he owned a garrison on the southwest shore of the river. His father, Peter, was a captain under Waldron, and well-respected in the community.

"I do it all the time," she retorted, slipping an escaped curl back into place. "No ill has come to me yet."

"There's always a first time," Tristan responded, adjusting the musket on his shoulder. "Allow me to make my rounds and I'll walk you back."

"Nay, Goodman Coffin," she said, grasping the rope that hung around Queenie's neck. "I want to get on with the morning's milking."

"As you please, Milk Maid," he said resignedly, resuming his fence inspection.

It is as I please. Bolt trotted up to his mother, nosing her udder. "Stop that, Bolt," Grace said, pulling on Queenie's lead and guiding her through the gate. She was in a hurry to get her milking done.

Queenie plodded along docilely while Grace ruminated over the day's plans. She had several finished cheeses that needed rubbing and turning. She hoped she could enlist the help of little Beth that afternoon. Eyes on the footpath, lost in thought, she was startled when Queenie all at once shied.

Moooo.

The cow had stopped short. "What is it, Queenie? Come along now!" Grace said, tugging on her lead. Bolt seized the moment and again tried to suckle, but Queenie was too alarmed and backed away.

"The cow fears for her calf," a familiar voice said from behind her.

Alarmed, Grace turned, tightening her grip on Queenie's lead. Before her stood Menane, three fat beaver carcasses slung over his back. His stern expression sent a myriad of conflicting feelings through her, and as she struggled to find words, he spoke again.

"I told you before--you should not walk alone. It is not safe."

She rolled her eyes in irritation. *Another man telling me what I can and can't do!*

"I make this trek morning and evening every day without incident, I'll have you know," she said, feeling her cheeks flush hot.

"I know you do," he said. "I watch."

Her mouth fell open. "You do?" A flare of resentment heated her face as she realized that her neckline was gaping open, adding to her indignation. As she hastily re-tied the string, an unruly curl sprang free from her coif like a tiny red serpent.

"I'm not a defenseless child who can't fend for herself," she insisted. "I don't appreciate every man I encounter telling me where I can and can't go--"

His bemused expression infuriated her even more, and just as she was about to demand he take her seriously, Menane reached for her face. His cool fingers brushed her cheek as he tugged gently on the curl, sending a thrilling shiver down her spine. It recoiled with a cheerful bounce as if it too were excited by his touch. Grace was instantly reminded of the similar sensation she had experienced when he had made the same gesture when they were children.

Bolt, who'd been nursing ever since Queenie stopped, ambled up to Grace and butted her arm with his head. Absently her hand fell between his eyes. Menane gestured at the calf, then at his own jagged scar.

"The calf and I have the same mark."

His words jolted her from her reverie. She looked again at Bolt's wide forehead.

"What, pray?"

"See?" he pointed again.

She regarded his scar, and Bolt's blaze, as if she had just noticed them, and was again struck by how similar they were. The realization sent another unexpected tickle down her spine.

"I do see," she murmured.

When she looked up, he'd disappeared. Finding herself alone on the footpath again, she continued on her way, sensing he was somewhere close, guarding her every step of the way.

Chapter Ten

Friday, June 21

Friday morning found Grace in her cheese house seasoning her cheese press's follower with saved bacon grease. After each individual cheese was removed from the press and hung to dry, the press barrel and follower needed to be seasoned. Shallow pans rested on what once had been Captain Heard's workbench. Cream floated to the surface in each one, ready to be skimmed off. The smell of her cheeses in their varying stages of ripeness delighted her as she burnished the oaken follower until it gleamed in the morning light that streamed in through the open door.

Besides the three rounds of cheese she had salvaged from the mud, she had five others aging on their cheese ladders. Next to the door sat her butter churn, the freshly-cleaned dasher resting paddle-end up against the barrel. Whey dripped into buckets beneath the freshest three cheeses as they hung from the rafters in their cheesecloths. Absalom had returned from the ferry landing the day before, and would escort her to the trading post on his way to the mill. So while she waited for her brother-in-law, she busied herself in her cheese house listening to the whey drip. Seated next to her sat little Beth. The child sat cross-legged on the floor, scowling in concentration as she burnished the press's interior with fervor.

"Not so hard, Beth," Grace admonished with concern. "You'll crack the wood."

Beth relaxed her rubbing, and as they continued their work in

127

companionable silence, Grace recalled her recent encounter with
Menane with guilty pleasure. She wished she could talk to Alice or
Sarah about her feelings. Was this what Alice felt for Absalom? What
Sarah felt for Jack? Oh, why did he have to be an Indian? The memory
of her childhood nightmare surfaced—the one about the Indian
attack on her home. Her pursuers turning into ravens, one carrying
a pair of burning arrows in its talons.

My life's been nothing but strife and turmoil, she thought with a wave
of self-pity. *Why should I expect love to come easily?*

Was she really entertaining love thoughts with an Indian? She
had never been smitten by any man like she was by Menane.

Wôbi Skog Wsizokw, she corrected herself silently. But the name
tangled clumsily on her tongue. When she thought of him, his
childhood appellation came to mind, and to her he would always be
Menane.

"What did you say, Miss Grace?"

Disturbed from her reverie, Grace saw Beth was peering at her
with a puzzled expression. When she didn't answer, Beth said, "You
said a funny word."

Grace's cheeks warmed when she realized she'd spoken the name
aloud. "Nay, I said naught," she insisted. Fixing a bright smile on her
face, she asked, "Are you nearly done?"

"Finished!" Beth cried in triumph, holding up the gleaming cheese
press.

Grace rewarded Beth with an approving smile. "Now take it to
the well and rinse it out."

"Aye, Miss Grace."

Beth sprang to her feet and ran out the door with a burst of
youthful energy. Grace smiled after her as she finished seasoning the
follower.

Beth's shrill scream shattered the morning's serenity.

"Miss Grace!"

Grace sprang to her feet, sending the follower crashing to the
floor. Instinctively she seized the churn's dasher, stubbing her toe

against the barrel. Cursing, she ran outside and stopped dead in her tracks.

A tall Indian was drawing water up from her well. She recognized Wahowah by the tattoos on his bare back; his muscles flexed beneath his tawny skin. The cheese press lay at Beth's feet, and the child trembled like a leaf.

"Beth, get in the cheese house," Grace ordered, grasping the child's fear-stiffened shoulder.

With a sob, the little girl retreated into the cheese house, slamming the door behind her with such force Grace's body shuddered at the impact. Alone, she clutched the wooden dasher, prepared to defend herself.

"Get away from my well, you nasty devil!" she cried, trembling with furor. "'T'is bad enough you soiled my cheeses and broke my wheel barrow, now you trespass on my property!"

The Indian set the bucket on the rim of the well before turning his shaved head to face her. To Grace's indignation, his hard scowl softened to one of amusement when he saw her poised to defend herself. Her chagrin intensified when he threw back his head and roared with laughter.

"Go away, I say!" she said, swinging the dasher at him.

He turned to face her fully, and took two swift strides toward her. Before Grace could think, he snatched the dasher out of her hands and flung it aside. It landed on the ground with a dull thud, several feet away. With his face mere inches from hers, he glared at her, the amusement in his eyes replaced by piercing hatred. Her rage gave in to fear as she felt his breath on her face.

"Foolish little woman!" he snarled.

She swallowed over the cold lump that blocked her throat as icy sweat ran down her spine. She could be in serious danger, and no one was around to rescue her. Gathering her remaining courage, she scowled back at him and pointed northward. "Go away!"

He continued to glower at her for a moment before he finally withdrew. Shooting her one last hateful glare, he stalked down Little Hill as silently as a shadow.

Only after he had disappeared did Grace release her suspended breath. Then her legs buckled beneath her and she slumped to the ground in a crumpled heap.

The alarming number of Indians entering Cochecho had increased in the past four years, setting the whites on edge. Sometimes they loitered along Cart Way, regarding passersby with stony silence. In the evenings, Pennacook women came into town with babies strapped in their *tkinogans,* often asking for a night's lodging behind the garrison's palisades. It was often granted because the women were considered passive and pleasant, and posed no threat to the settlers. Even as tensions escalated regarding the number of warriors entering Cochecho, no concern was given to the Indian women.

With this in mind, Kancamagus sat with Masandowit and other prominent members of the Pennacook council. Council was usually held in the evening, but Kancamagus had called for a special meeting to discuss what to do about the whites.

Since the day before, Kancamagus had become aware of a recent change in Wôbi Skog Wsizokw's disposition. He knew Wôbi Skog Wsizokw favored peace with the whites, like Wanalancet, and Passaconaway before him. Wôbi Skog Wsizokw reveled in a good battle and was not opposed to bloodshed. Now around the council fire, Kancamagus listened as Wahowah relayed his earlier confrontation with Waldron, which had prompted Masandowit to make an attempt to smooth things over with the major.

"He cheats us every time," Wahowah complained. "Doesn't he think we know he can manipulate the scale when he uses his fist for a counterweight? Next time I see him, I'll cut off his fingers and stuff them down his throat!"

"And the corn tributes he demands," a warrior called Bomazeen reminded the others. "Such an outrage!"

"Telling us where we can and can't hunt," grumbled another.

"Even their women need to be put in their place," Wahowah

went on. "A stupid little woman with spots all over face tried to stop me from getting a drink at her well this afternoon." He chuckled. "Threatened me with a big stick! I'll enjoy slitting her throat when we attack."

As others laughed at the vision of a woman wielding a stick at the warrior, Kancamagus looked again at Wôbi Skog Wsizokw. The young warrior was staring intently at Wahowah, flexing his jaw muscles. His brother and Wahowah disliked each other, but something besides contempt flashed in Wôbi Skog Wsizokw's eyes. A suspicion began to wriggle like a worm in Kancagmagus's heart, and he decided he would have to have a talk with his little brother.

Wahowah's account fueled the others, and they demanded Waldron be given his just punishment. Treaties had been made and broken, and the incident of the sham battle still hadn't been suitably vindicated.

"Too many innocents could get hurt," Wôbi Skog Wsizokw said, somewhat to his brother's surprise. "I want no part in the siege."

"Coward," Wahowah muttered under his breath, and Kancagmagus tensed in anticipation of his brother's response. Wôbi Skog Wsizokw only glared at Wahowah with hatred.

Kancamagus was still digesting Wôbi Skog Wsizokw's unwillingness to take part when Masandowit, who was usually quiet during council, spoke up.

"The whites might expect us to attack during the full moon. Waldron has invited me to sup with him six nights from now. They will have let their guard down. That could give us the opportunity we're looking for."

Kancamagus considered Masandowit's words. "Then tell the women to go into the town that night and ask for lodging. This has been a long time in coming. When the whites are all asleep, that is when we'll attack."

"The whites need to be warned," old Wanalancet whispered,

drawing a woolen blanket around his thin shoulders. Kancamagus
had just dismissed the council, and Wôbi Skog Wsizokw and his
uncle were alone. "Nephew, summon me two runners. I'll send them
to Chelmsford. There's a military headquarters there. I'll tell them to
find Major Thomas Hinchman."

Wôbi Skog Wsizokw nodded. While he agreed with Kancamagus
that the whites—at least Waldron—deserved to be punished for their
transgressions, he didn't like the idea of killing innocent women and
children—especially Grace.

He considered his uncle's request thoughtfully. The two fastest
runners went by the names of Job Maramasquand and Peter
Muckamug, and could be trusted to deliver the warning the quickest.

"It would take them half a day to make that distance," Wôbi Skog
Wsizokw ruminated aloud.

The old sagamore looked up into his nephew's youthful face.
"Then send them, Nephew. Hopefully we can prevent unnecessary
bloodshed."

Job Maramasquand and Peter Muckamug were lean young men
with long legs that covered over fifty leagues in a day. Heads shaved
clear of all hair, they were esteemed for their speed and alacrity. They
were also friends of Wôbi Skog Wsizokw. Like him, they opposed
Kancamagus's actions toward the whites, especially the killing of
innocents. They regarded Wanalancet's plea solemnly and agreed
to take the warning to Major Hinchman. Chelmsford was less than
eighteen leagues from Cochecho, and Wôbi Skog Wsizokw hoped
they could convey the warning in time.

"What if this Major Hinchman refuses to listen to us?" Job
Maramasquand asked.

"Do what you must to see that he does," Wanalancet replied.
"Now go."

Wôbi Skog Wsizokw stood next to his uncle as he watched the
two take off in the direction of Chelmsford, fingering his medicine

bag. The rock clattered softly against another object. This one was disc-shaped, a length of tow linen strung through its pierced center.

Grace's freckled face formed in his mind. For her sake and those of the other innocent whites, he hoped Kancamagus and Wahowah wouldn't notice the runners' absence.

The creases in Wanalancet's face deepened, and Wôbi Skog Wsizokw sensed the old sachem held little hope that the message would reach its recipients in time. With a resigned look, Wanalancet turned back to camp, leaving Wôbi Skog Wsizokw alone with his thoughts.

"*Nijia .*"

Wôbi Skog Wsizokw's shoulders tightened when he heard his brother behind him. Hoping he hadn't witnessed the exchange with the runners, he turned to face Kancamagus.

"Aye, *Nidokan?*"

"Where did you send the runners to?"

Wôbi Skog Wsizokw cursed his luck. It was not in his nature to lie, especially to Kancagmagus, so he swallowed, squared his shoulders and said, "To Chelmsford."

Kancagmagus's eyes narrowed. "Why?"

When he didn't answer immediately, Kancagmagus stepped closer. Wôbi Skog Wsizokw surpassed his brother in height enough that Kancagmagus had to look up into his younger brother's face. "You sent them to warn the whites, didn't you?"

Wôbi Skog Wsizokw realized he was holding his breath and exhaled. "Nidokan," he said, choosing his words carefully. "Not all the whites deserve to die."

"The ones that don't, we capture."

The brothers locked eyes, regarding each other with cold antagonism.

"Waldron is the only one who deserves death," Wôbi Skog Wsizokw insisted. "I don't want to take innocent lives."

Kancamagus remembered his brother's reaction when Wahowah talked about the woman at the well.

"You have feelings for a woman there."

Wôbi Skog Wsizokw remained silent.

Kancagmagus held his steady gaze. "Then stay home, Nijia. That is your choice. But I won't allow you to warn them."

———◇———

Saturday, June 22
Full Moon

Absalom Hart locked the mill door behind him and shouldered his musket. He was anxious to get home to Alice. For the past few nights, he hadn't slept well and insisted he and Alice bed behind the Heard garrison's walls. The moon would be full that night, and it was generally accepted that Indians didn't attack during such times, but Absalom couldn't ignore his pestering intuition.

Striding purposefully homeward, he saw two Pennacook warriors transporting a bundle of beaver pelts suspended on a sturdy tree branch. Heading toward Waldron's trading post, the two Indians were just yards away from Absalom. He recognized the Indian in front as Wahowah, and his suspicion unfurled. Wahowah regarded Absalom with dismissive coldness when they met on Cart Way.

The second Indian was younger, with a prominent scar darting across his face. Wahowah was one to be watched, Absalom knew, and certainly not one to be trusted. Young Wôbi Skog Wsizokw, however, was looked upon by the whites as nonaggressive, and so it surprised Absalom when, as he came abreast of the young warrior, Wôbi Skog Wsizokw dropped his end of the pole and collided into Absalom's shoulder.

"You try to trip me!" Wôbi Skog Wsizokw accused, his face set in a vicious snarl as he lunged at Absalom.

Taken by surprise, Absalom was thrown off balance and tumbled to the ground with Wôbi Skog Wsizokw's hands around his throat. The force knocked Absalom's hat off and sent it rolling. Wôbi Skog Wsizokw straddled him, his back to Wahowah. Absalom for his part brought the musket's barrel against his attacker's chest. Looking into the Indian's eyes, he realized that although Wôbi Skog Wsizokw's hands held firm, they weren't tight around his throat. His young face took on an urgent look and he mumbled in a low voice. "Keep close watch."

"Wôbi Skog Wsizokw!" Wahowah called, setting his end of the pole down and pulling Wôbi Skog Wsizokw off Absalom's chest. "Stop it!"

Wôbi Skog Wsizokw's intent glare bore into him, as if waiting for confirmation that his message had been received. Absalom slowly got to his feet, giving his attacker only the slightest nod.

"Pick up the pole!" Wahowah ordered. "The trading post will be closed before we get there."

While the two Indians took up their pelts, Absalom retrieved his hat from the road and resumed his trek home. He suspected other Indians observed him from the woods, and to avoid suspicion, he maintained his usual pace.

Keep good watch.

An attack was imminent, just as he feared. *But which night?*

He suspected that, if given the opportunity, Wôbi Skog Wsizokw would have told him when.

Full moon or not, Absalom would maintain a close watch.

The Indians had disappeared down the road, and Absalom backtracked to the meetinghouse. He needed to summon a meeting of the selectmen.

"This is the last time you sell me stale tobacco!"

"I've never sold stale tobacco, you cranky old skinflint! You're just too cheap to buy the freshest!"

Elsie watched this exchange from the storeroom. She was taking inventory, and the loud bickering caused her to lose track of her counting. Elder Wentworth glared at Waldron beneath his bushy white brows. Waldron matched his animosity across the counter. The two elderly men were the wealthiest in Cochecho, and despised each other greatly.

"'Tis one thing to cheat the savages," Wentworth grumbled, "but to swindle a fellow Englishman—"

Bong! Bong! Bong!

Both men fell silent, and turned toward the sound. As the peals faded, Wahowah and Wôbi Skog Wsizokw walked in with their cache of pelts. Wahowah forced Elder Wentworth to step aside as he and Wôbi Skog Wsizokw set down their load.

"What the devil could that be about?" Waldron muttered as another series of three chimes rang in the late afternoon air. Three bells were a signal for an emergency selectmen's meeting. "Elsie! Come tend to their transaction, then lock up. I've been summoned."

Elsie's stomach plummeted. Nothing scared her more than when Indians—especially the one called Wahowah—entered the store. With great reluctance, she emerged from the storeroom, hiding her trembling hands beneath her apron.

"Aye, sir."

As she drew closer, Wahowah glowered at her and muttered, "*W8bikwsos!*" Mouse.

She didn't know what the word meant, but by his disdainful look it was some sort of insult. She squeezed past Elder Wentworth and slipped behind the counter while Waldron grabbed his hat from its peg.

"No refund on Wentworth's tobacco," Waldron instructed, heading out the door. "And be sure to weigh those pelts."

"Aye, sir."

"We're not done here, Waldron," Wentworth insisted, waving his cane at Waldron's retreating back. Then to Elsie's horror, he too turned to leave.

Don't leave me alone with them! Elsie wanted to beg. Even the presence of an elderly curmudgeon like Wentworth was better than facing a pair of warriors alone. But he seemed not to care that he was abandoning her, and after both old men left, she stared glumly at the open ledger.

Bang!

Wahowah slammed his palm down on the counter, jangling the pair of brass scales. Elsie jumped, her heart almost leaping out of her chest as the big Indian laughed.

With a trembling hand she reached for the quill. Fighting back tears, she felt a warm wet stream flow down her legs. As it hit the wooden floor with a *hiss,* Wahowah's laughter at her embarrassment jarred her nerves further. Her trembling hand upset the ink pot, and black ink splattered onto the pages of the open ledger.

To her stunned disbelief, a tawny bare arm reached across the counter and set the ink pot aright. Surprised, she looked into the scarred face of the other Indian. No menacing hostility flashed in his eyes. Instead, she detected something like benevolence. He spoke no words, but the look of compassion he offered was like a balm to her frayed nerves as the sour stink of her own urine rose to her nostrils.

Chapter Eleven

"The Indians won't be attacking us," Waldron insisted after Hart repeated the cryptic words of Wôbi Skog Wsizokw. "We're well-armed, well-fortified, and everyone knows they won't attack on a full moon night when they could be so easily seen."

As the other selectmen mumbled words that ranged from skepticism to alarm, Absalom Hart raised his hands in a plea for silence. "I'm not saying 't'will be tonight," he said. "I was warned by a friendly warrior. His very words were *keep good watch*," and that's what I intend to do at the Heard garrison. I advise the other garrisons do the same."

Waldron snorted derisively. "You're trusting the vaguest of warnings about savages *from* a savage?"

Absalom bristled at the chuckling that ensued. Most times, his sensible voice was received with respect and consideration, but this day Waldron's disparaging remarks were blocking the urgency of his message.

"I am simply proposing that we heighten security for the time being," he said, glancing from man to man. He swallowed a lump of frustration as Waldron shook his head.

"I've invited Masandowit over to sup and play a game of noddy this Thursday," the majorwent on. "He's accepted, and if that doesn't bespeak complacency I know not what does."

"Masandowit travels with a number of attendants," Jack Meader reminded the group. "Mayhap that very night he might raise arms against us."

Waldron shook his head dismissively. "Cowardly talk! Masandowit travels mostly with women. Are you all afraid of a bunch of heathen women?"

As other men voiced their opinions loudly, Stephen Otis threw Hart a supportive glance. "Well, I think Hart has a good point, and I intend to bring the family to Pa's garrison this night and any night there may be a threat."

Absalom Hart exhaled in gratitude. "Thank you, my friend," he said. *Someone* was listening to him! Stephen reached out and placed his hand on Absalom's shoulder. "I've learned 'tis wise to listen to you and your premonitions," Stephen said, nodding in the direction of his injured arm. "Had I three and ten years ago, I'd have *two* sound arms!"

The other men confirmed this with nods and mutterings, and Absalom sensed that the group's mindset had shifted in his favor.

"Papa, smell it!"

Richard Otis sensed that Hannah had thrust a bouquet of wildflowers under his nose, and he breathed in their sweet scent. Hannah seemed to understand he was unable to see, and she delighted in holding up fragrant items for him to smell. One of his greatest delights was pressing his nose against the top of her head. The precious scent of baby sweat and rainwater emanated from her pudding cap, and Richard inhaled it deeply like parched earth absorbed rain.

"Very nice, love," Richard said, reaching for her little hand. "Have Mama put them in a bowl of water and set them on the board."

"Aye, Papa."

The little hand withdrew from his and he listened as her footfalls faded into the hall. He was sitting outside with Stephen and Eb, and wanted to discuss the selectmen's impromptu meeting. He heard Grizel, Margaret and Maggie talking quietly among themselves as they cleaned the supper dishes. The scent of lamb stew wafted through the open door, and he drew a deep puff on his pipe before he spoke next.

"So Hart has you convinced an attack is imminent, son?"

"Aye, he has, Pa," Stephen replied. "You know he has a keen sense for these things, and he claims a friendly Indian attempted to warn him this very afternoon."

Richard digested this information. Hart's premonitions often proved uncannily accurate, but he had to consider the validity of Waldron's insistence that Indians did not attack during a full moon. "'T'is always wise to be cautious," he commented, taking a puff on his pipe.

"And so we shall," Stephen said. "I may not be able to shoot as well as most with this arm, but I can still defend my own. What say you, Eb?"

The Quaker nodded. Although he abhorred violence, he realized the necessity of protecting his own. "Permit me to take first watch this night, Stephen Otis."

"Then that's settled," Stephen said. He slapped a hand on his father's bony knee, and Richard knew Stephen's blue eyes were twinkling. "Be of good cheer, Pa. All will be well."

"Let us in! We have an urgent message for Major Hinchman!"

Major Hinchman's secretary opened the peephole to discover two lean and panting savages outside the major's door. Sweat glistened on their hairless bodies and he grimaced in disgust at their savage appearance.

"Go away. The major's dining just now. Come back in the morn."

"It is of great importance," insisted the taller Indian. "A matter of life and death."

Despite his general distrust of natives, the secretary acknowledged the urgent nature of their expressions. Setting aside his prejudices for the sake of precaution, he unlocked the door and with guarded reluctance let them in.

Grace glanced upward as a raven soared in the clouded sky, a blazing arrow clutched in each talon. It swooped low, regarding Grace with a soulless eye before once again ascending. An overwhelming sense of dread seized her as the bird released its grip on the arrows' shafts. She watched helplessly as the flaming pair plummeted to earth.

"No!" she screamed, running to catch them.

One pierced the riverbank, still aflame. The second plunged into the Cochecho with a searing hiss before the fire was extinguished. Stricken with grief, Grace fell on her knees and wept.

Grace awoke from the dream to find her cheeks moist from tears. She sat up and wiped at them with the base of her palm. Her heart thundered in her chest as if she had run a great distance.

There was something strangely familiar yet disturbingly urgent about this dream, but she failed to decipher any meaning from it.

Near the hearth, Elder Wentworth and Dog snored in unison. Without donning shoes and socks, Grace rose and tip-toed quietly around the sleeping figures on the floor. A quiet moment of stargazing from the cheese house roof was in order, and she opened and closed the garrison door as quietly as she could.

The cool, damp grass beneath her feet exhilarated her as she ran across the moonlit courtyard. Within minutes she had propped the ladder against the side of the cheese house and shimmied up it.

Seating herself on the rough shingles, she hugged her knees to her chest and shivered. The dream was evaporating from her memory but not its lingering, disturbing aura.

Two burning arrows? What could they mean? At once she admonished herself. She didn't have meaningful dreams like Absalom was known to do. Alice had often told her of her husband's premonitions that had subsequently come to fruition. *'T'is just a silly dream*, she assured herself.

Just then, a pair of falling stars arched downward, one following closely behind the other. She gasped with the shock of the chill running down her spine. Perhaps the heavens understood her dreams more than she.

From a corner watchtower, Absalom Hart scanned the moonlit area surrounding Little Hill. The oakey scent of chimney smoke wafted in the humid summer air, bringing to mind Alice lying alone in Widow Heard's string bed. Being with child, Alice was spared having to sleep on a pallet on the hard floor—he hoped she was sleeping well. Despite a full day at the mill, Absalom had spent a good hour in the shed, crafting a narrow cradle for their child. It only needed a good sanding before he would present it to his wife.

He shifted the musket in his arm and chewed the inside of his cheek. He longed for his pipe, but the very scent of the tobacco would give away his location to any lurking Indian.

Not that the bright moonlight hasn't done that already. Waldron's dismissive comment rang in his head.

"The Indians won't be attacking us. We're well-armed, well-fortified, and everyone knows they won't attack on a full moon night when they could be so easily seen."

That was likely the case. But why would the young Indian warn him if no threat loomed?

Some creature in the near distance—a bear, he guessed—emitted a rumbling growl that jarred his nerves.

He detected movement near Grace's cheese house. He watched his sister-in-law place a ladder against it, then quietly ascend to the sloping roof. She was prone to perch there on warm summer evenings, but her disregard for her own safety irked him.

"Hart, I'm here to relieve you."

The unexpected voice startled him and he bit his cheek too hard, drawing blood. He cursed softly and glanced down to see Jack Meader gazing up at him, cradling his musket.

Absalom descended the watchtower and pointed with his chin at the cheese house. "Yonder she sits."

Jack Meader glanced over his shoulder. "She's a strange one, your sister-in-law."

Absalom merely nodded as Jack clambered up the watchtower.

Rubbing his eyes, he shouldered his musket and strode across the yard to the cheese house.

At his post at Otis garrison, Eb Varney rubbed his stiff neck and yawned. He had taken first shift and was eager to be relieved by Stephen Otis. Despite the disquieting threat of attack, it had been a pleasant evening. After the supper dishes were washed, corn was popped. The treat was devoured by the handful until all that remained were the greasy butter stains on faces and hands.

"Eb, start with *Come Live With Me*," Grizel Otis had requested, jostling little Hannah on her knee.

He had obliged, and nodded to Maggie that she might sing the heart-rending lyrics:

> *Come live with me and be my love,*
> *And we will all the pleasures prove*
> *That hill and valley, dale and field,*
> *And all the craggy mountains yield.*
>
> *There we will sit upon the rocks,*
> *And see the shepherds feed their flocks,*
> *By shallow rivers to whose falls*
> *Melodious birds sing madrigals.*
>
> *There I will make thee beds of roses*
> *And a thousand fragrant posies,*
> *A cap of flowers, and a kirtle*
> *Embroidered all with leaves of myrtle;*
>
> *A gown made of the finest wool*
> *Which from our pretty lambs we pull;*
> *Fair lined slippers for the cold,*
> *With buckles of the purest gold;*

A belt of straw and ivy buds,
With coral clasps and amber studs:
And if these pleasures may thee move,
Come live with me and be my love.

Thy silver dishes for thy meat,
As precious as the gods do eat,
Shall on an ivory table be
Prepared each day for thee and me.

The shepherds' swains shall dance and sing
For thy delight each May morning:
If these delights thy mind may move,
Then live with me and be my love.

He smiled now, remembering the shy looks young Maggie gave him as her voice melded with the violin's notes. She really was a delightful young woman, and sometimes he entertained the thought of courting her when she came of age.

Thinking of Maggie Otis brought to mind Alice Hampton Hart. He had resolved himself to the fact she had never returned his feelings, but whenever he thought of her, an old ache would poke his heart.

His dear friend William Adams, now well in his eighties, had remained a bachelor, and would often console Ebenezer, insisting that lifelong bachelorhood was not as bad as one often thought.

Nonetheless, the concept of never finding a wife saddened him.

Tears of self-pity blurred his vision and he blinked them away as he scanned the moonlit forest from his post.

All at once a distant scream, and then the report of musket fire. *Bang!*

He readied his own musket. Had the foreseen attack begun? His body tensed as he surveyed the trees.

He caught his breath when he saw a large figure running toward the Otis's palisade gate.

Grace reclined on the sloping roof, cradling her head on her hands, contemplating the dream further. She relished the escape from Elder Wentworth's and Dog's snores. She would rather listen to the crickets and the far-off hoot of an owl. Even a distant wolf's howl was preferable to the incessant snoring.

Only a handful of stars glimmered strong enough to penetrate the moon's luminous glow. She relished moonless nights, when the sky was so star-filled it appeared as though only a thin gauze separated this world from the Heavens.

But the moon was nice too.

It reminded her of the mother-of-pearl button she so cherished as a child. She would pretend it was the moon, and that she had the moon on a string.

Silly child, I was. A gentle breeze goosefleshed her skin. Had she ever dreamed she would grow up to be a spinster cheesemongress?

She had worked hard that day, and had four new cheeses dangling from the rafters, with one still in the press, dripping whey into the pan beneath. Widow Heard's garden needed weeding and the barn needed mucked, but right now all she felt like doing was drinking in the moonlight.

Menane's—no, Wôbi Skog Wsizokw's—handsome but scarred face drifted into her mind's eye. "Grace."

Grace bolted upright to find Absalom Hart standing on the ladder, his musket slung over one shoulder. His expression was stern in the moonlight.

"Go inside, Sister," he ordered firmly. "'T'is not a safe practice, lying on the roof thus."

"But I'm within the palisade walls," she argued. Her private thoughts lingered in her head and she hoped he couldn't see the embarrassing flush that heated her face.

"Pray, don't argue," Absalom said. "Come on down and go into the garrison. Meader's got watch now."

"But it's such a peaceful night, and the moon—"

"Grace." His tone was that one would use on a stubborn child.

Grace scrambled to her feet. She wanted to argue further but his determination exceeded hers, and she acquiesced with a heavy sigh. Reluctantly she turned her back to him and placed a foot on the top wrung. He descended the ladder and held it steady as she made her way down. Once she joined her brother-in-law on firm ground, she turned to tell him that he need not worry when from the opposite side of the palisade came a horrifying scream.

Chapter Twelve

Although it was early in her pregnancy, Alice was certain she felt a stirring within her womb. Smiling, she put a hand on her abdomen.

It will be a girl, she thought, envisioning a baby with Absalom's dark curls and intense brown eyes.

She knew Absalom was concerned about the Indians. She had heard the church bells and knew a selectmen's meeting had been called, so she didn't allow herself to worry when he arrived home late. Worry creased his handsome face, and he had held her especially tightly the moment he entered their small home.

"We'll spend this night in the garrison," was all he said.

It was all he needed to say: she trusted her husband to keep her safe.

Jack Meader returned to the garrison. She heard him enter and set his musket down before sitting on his pallet. He took off his boots and slipped beside Sarah and Beth with a relieved sigh. Closer to the hearth, Elder Wentworth and Dog's snoring comprised a raucous duet.

BANG!

Dog rose on his haunches and started barking at the door.

"What the devil now!" Exclaimed Elder Wentworth, rising from his pallet.

Alice sat up, her heart jumping into throat. She and Sarah Meader exchanged anxious glances. "Beth," Sarah said evenly, "run along up to the loft now."

"Mama, is it Indians?" the child whimpered nervously, crawling from beneath her blanket.

"I know not," Sarah replied as Jack Meader scrambled to retrieve his musket. "Pray, run up to the loft—"

The door burst open, sending Dog into a fresh frenzy of barks.

"Clear a space!" Absalom demanded, cradling a bloodied and broken figure in his arms. Beside him Grace stood, pale and stricken.

"Absalom! What—who?" Alice abandoned the bed clumsily as Absalom carried his burden to Widow Heard's bedstead and laid it down. She gasped at the bloodied, unrecognizable face. The coppery smell of blood sickened her and she clamped her jaw against the gorge that rose in her throat.

Sarah enveloped a weeping Beth in her skirts, shielding the child from the bloody spectacle.

"Adams," Absalom said as the broken body moaned and blood seeped onto Widow Heard's thin mattress. "A bear came upon him, poor devil. I shot the bear. Seems the bear killed a lamb—"

"Lamb..." the old Quaker moaned from the bedstead as Alice and Sarah knelt to apply pressure on the most profusely bleeding wounds.

"Adams and Eb are close," Sarah said. "Mayn't someone summon Eb?"

"I'll go," Grace offered. "I'm fast."

"Nay," Absalom said, slinging his musket from his shoulder. "I'll do it."

Alice's heart leaped. "Have a care, Husband!"

He gave her a quick nod before he darted past Wentworth, who held a barking Dog by his rope collar. Alice felt as though her heart was being torn asunder as he slammed the door shut behind him.

"Ho, Otis garrison!"

Eb rubbed his gritty eyes as he recognized the lumbering figure outside the palisade.

"Absalom Hart?"

"Aye," Hart replied, bracing his musket against his chest. "Summon your relief and come with me. Elder Adams has been attacked by a bear. He's bad off, and we thought best to fetch you."

The shock of the news gave way to urgency as Eb saw Stephen Otis crossing the courtyard to relieve him. He shimmied down the ladder quickly as Stephen, who had apparently heard Hart's words, unbarred the gate, his usually merry face uncharacteristically somber.

"Go along and God be with you, Eb," Stephen said, his hand on the gate.

As Stephen Otis closed and barred the gate on the opposite side, Eb and Absalom broke into a run back to the Heard garrison. Eb had avoided Absalom in the past on account of Alice, but due to the acuteness of the situation, the old hurt seemed minor, and he was glad the big man had come.

Jack Meader had the palisade gate opened as they clambered up Little Hill. Breathless, Eb burst into the Heard garrison, ignoring Dog's frantic barks. The women removed themselves from the bedside, revealing William Adam's torn and bloodied body.

"He's breathing his last, I fear," Eb heard Sarah Meader say as he fell to his knees and clasped one of the old man's cold, limp hands.

"Willam Adams," Eb whispered over the cold lump that swelled in his throat. "'T'is I, Ebenezer Varney."

The old man's pale gray eyes fluttered open briefly before they closed again.

"I heard the wayward lamb," whispered Adams weakly. His words were hard to hear over the incessant barking. *Couldn't Elder Wentworth remove that accursed dog from the premises?* "Thought I could secure it, but a bear—"

"Wentworth, silence that damn beast of yours!" Absalom bellowed.

"Don't speak," Eb implored, patting the old man's hand as Alice Hart drew the bloodied woolen blanket up to the shivering man's chin. Eb looked from William's mauled face to Alice's, and for a brief moment he saw the girl he had once been in love with. She gave him a sad smile before stepping away again to join Grace, Sarah Meader and Sarah's weeping daughter.

Eb glanced back at his dying friend and realized the old man was crying. Tears blended with blood as they traversed down his mangled face.

"Poor lamb," Adams sobbed, invoking such sorrow in Eb that he felt as if his anvil had fallen on his chest.

William Adams drew another shallow breath, and then lay still. Tearfully, Ebenezer released the cold limp hand and allowed Alice to pull the blanket over the old man's face.

Rising to his feet, Ebenezer thumbed tears from his whiskered cheeks and faced Absalom and Alice Hart. He offered his hand to Absalom, and the big man took it readily.

"Thank thee for summoning me, Absalom Hart," he said in a quavering voice. He glanced at Alice, whose pretty face was also tear-streaked. "Thank thee also, Alice Hart. Thou art the best of humanity."

"Grace and Sarah and I will prepare the body for you, Eb," Alice said softly. "You can stay here until morn. You're in no state of mind to walk back to Otis's."

He knew he couldn't remain among them, and suddenly felt the need for fresh air. The thickening lump in his throat prevented him from speaking, and he tipped his hat to them before giving his leave.

Monday, June 24

The stench of death lingered in the Heard garrison despite every door and window being left open. Candles glowed constantly and the bloodied blankets had been burned and replaced. The dried corn husks were removed from the ticking, which was washed and left to dry in the sun. By Monday afternoon it had dried, and Grace sat in the dooryard with Sarah Meader and the Otis women. Her neighbors had brought wheel barrows full of dried corn husks and sprigs of lavender. While the women sat in a circle filling the ticking,

Beth Meader and Hannah Otis trailed after the women, entertaining themselves by playing tag.

"'T'was so like Major Waldron to remind us all he was right about the Indians not attacking," Sarah Meader said, reaching for a handful of lavender. "After services yesterday, that's all he talked about. 'I told you so! There's nothing to fear!'"

The other women nodded. Grizel Otis's pretty face contorted with concern as she watched little Hannah trip on the hem of her smock. The child met her mother's gaze with a guilty pout. "Have a care, Hannah!" she called anxiously.

Sarah looked up from her work. "Beth, watch Hannah more closely."

"Aye, Mama," Beth replied.

Margaret Otis eyed the sole of Grace's shoe. "'T'is high time you have Stephen mend that sole, Grace," she said.

"And your drawstring needs replacing," Alice commented, gesturing at Grace's loosened neckline. "That one's worn through."

"I haven't had the time," she replied a little too sharply, a curl swinging against her cheek. She glanced down at her gaping bodice with irritation. She hadn't slept in two nights. Dark circles had formed under her eyes and she was in a sour mood. The hot afternoon sun beating on her back only made her sleepier, and although she was glad for the help, she was anxious for the ticking to be filled so she could be left alone.

The mood turned gloomy, and the women grew quiet for a time. Only the children's laughter and the crinkling of corn husks filled the late afternoon air.

"Elder Adams was laid to rest this morn, Eb told us," Maggie Otis said somberly "Poor soul. Not one family member to claim him."

"What will happen to his flock?" Grizel Otis questioned, keeping a close eye on Hannah who toddled happily after Beth.

"Old Dick will confiscate it, I'll wager," muttered Grace bitterly, shoving the curl inside her coif.The other women exchanged curious glances.

"Sister, are you all right?" Alice asked.

Grace was only half-listening to the women's conversation. "Just tired, is all," she replied, rubbing her dry eyes."And I still have yet to milk Queenie."

"Mayhap you can let Bolt nurse this night," Sarah Meader suggested. "You look as if you could fall asleep where you sit."

"Nay, I'll do my milking," Grace insisted around a yawn.

The women continued stuffing in silence until the sun glowed orange behind the trees. The sundial showed six o'clock by the time Jack Meader and Stephen Otis strode through the palisade gate to collect their women.

"Have you finished, ladies?" Jack Meader asked, catching Beth as she ran up to him and lifting her in his arms. Hannah toddled toward her half-brother, Stephen, who carefully lifted the child with his good arm.

"Just a few more stitches—ow!" Grace held back a curse as she pierced her own thumb with the needle. She thrust it into her mouth while Alice commandeered the needle and thread and finished for her.

"Jack, will you carry it in for Grace?" Sarah asked. "She's worn herself out."

"By all means," Jack Meader agreed, setting his daughter down and taking up the newly-filled ticking. Like Stephen Otis, he was a pleasant, good-natured man, and always willing to help.

The scent of death inside the garrison had diminished, but not entirely. Grace's sensitive nose still detected the redolent metallic edge of dried blood. *I'd rather sleep in the barn*, she thought as Jack placed the ticking on Dame Heard's bedstead.

"There you are, Grace," Jack said with a smile. "Now take advantage of that clean mattress afore you drop where you stand!"

"I have milking to do," she grumbled irritably. "Thank you, just the same."

The women hugged and kissed her and wished her a good night before they followed their men through the palisade gate, and Grace was left standing in the dooryard alone.

Hot and tired, she went inside and removed her stays and skirt. With a groan of irritation, she saw that the drawstring to her shift had become undone, and she re-tied it in a careless knot as she headed toward the barn. Without the support of her stays, the gaping neckline repeatedly slipped from her shoulders. In exasperation she allowed the shift to fall where it may and despite her exhaustion headed for the barn.

Ever since the bear attack, Grace had insisted on keeping Queenie and Bolt in the barn overnight, and when she opened the barn door, a restless young Bolt mooed at her impatiently. Secured in his calf pen with a rope around his neck, he pranced on his long legs, full of youthful energy.

"Forgive me your confinement, Bolt," Grace said wearily as she scratched the jagged white blaze between his eyes. "But you'll just have to spend your nights in the barn with your dam until I feel it's safe to pasture you again."

Both animals had relieved themselves, but Grace much preferred the odor of fresh manure to the stench of death. She would have to muck the stalls, but that could wait until morning.

She hadn't slept since William Adams died. She fell asleep during Sabbath services more than once, and would have received a knock on the head by the tithingman's pole had it not been for Alice jabbing her several times with a finger.

She grabbed an armful of fresh hay from the hay pile and threw it in Queenie's trough, then retrieved her buckets and stool. The rhythmic hiss of milk hitting the bucket soothed her as she pressed her cheek against Queenie's tawny flank. She breathed in the earthy scents of milk and manure and tried to erase the image of William Adams's mangled body from her mind. Her eyelids grew heavier and she almost fell off the milk stool.

Before long, both buckets were filled with fresh, frothy milk, and as Grace passed the calf pen to get the yoke, Bolt bellowed plaintively.

With a sigh of resignation, Grace relinquished her resolve to keep mother and son separated. "All right, but I daresay she won't have that much milk left for you," she said, unlatching the pen's little gate. The freed calf scampered over to his mother gleefully, kicking up his legs before dipping his head to her udder. He was growing fast, and would make a nice bull someday.

"There now, I'll see you both in the morning," Grace said over another yawn as she adjusted her shift and attached the milk buckets to the yoke. Her pricked thumb throbbed and her arms ached from the day's previous chores. Curls from both sides of her head had escaped her coif, but she was too tired to bother tucking them in.

She shouldered the yoke and lumbered beneath her burden, leaving the barn door ajar as she headed for the cheese house. Foam on the milk's surface sloshed over the rim, sliding down the buckets with each weary step.

Inside the cheese house, four wide pans rested on the work bench. She was glad to remove the heavy yoke from her shoulders. The light was growing dim, and she cursed under her breath when she spilled some of the milk. With the pans filled, she set the last emptied pail down with a grunt of satisfaction.

Mooooo-oooo!

Queenie's bellow, louder than normal, sounded agitated. Rubbing her tired eyes, Grace turned to exit the cheese house only to bang a shin on the butter churn near the door.

With a curse, she stumbled toward the barn, then gasped.

The barn door stood wide open.

Mooo-ooo

Suddenly alert, Grace ran to the barn to find Queenie straining at her tether, her eyes wide.

Bolt was gone!

Oh dear Lord, I forgot to shut and lock the door! Grace's heart plummeted to her feet. "T'will be a'right, Queenie! I'll find him!"

Running across the compound, she saw the little bull calf heading for the open palisade gate, trailing his lead behind him.

"Bolt! Get back here!" Grace cried. But when Bolt saw her running towards him, he bounded out of the gate and into the woods beyond.

Chapter Thirteen

Wahowah relaxed his vigilance over Wôbi Skog Wsizokw enough for the younger warrior to check his beaver traps and go hunting alone. Whenever possible, Wôbi Skog Wsizokw scanned the settlement for Grace, and was glad to see she was mostly confining herself to the safety of the Heard garrison. Some nights he climbed a beech tree on Little Hill that gave him a clear view into the compound. He knew what time she milked her cow in the evenings, and watched her carry two buckets of fresh milk from the barn to the cheese house. Many nights she clambered up to the cheese house roof and sat there, gazing into the night sky. In her white shift and cap, she looked like a spirit contemplating the Heavens. Together, yet apart, they watched the same moon. Sometimes a star would plummet to earth in a thin trail of crystalline dust against the darkened sky. He would wait until she returned to the garrison, then make his way back to the Pennacook camp.

Tonight, however, she looked especially fatigued and he wondered if she would make her customary sojourn to the cheese house roof. He shifted more comfortably on the tree limb, watching her carry the two heavy buckets to the cheese house. Frothy milk sloshed onto the grass as she lumbered from barn to cheese house. The heavy yoke rested on bare shoulders as pale as the milk. *She is a hard worker. She would make a good wife.* His thoughts at once became protective. He needed to warn her about the upcoming attack, somehow.

Movement caught his eye as the barn door opened slightly. He watched with interest as the calf emerged, exploring his surroundings and prancing jubilantly. He heard the cow call to her calf, but the curious little animal wandered the yard, drawing farther and farther away from the barn. A length of rope dangled from the calf's neck. By the time Grace returned to the barn, the calf was on the other side of the compound, heading toward the unlocked gate.

He heard Grace cry out. "Bolt! Get back here!"

When the calf disappeared through the open gate, Wôbi Skog Wsizokw jumped down from the tree.

Grace's feet were heavy as she trailed after the calf. It was nearly dark and if Bolt disappeared into the forest, she might never find him. She could hear Queenie's restless lowing back at the barn. It was too much for Grace in her exhausted state and she began to cry.

"Please! Enough of this, Bolt!" she pleaded when the calf finally stopped long enough to sniff a dandelion. She chose that moment to seize his lead rope, and yanked his little head up from the ground.

"Let's get back inside or we'll both be a bear's meal," she said, glancing into the darkening woods. The sun had almost dipped below the horizon and she swore she heard some animal lurking in the trees. She shivered and turned to run back to the garrison. Bolt stubbornly jerked his head, yanking the rope from her grasp.

A naked arm reached from behind her and seized the rope before it hit the ground. If she hadn't been so exhausted she would have cried out.

To her astonishment, Menane stood next to her, taking a firm hold on Bolt's lead. His black scalp lock fell across one bare shoulder and the old scar gleamed in the fading twilight while his dark eyes regarded her with urgency.

"Menane!" she managed, wiping tears from her cheeks. "Why are you here?"

"I told you before, I watch. You should not be out here."

Wearily, she covered her face in her hands and sobbed. "Menane, I am so tired."

She felt him place both hands on her shoulders, with Bolt's rope gripped securely in his right. "Listen to me, Grace," he said, and when she looked up at him his stern look frightened her.

"There will be an attack in three nights."

An attack? What was he talking about? "Wh-why?" she blubbered, more hair emerging from her coif.

"Kancamagus and the others seek revenge on Waldron," he explained. "I can do nothing to stop it. Your garrison may not be struck, but I want you to be prepared."

She burst into fresh tears. "What am I to do?"

"Tell your men."

"They won't believe me," she protested. "And how am I to explain that an Indian spoke to me in private?"

"Tell them you heard it from a Pennacook woman."

"'Tis doubtful they'd believe even that."

"Can you fire a musket?"

"Aye." All grown women were taught to defend themselves in case they were attacked when the men were not home. "But no one will believe me—"

He shook her slightly, sending her weary head bobbing. "You must get them to believe you."

Forgetting herself, she crumpled against his hairless chest, dampening it with her tears. His arms went around her and she breathed in the scent of bear grease and sweat. In her exhaustion his strength comforted her. No man had ever offered his embrace before, and she didn't want it to end. Her head throbbed and Queenie's incessant, mournful lowing made her nerves raw. She sniffed and looked up into his broad, scarred face. "Menane, I'm just so tired." The weight of fresh and overwhelming emotions pressed down on her tired frame and she could withstand no more. Her knees buckled and she collapsed, only to feel her feet leave the ground as Menane swept her up and cradled her limp body in his arms.

She felt no bigger than a child as he carried her back to the garrison with the calf trottting behind them. Her relaxed features conjured up the young girl he had met thirteen years before. She looked the same, save for the dark circles that shadowed her eyes. Several red curls fell across her face like vine tendrils. Tears still glistened on the freckled cheeks, and her lips parted slightly as her chest rose and fell. The drawstring of her neckline had loosened, exposing the swell of her bosom. She smelled of cow and cheese, and although those odors normally repulsed him, he breathed them in willingly.

He hadn't minded when she called him by his boyhood name. After all, he would always think of her as Turkey Egg Girl.

The watchtowers were unmanned, and the palisade gate was still slightly ajar. *How could the whites be so careless?* With a foot he nudged the gate open farther in order to gain entry. Looking from the garrison to the barn, he decided he would deposit both Grace and the calf in one of the stalls. Surely someone would be roused by all the noise the cow was making, and he didn't want to be discovered.

He heard the cow's sorrowful cries as he approached and Bolt replied with wails of his own. When Menane entered, the cow strained at her leash, showing the whites of her big eyes. She mooed anxiously and moved away from him, pressing herself against the barn wall.

"*Tabat,* cow!" he admonished. "I'm bringing back your son."

The stink of manure assaulted his nose, and he grimaced in disgust. Filthy animals! With one foot, he closed the barn door behind them and dropped Bolt's leash. The little calf trotted happily next to his mother and began nursing, while Queenie continued to ogle the stranger with suspicion and fear.

It was dark in the barn, and he paused with the sleeping woman in his arms while he waited for his eyes to adjust. He discerned a pile of sweet-smelling hay along one side, and gently laid her down on it. She sighed, and the soft exhalation met his chest in a warm puff.

Squatting on his heels, he observed her thoughtfully. Her neck and shoulders were dusted with fewer freckles than her face. Delicate blue veins meandered beneath skin as pale as her cheeses. Her blatant vulnerability unsettled him. Could she survive the attack? Certainly not without his help.

"I want to tell you about my visions," he muttered softly. "You have to survive, because we are meant to be together. We are twin flames."

And then he reached for his medicine bag and opened it.

He withdrew the mother-of-pearl button, still on its original tow linen string, and held it in his hand. He remembered how she had worn it on her wrist as a child. Gently, he took her left wrist in his hands and secured the button to it. Her pulse beat rhythmically beneath his fingers, and he prayed that the talisman that had kept him safe for thirteen years would now do the same for her.

"Stay safe, Turkey Egg Girl," he implored. "I will do what I can to protect you, but if I die, remember you are my twin flame."

The light from an approaching torch flickered through the panels of the barn door, and he heard footsteps. Wôbi Skog Wsizokw sprang to his feet. It would do neither he nor Grace any good if he were found here. He darted to the rear of the structure and found a back door, disengaging the latch just as the opposite door was opening. A wave of torch light broke the darkness of the barn's interior and a voice cried out, but Menane was already several steps ahead, disappearing into the dark forest.

At the base of Little Hill, Absalom and Alice were preparing for bed. Absalom sat and watched Alice brush her long brown hair in the firelight. She sat upright next to him in the bed. Her soft features, sweetened by impending motherhood, never looked lovelier to him. Reclining on one elbow, he regarded her with adoration.

"I'm worried about Grace," Alice said, setting down her brush. "She works so hard, and I fear she'll end up all alone in life."

"She appears happy being a single woman," Absalom remarked with disinterest.

Alice swung the entire length of her hair over one shoulder and began braiding it, as was her nightly custom. "But to never know a man's love," Alice said wistfully. One of her hands fell lightly on her rounded abdomen. "Nor to ever have a child. That sounds like such an empty life to me."

From behind the garrison walls came an agitated *moo.*

Absalom thought for a moment and agreed with his wife. Having been single for so many years, he was grateful for his married status. "Grace is a grown woman, and the choice is hers to make," he reminded his wife, gently stroking her back.

Mooo!

Alice sighed, the firelight accentuating her pretty face in a golden glow. "Aye, that's true, but still—"

Mooo—ooo! "Why is Queenie making that ruckus?" Alice asked as she secured the braid with a length of thread. "Mayhap Grace didn't milk her after all, and Bolt is in his calf pen. Grace was more tired than I'd ever seen her."

Absalom rose from the bed with reluctance. "Methinks some fox got into the barn. I'll check just to make sure."

"Do take care," Alice said anxiously as Absalom put on his breeches and pulled on his boots. "'Tis dark as pitch out there."

He threw a cloak over his shoulders and slapped his felt hat on his head. He kissed her before reaching for a pine knot that rested near the hearth. One touch to the embers in the hearth, and the torch was ablaze.

"Lock the door behind me, Wife, just in case," he said. Her worried look needled his heart.

He reached for his musket over the door and headed into the darkness, up Little Hill. The sky was cloudless and encrusted with stars. The night air was thick with the mingled scents of woodland flora. Some animal disappeared into the shadows, putting Absalom on high alert. *'T'is the creatures one doesn't hear nor see that are cause for concern,* he reminded himself.

The Heard palisade loomed darkly before him, and Queenie's demanding cries grew more frequent. His heart sunk heavily when he saw the palisade gate was ajar. He hoped no intruders—human or otherwise—had entered.

The garrison itself, along with the cheese house and other outbuildings, appeared tranquil, but from within the barn Queenie continued to bellow. Absalom drew in a deep breath as he approached the barn door. Cradling his musket and holding the torch aloft, he nudged the door open with an elbow. He entered warily, wrinkling his nose at the smell of fresh manure. As his eyes adjusted, he saw Queenie regarding him with her soulful brown eyes. The calf stood next to his dam, swishing his ropy tail.

He thought he detected movement near the back door.

"Halt!"

He sprang forward, flinging the door open, but whatever or whomever had vanished into the darkness.

In the torchlight he inspected the cow and calf, who withdrew from the flame. They appeared unharmed. Quickly he scanned the rest of the barn, then stopped when his torch illuminated the hay pile. There lay his sister-in-law, fast asleep. Her shift had gaped open, partially exposing her bosom. Absalom averted his eyes while he removed his cloak and covered her.

Should I carry her into the garrison? Likely she would be safe sleeping where she was. She looked peaceful and unharmed. Tears had dried and left trails on her flushed cheeks. He looked over in the direction of the rear door, then back again to Grace's relaxed, peaceful face. His wife's earlier words gave him pause. If someone had been here with his sister-in-law, then Alice, as well as he, would be quite curious to know just whom.

Chapter Fourteen

Tuesday, June 25

The rooster crowed, and Grace awoke to sunlight streaming through the barn window. Her eyes felt gritty and her tongue was dry as tree bark. She stretched languorously, yawned and opened her eyes—and then sat up with a start. Her head spun as she looked left and right. Putting her hand to her chest, she fumbled nervously with the loose drawstrings. *I must have slept here to avoid the stink in the garrison*, her foggy mind decided. Then she noticed the man's cloak that lay over her. *Who covered me?*

Confused, she tied the drawstring securely. Something dangled at her wrist, and she gasped in disbelief.

Her whirligig! She began to giggle and sputter at the same time. *Where* had it come from?

Queenie gave a low *mooo* and regarded her curiously while Bolt nursed.

"Stop nursing, Bolt!" she exclaimed, scrambling to her feet. "I have milking to do! And why aren't you in your pen?"

Brushing off hay that clung to her clothing, she seized Bolt's lead and struggled to pull him from the teat. The little calf complained loudly when she led him into his pen. "I'll give you your share," she promised the calf. "But first allow me to wake up."

She felt peculiar this morning, the way she felt after having the old nightmare. Did she have the nightmare last night? She couldn't remember.

But she was certain she had dreamed about Menane. Or was it a dream?

They had met at twilight in the woods. The memory of his dark, penetrating eyes warmed her skin anew. He had placed his hands, firm yet gentle, on her shoulders and she recalled the scent of sweat and bear grease. At one point his arms encircled her. He was telling her something very important. He wanted her to remember something. *An attack! The Indians are going to attack! But when? Did he tell me when?*

Grace paused by the barn door and looked back at the pile of hay. There was something else…the feel of his touch, the sound of his voice…. "We are twin flames."

Twin flames.

The odd term conjured up her nightmare of the raven grasping flaming arrows in its talons. Shivering at the memory, she shook her head to clear it. Fondling the whirligig, Grace opened the barn door and headed to the well. The morning air smelled fresh and cold dew seeped through the hole in her shoe.

A multitude of birds joined the rooster's crowing, and although the morning glistened with promise, Grace couldn't shake the unsettling feeling.

She remembered being so exhausted while stuffing the ticking with the other women, and she certainly wouldn't have neglected to milk Queenie no matter how spent she was. She must have finished the milking and fallen asleep in the hay pile.

But how to explain the man's cloak?

And the dream about Menane felt so *real*. She could still feel his arms around her, could still smell his scent.

No, she was certain it hadn't been a dream. The reappearance of her lost whirligig proved it. Could Menane have found it, and kept it all these years, only to return it to her now?

She drew up the water bucket and took a refreshing sip before plunging her hands into its cool depths and splashing her face. She removed her coif and rearranged her hair, tucking every curl beneath the white linen. She had to get to her milking, but before anything else, she needed to talk to Alice and Absalom. Queenie and Bolt would have to wait.

She ran into the Heard garrison, found her stays and laced them. Then she plucked her cloak from its peg and threw it over her shoulders.

What am I going to tell them? She opened the palisade gate and hurrying down Little Hill to her sister's small clapboard dwelling.

She found Alice in her garden pulling radishes, her pretty face shaded by a straw hat despite the fact the sun hadn't cleared the tree line. Alice looked up and gave Grace a bemused smile.

"Good morn, Sister," Alice said. "How was your night in the barn?"

Grace scowled in puzzlement. "How do you know I slept in the barn?"

Alice placed a radish in her basket and wiped her dirt-stained fingers on her apron. "Last night Queenie was making such a commotion Absalom went to check, and found you sleeping in the hay pile." Alice's face sobered with concern. "He also thinks he saw a man fleeing the barn just as he was entering."

So it had been Absalom who had covered her. Abruptly, Grace thrust out her left arm. "Alice, look."

Now it was Alice who looked puzzled, and her eyes widened in recognition when she saw the mother-of-pearl disc dangling from her sister's wrist. "Is that—?"

"'T'is my old whirligig I lost so long ago!" Grace confirmed.

Alice got to her feet, groaning slightly. "Grace, what happened last night?"

Grace felt like crying. "Do you remember the Indian boy, Menane?"

Alice gave Grace an accusatory look. "Oh, Grace, for shame!"

"Nay, listen to me!" Grace pleaded, seizing her sister's arms. "Bolt got out last night and Menane helped me retrieve him. I was so exhausted last night he must have carried me back to the barn and laid me in the hay—"

"Grace, I'm surprised at you!"

"He didn't molest me, Alice! Truly he didn't! He was there to warn me."

"Warn you of what?"

"The Indians plan to attack."

Alice gasped. "When?"

"That I'm not sure, I was so sleepy I don't remember what night. Oh, Alice, what are we to do?"

Grace watched her sister's face crease with worry. "Absalom has already left for the mill. We'll bring him his noonday meal together and you can tell him yourself."

"He'll look at me like you did just now. He'll think I've lost my virtue."

It was Alice's turn to put a hand on Grace's arm. "Forgive me for that, Sister, but 'tis hard to accept that a savage—"

"Wôbi Skog Wsizokw is not a savage!" Grace contradicted with so much passion she surprised even herself. "He's a friend."

"Who? I thought his name was Menane?"

"He goes by Wôbi Skog Wsizokw now," Grace explained, thrusting the curl in place with growing impatience. "Oh, Queenie will just have to wait a bit longer! I need to speak with Absalom."

Alice retrieved her basket of radishes and took her sister's hand. "Then we'll go now."

Over the roar of the water wheel, Absalom couldn't be certain he heard his sister-in-law correctly. She stood next to Alice, keeping a tight grip on his spare musket. He was glad the women had the presence of mind to travel to the mill armed, and glad that it was Grace who handled it, because Alice was not a good shot.

"'T'was the young buck with the scar on his face?" Absalom questioned.

"Aye," Grace confirmed, her face red after explaining last night's encounter once more. She rested the butt of the musket on the ground, her eyes pleading with him. "He's called Wôbi Skog Wsizokw now. Oh, please believe me, Ab!"

Absalom nodded. *The same Indian who warned me.* A cold feeling of dread drizzled down his spine. Anyone else would have dismissed Grace's story as the ramblings of an hysterical woman, under the spell of some Indian's charms, but Absalom knew Grace, and he believed her.

"I fear 't'would be folly to summon another selectmen's meeting," he said thoughtfully. "Waldron and the others are even less likely to believe we're under threat after nothing transpired at the full moon."

"What are we to do, Husband?" Alice asked anxiously, cupping her rounded abdomen with trembling hands.

Rubbing his bearded chin, he observed the frightened women with a growing sense of urgency. "I'll tell Wentworth and the Meaders to spend the next few nights in the garrison. Come Thursday, I meet the ferry to retrieve Widow Heard and her clan," Absalom said. "That will leave the garrison down one man that night."

Absalom knew no one got any sleep when both Wentworth and his dog spent the night in the garrison due to their combined snoring. Some nights the noisy pair was banished to sleep in the barn. Even then, their snores could be heard from across the courtyard.

"I can take watch that night," Grace offered. She had keen eyesight and had proved herself a good shot on many occasions.

"You'll have to," Absalom agreed, turning his gaze on Alice's anxious face. "As will you, Wife. Wear men's hats so it looks like more men are there. Everyone will need to be alert." To Grace, he said, "Go now to Otis's. For the sake of your own reputation, tell them it was I who spoke with the Indian."

"I shall," Grace agreed.

Absalom gave his wife a quick embrace before watching both women make their way to the Otis garrison. He chewed his bottom lip anxiously as a sense of impending disaster gathered over him like a darkening thundercloud.

Stephen Otis straddled his cobbler's bench, draping a leather insole over a wooden last. He heard Margaret and Maggie conversing in the garden, no doubt gathering plants from which to make their dyes. Despite his almost-useless right arm, he was happy with his lot in life. Although he couldn't shoot a musket anymore, he practiced throwing his knife with his left hand until he was almost as good as his friend Absalom Hart. Margaret was opposed to him using what she considered "the devil's hand," but the necessity to defend his family overruled her superstition, and he continued to practice every day.

With his hat brim pulled low over his eyes against the rising sun, he smiled in greeting when the Hampton sisters arrived.

"Good morn to you, Hampton sisters," he said, his blue eyes squinting against the rising sun. "Finally come to repair that shoe, Miss Grace?" When his cheerful greeting didn't get the light-hearted response he expected, his smile fell. "What's wrong? Has something happened?"

The women shared an anxious look and they murmured a quick "good morning" to him and to his wife and daughter, who came around the corner with baskets full of yarrow and sumac.

"Absalom fears an attack is truly imminent," Alice explained, twisting her apron as Grace once again rested the butt of the musket on the ground.

Stephen heard his wife gasp behind him.

"Has he had a premonition?" Margaret asked anxiously, putting a hand to her delicate throat.

"Nay, but the same Indian who warned him bespoke of it again last night," Alice said in an odd tone, glancing at her sister, whose freckled face reddened curiously.

"Does he know when?" Stephen asked, rising from his bench.

"Nay," both sisters answered together.

"But he is adamant that everyone take cover in the garrisons and be on the alert," Alice insisted.

Stephen exchanged looks with his wife and daughter. Absalom was an excellent judge of character, and if he believed the Indian was being truthful, there was likely some merit to it.

"Thank you, then, for the warning," Stephen said. "I'll tell Pa and Eb."

Both sisters' shoulders sagged in relief that he believed them.

"I've got time to repair that sole if you like, Miss Grace," Stephen said.

"Another time," Grace said, a rust-colored curl springing from her coif. "'T'is growing late and I have yet to milk Queenie."

He nodded. "God be with you, Hampton sisters."

"And you, Otis family," Alice replied.

As the two women hurried away, Stephen draped his good arm around his wife as she stepped closer, still holding her basket of yarrow.

"When do you think the attack will come, Papa?" Maggie asked in a quaking voice.

He looked from his wife to his daughter. Maggie was but a younger version of her mother, and he loved them both so much his heart ached. He wanted to whisk away the fear with reassuring words, but none came to him.

"I know not, daughter," he said.

The sun was well past the tree line by the time Grace returned to the barn. Queenie appeared agitated and Bolt pranced impatiently in his pen. She mumbled apologies to the disgruntled beasts, milking as quickly as she could. But her mind was elsewhere, and she almost upset the first milk bucket.

What am I to do? Her frightened mind refrained, pressing her cheek firmly against Queenie's solid flank. Every garrison had a well-choreographed defense plan, but the foreknowledge that an attack was pending chilled the blood in her veins.

And why did Menane warn her? *"We are twin flames"* echoed in her memory. Did that mean they were meant to be together? Did he love her? For that matter, did she love him? In any case, what good would having a love do if one faced imminent peril? She had good eyesight and could shoot a musket, but she never really had to fire one before.

"All we can do is keep a keen eye out each night," she said to Queenie, who glanced at her noncommittally, chewing her cud. Grace's stomach rumbled as she realized it was probably almost noon, and she hadn't eaten anything since the night before.

Bolt released a strong stream of urine that hissed onto the hay in his pen, reminding Grace the barn needed to be mucked badly. With the second bucket filled, she set them safely aside to take to the cheese house later. She decided she would take Queenie and Bolt out to the common pasture before they were driven mad from being in the barn so long.

"Come along now," she said, hoping they didn't sense the fear in her voice as she took their leads and opened the barn door. "Off to the pasture with you."

The gutted deer carcass swayed on its pole as Wôbi Skog Wsizokw and Wahowah made their way back to their camp, their bows and quivers slung across their backs. Wahowah took the lead, muscles taught under his tattooed skin. Wôbi Skog Wsizokw glared at his companion's bare back with resentment. Against his wishes, Wahowah had insisted on accompanying him that morning.

The sun reached its apex in the cloudless sky as the whites' common pasture came into view. The zigzag of the snake fence demarcated the meadow from the woods with stark ugliness while the stench of cow manure wafted in the hot summer air. Wôbi Skog Wsizokw idly contemplated the repulsive ways of the whites until he heard the fence open with a groan.

Grace was leading her cow and calf through the fence. She was less than half a league away, alone and defenseless. *She should have finished her morning milking hours ago.* Wahowah thrust his chin in Grace's direction.

"That foolish little woman dies in two nights," Wahowah said without breaking his leisurely stride. "And guarding her from that tree each night won't save her."

Wôbi Skog Wsizokw's heart chilled. He never liked the hottempered older warrior, and he had been naive to think Wahowah had slackened his vigilance. The knowledge that Wahowah was aware of his nocturnal observations in the beech tree both angered and frightened him. *If Wahowah knows, he's most likely told Kancamagus.* Wôbi Skog Wsizokw was at a loss for how to react to this unsettling discovery. While he silently admonished himself for not being more careful, Wahowah chuckled coldly.

"Look, she sees us."

Grace was watching them, untying the leads from her beasts' tawny necks. She looked so small and defenseless from this distance, but he was certain she recognized him. Sunlight set red curls ablaze against her freckled face. Coiling the hemp leads around one arm, she returned his gaze steadily.

Retreat back to the settlement! He implored her silently, his stomach clenching. His hatred for Wahowah bubbled from within until it burst from his throat in a snarl.

"Only a coward would kill a defenseless woman!"

Wahowah glanced back and grinned with a serpentine gleam in his eye. "I would do it without a second thought if I felt she deserved it."

Rage threatened to seize Wôbi Skog Wsizokw. His right palm itched to grab the knife at his waist and plunge it into the other man's neck. He could think of no reason why the freckle-faced white woman should mean so much to him, other than the dreams and visions he had had. He met her gaze again, and now she had her left hand over her heart. The bright sunlight glinted off something shiny at her wrist, and he knew it was the whirligig.

He had told her when the attack would come, and it gave him some solace that she likely had warned her men.

With all the restraint he could muster, he remained silent while

Wahowah's mocking laughter sent birds fleeing their perches to soar into the cloudless sky.

She knew he had seen her. But he was with that hateful savage who had broken her wheel barrow and drank from her well. Her heart fluttered as if it had grown wings and she pressed her left hand to her chest in an attempt to ease its palpitations. She hoped he saw the whirligig dangling from her wrist.

She heard them speaking in their own tongue, and the stern expression on Menane's face contrasted sharply to the other man's mocking laughter. *They are discussing me.* She all at once felt vulnerable as Bolt butted her gently with his head. She drew her cloak tighter around her shoulders and waited until Menane broke eye contact. Then, with a renewed sense of urgency, she turned and hurried out the pasture, securing the gate behind her.

Oh, what night did he tell me? She tried desperately to recall. The memory of their encounter was growing dimmer and more dreamlike. The clearest memory was the sensation of his arms embracing her while she wept against his hard chest.

Dog announced her arrival at Little Hill with incessant barks as he strained against his chain. The barking jarred her nerves and her head began to throb as she reached Alice's door. When she burst in her sister was stirring coals in her hearth. Alice's pretty face settled into lines of concern when Grace entered. "What's happened?" she gasped, straightening from her stooped position among the ashes.

Grace bit back a sob of anxiety. "I fear the attack is nigh."

Alice's face blanched. "Did you speak with your—friend— this day?"

Shaking her head, Grace glanced around for the musket Absalom always left for Alice. "Nay, but I saw him just now while I was returning Queenie and Bolt to the pasture—"

"Grace, you must stop going out alone!" Alice admonished.

"Nay, listen!" Finding the musket hanging above the door, she stood on tiptoe to reach it. "Menane was there, and he saw me, but he was with that hateful Wahowah, and I sensed he wanted to warn me yet again but couldn't." She reached for the bag of shot and the powder horn. "Alice, come stay in the garrison with me. They may even attack in the light of day, for all we know!"

Alice rested the iron poker against the hearth and gripped Grace's trembling shoulders. "Compose yourself, sister!" she said, giving Grace a little shake. "I've too much to do here. And I sincerely doubt any attack will occur in the light of day."

Grace looked gravely into her sister's eyes. "Alice, daylight matters not. Just last week, while Beth was helping me, that hateful Wahowah was at our well."

Alice's face blanched. "Why didn't you tell me? Why didn't you tell Absalom?"

"Because he didn't hurt us," Grace replied. *But he frightened me more than I care to admit.*

"Oh, Grace, you should have said something!" Alice admonished, wringing her apron. "We'll sup at the garrison this eve, and the Meaders and Elder Wentworth will join us—what are you doing with that musket?"

Grace sat on the table with the musket between her knees and tore open a cartridge of gunpowder. Placing a small amount in the flash pan, Grace closed the frizzen and dropped the rest of the cartridge down the barrel.

"I'm out of practice, as are you, sister," she said, freeing the ramrod and plunging it down the barrel. "Come with me and we'll fire some shots."

Alice's face paled. "You know I'm no good with a musket. Besides, 'tis unwise to waste ammunition."

"We've plenty," Grace insisted, returning the ramrod to its place alongside the barrel. "And what good would ammunition do if we're ill-prepared?" Rising, she grabbed her sister's limp hand and stepped into the bright afternoon sunlight.

They stopped in a clearing, several yards from a large oak that had been cleaved in two by a lightning bolt. Half of the once-great tree remained erect, but its interior had decayed, forming an alcove big enough for a bear to sleep in. Even at this distance, Grace could smell the odor of rotting wood. The other half sagged at an angle, its bare branches almost touching the ground. An abandoned squirrel's nest rested in the dead limbs, and Grace pointed at it.

"Behold, Alice!" she said as birds serenaded them from the treetops. "Before us stands a savage. You take the first shot, and then I will take the next."

Alice accepted the musket with reluctance. The heavy weapon wobbled in her arms as she cocked it, and Grace stopped her ears with her fingers in preparation.

BANG!

Alice fired and missed. The recoil thrust her backward, almost knocking her down.

From Elder Wentworth's property, Dog began to bark with alarm. Choking on the cloud of smoke, Alice looked dismayed. But Grace gave her sister an encouraging smile. "We'll practice some more. Hand me the musket."

Alice complied readily, prematurely stopping her ears as Grace once again prepared the musket for firing. Tucking a curl out of the way, she squinted into the sites and took aim. The squirrel's nest transformed into the hateful Indian's face, and she braced herself as she cocked the gun and squeezed the trigger.

BANG!

The kick thrust her backwards and the smoke stung her eyes, but she could see that the squirrel's nest had been destroyed.

Alice withdrew her fingers from her ears, her expression one admiration.

Grace smiled at her accomplishment. "Now you again, sister," she said, handing the musket back to Alice. "We'll practice until you hit the mark."

Distant musket fire could be heard from the settlement as

Wôbi Skog Wsizokw and Wahowah entered the Pennacook camp. Glowering hatefully at Wahowah with every step, he hoped the reports he heard meant Grace—or someone—had heeded his warning and was practicing their defense.

His Aunt Toloti stepped out of her wigwam as the two hunters deposited their quarry. She and the other women would skin the carcass and prepare the meat for drying. She was several years younger than his uncle Wanalancet, and gave her nephew a curious look after Wahowah ambled off to join Kancamagus and some other men who sat cleaning their muskets.

"They don't trust you, nephew," Toloti said, watching Wahowah join the circle of men. "But I am glad you refuse to take part in the siege. I remember *Nigawesega's* vision. She feared you would die if you went to the settlement."

Wôbi Skog Wsizokw remembered. *I saw you at the white settlement and a big red hawk swooped down and tore out your heart.* The warning echoed in his memory even now. For the past several nights, he had dreamed of a red hawk grasping a flaming arrow in each talon as it soared into a starry night sky. He awakened troubled, fearing the dream's portent.

His aunt's expression was one of relief. Wôbi Skog Wsizokw forced a reassuring smile. "All is well, Aunt. Have no fear for me."

Apparently pacified, she turned from him and withdrew a knife from her belt as she approached the deer carcass. As she skillfully skinned the deer he was reminded of the hunt and how he had hated every moment he was forced to spend in Wahowah's company. He glanced at his nemesis, who sat next to Kancamagus, laughing with the other warriors. With a grunt of disdain, he strode past the group of men cleaning their weapons, keenly aware that their conversation ceased as he approached.

"So have you said your goodbyes to your white woman?" Wahowah jeered as he walked past.

He heard laughter from the other men, and all sense of reason left him in a white-hot rage. Retracing his steps, he lunged at his tormenter with a frenzied cry. His hands went around the other man's throat as they wrestled in the grass, cheered on by their spectators. Wôbi Skog Wsizokw got the upper hand, straddling his opponent and landing two hard blows to Wahowah's jaw before Kancamagus and another warrior pulled him off.

"Nijia!" Kancamagus yelled, leaping up from where he sat.

"Your brother is crazy, Kancamagus!" Wahowah accused, wiping blood from his mouth as he got to his feet.

Wôbi Skog Wsizokw seethed against the restraints of his brother's arms. "I won't have you speak of her!"

The silence that followed chilled the summer air, and Wôbi Skog Wsizokw glowered at Wahowah even as Kancamagus shook him.

"Stop this, Wôbi Skog Wsizokw!" Kancamagus demanded. "You are talking crazy."

Masandowit had approached. "He'll have to be restrained the night we strike."

Wôbi Skog Wsizokw shook himself loose from Kancamagus's grip.

"Make peace," Masandowit instructed.

Wahowah smiled nastily, extending a hand to Wôbi Skog Wsizokw. Wôbi Skog Wsizokw accepted it with revulsion and when the two leaned in close enough, he hissed into Wahowah's ear, "If you harm her, Wahowah, I swear to Kitchi Manitou I'll kill you myself."

Chapter Fifteen

ine wood shavings littered the plank floor like dry autumn leaves as Absalom finished sanding the birchwood cradle. The only time he could work on it was at sunup before he left for the mill. The east-facing door was open, flooding the shed with soft pink light. When he wasn't working on it, he stowed the cradle in a corner with sackcloth draped over it. Alice presumed their child would borrow the cradle Beth Meader had outgrown, and Absalom anticipated surprising her with his handiwork.

Absalom loved carpentry. Like Captain Heard, his father had been a carpenter. His boyhood intention was to embrace the trade, but when his hands grew too big for the fine, intricate work his father had mastered, he took on the heftier tasks. Impressed with Absalom's size, Richard Waldron offered him a job at the mill. Although Absalom's strength enabled him to do the work of three men, Waldron paid him no extra.

With the child coming, Absalom considered demanding a fairer wage. Stephen Otis encouraged him to do so, joking that if the child inherited his father's appetite, Absalom would spend half of his pay on food alone.

Absalom ran a calloused hand over the fine grain and gave the cradle a gentle push on its crescent-shaped rockers. It rocked smoothly and he smiled with satisfaction.

When he tried to envision his child swaddled and sleeping in the tiny bed, however, his mind's eye only conjured up emptiness. That disturbed him deeply, and he was afraid it bespoke of an ill fate.

The encounter with the young Pennacook had shaken him greatly. For the past two nights he had been plagued with the same nightmare. He would call Alice, looking for her everywhere but to no avail. The nightmare would leave him waking in a cold sweat, causing him to hug his sleeping wife close to him.

The front door of the house creaked open, and he hastily threw the sackcloth over the cradle. He shoved the little bed back into its corner just as Alice's approaching footfalls hit the flagstones. On her way to the garden, she would pass the shed's open door within minutes. He turned to see her standing just outside the shed door, an empty willow basket in her hands. A straw hat cast a shadow over her shapely brow.

"Husband, you've not left for the mill yet?" Alice inquired with a hint of surprise in her voice.

"Stephen Otis asked to borrow an awl," Ab said hastily, snatching up the small implement and holding it up as proof of his delay. He had always been a poor liar, and he suspected she detected his deception. She smiled up at him, and he knew she had not been fooled.

"Methinks a cobbler would own plenty of awls and not be in need of borrowing," she teased as he swung his musket on his shoulder and closed the shed door behind him.

"He lost his."

"I see."

He smiled down into her beautiful violet eyes. Lifting her chin with his free hand, he kissed her soft mouth and when he withdrew, her face flushed prettily.

"Pray, don't go into the shed."

"The garden's covered with weeds. I may need the hoe."

"Have Grace get it for you, or wait until I return."

At last she relented. "Very well, husband."

As canny as she is beautiful, he thought with pride. Then, he had another thought. "Let me get the other musket for you." His wife looked at him with gentle admonishment. "I'll only be in the garden, and you know how poor a shot I am."

That was true, but at least the presence of a musket would give the illusion she was capable of defending herself.

"Be safe, Wife."

He gave her a last kiss before leaving for the mill, the taste of her sweet lips still on his tongue as he strode down Cart Way.

Alice watched him until he disappeared from her sight. When they were apart, she felt as though invisible bonds joining their hearts were pulled taut. Only when they were together did she feel complete.

She smiled and splayed a hand over her swollen abdomen. Saying a silent prayer of gratitude, she resumed her walk to the garden and knelt in the moist soil. She plucked a few tufts of crabgrass from between the peas and radishes, inhaling the fecund scent of the soil.

The rising sun warmed her shoulders and soothed an ache in her lower back. A busy day lay ahead of her, and she hoped the morning sickness would abate long enough for her to get her chores finished. She had left a pot of water boiling over the fire. While the vegetables boiled, she would cut up the salt pork and season it with black pepper.

When her basket grew laden with fruitage, Alice got to her feet with a groan and shook dirt from her apron. Grasping the basket's handle, she paused, sensing she was not alone.

Out of the corner of her eye, she detected movement. She slid her eyes to the tree line, and stifled a gasp.

Less than twenty feet away from her stood the Pennacook warrior, Wahowah.

Terror iced her veins as she tried to think what to do. Clutching the basket, she bit back a whimper of panic as she took one, then another, step toward the house. The radish tops quivered in the basket and she realized her hands were trembling. Her heart knocked wildly against her ribcage, urging her to move faster.

In the corner of her eye, she saw that he matched her step for step, keeping adjacent to her.

Just a few more steps and she would be in the house. Then she would bar the door and arm herself with the spare musket.

She dropped the basket, her feet hitting the flagstones as she reached for the doorknob. Praying an arrow wouldn't strike her from behind, she pushed open the door and ran in, slamming and locking it securely behind her. Standing on tiptoe, she opened the peephole and peered out at the tree line, but the fearsome warrior had disappeared.

With her back pressed against the door, she dropped her head into her hands and released sobs of fear and relief.

"Absalom, hurry home!"

The beheaded duck's limbs spasmed as Elsie carried it by its severed neck. Such twitching death throes always spooked her, and she was certain she would be chased by headless fowl in her dreams the coming night.

"Elsie, be sure you clean that bird fully!" Waldron bellowed from the bench. "If Masandowit finds one hair on his portion, I'll have you flogged."

"Aye, sir," she replied wearily, grasping the bloodied little hatchet in one hand. The unfortunate bird's blood stained her apron and bodice, and when she wiped her brow on her sleeve, it came away stained likewise. She could never decide what part of this chore was worse: the blood and gore or Waldron's criticisms. *I can bear this*, she reminded herself as she struggled to keep her gorge down.

"Mind you, don't toss away the neck and gizzard this time!"

"Aye, sir."

Elsie sat on the stoop, wearing her oldest and most worn garments. She loathed the impending shower of down and feathers that would cling to her with relentless persistence. Waldron derived malicious satisfaction from supervising her labor on the bench. He insisted she sit on the stoop so he could look down upon her. Whenever she was placed in such a lowly position she wanted to cry. Biting back a sob that swelled in her throat, she set down the hatchet and picked up the knife with which to slit the duck's belly.

"Worthless girl! Where's the canvas? If you don't put down the canvas, you'll have to gather the innards in your apron. Is that what you plan to do?"

"Nay, sir."

"Oh never mind," Waldron barked. "That apron's so soiled now it doesn't matter. Just lay it out before you and wrap the innards in it."

Hot tears scalded the backs of her eyeballs as she set the carcass down and untied the apron from her waist. *I can bear this*, she told herself again. *I can bear this, for I've borne far worse.*

Thursday, June 27

When Thursday morning dawned with the promise of another peaceful day, the citizens of Cochecho began to be less wary. The consensus was that if the Indians were going to attack, surely they would have before now.

In the soft light of the rising sun, Absalom Hart stood on his stoop, shouldering his musket. He heard Alice's soft weeping from within. After breakfast, he told her that he would leave for the ferry landing directly from the mill. As he did before, he would borrow Jack Meader's ox and cart, and didn't know what time Alice could expect him home.

"It tears at my heart to have you gone so long," Alice whimpered into his chest.

In their eleven years of marriage, the only time they were apart was when he worked at the mill or trained for the militia. Tears glimmered in her violet eyes, and he blamed the fickle humors said to run rampant in a breeding woman.

"Extinguish the hearth and take your knitting along to the garrison," he suggested, eyeing the basket of yarn she kept at the side of their bedstead. She had begun knitting a bunting for the baby from cream-colored yarn she had spun herself. "Take the spare musket with you also."

She glanced nervously at the weapon he always left for her, resting on its pegs above the door. "You know what a poor shot I am, Husband," she said, and he felt her tremble in his embrace. "Do you think something will happen tonight?" She looked up at him with frightened eyes. "Have you had a premonition?"

He hesitated, not wanting to frighten her further. *I fear if I leave I may never see you again.* A foreboding chill slithering down his spine. "I don't think the threat has passed," he finally said. "You will be safe in the garrison."

When he kissed her goodbye, he tasted the salt from her tears, and he murmured encouragements against her coifed head before taking up his hat and musket and stepping out into the newborn day.

His concerns increased as he watched a pair of Indians ambling into the shadowy recesses of the woods. The one who had warned him—and Grace—was followed by the tall one called Wahowah, whose belligerent reputation was regarded with fear by Cochecho's residents.

He heard footsteps and saw Grace descending Little Hill on her way to return Queenie and Bolt to the common pasture. As she passed by his dwelling with the docile animals in tow, he stepped off the stoop and approached her.

"Sister, you shouldn't take them to pasture alone. I've just spotted Indians lurking yonder."

He detected a hint of defiance in her blue eyes as she looked up at him. "They need pasturing and I have no one to escort me. If you escort me, you'll be late to the mill and Old Dick will dock your pay."

That was true. He glanced back at the pair of Indians who reemerged briefly in a clearing. As he watched them warily, Grace murmured with contempt, "I despise that tall one. Had I a pitchfork, I'd have willingly speared him with it last week when he was at my well."

He spun and glared at her, his eyebrows raised in alarm.

"Why didn't you tell me?"

"I told Alice two days ago," she replied, her tone defensive.

Why hadn't Alice informed him? His shock blossomed like bloodstain on linen. He glanced back at the clapboard house. He no longer heard Alice's sobs, but knowing he was abandoning her in such a state distressed him. Alice did not share her sister's boldness, and her delicate nature was a constant worry for him.

Absalom watched Bolt dip his tawny head to Queenie's udder. He didn't like Grace's predilection for walking alone, but she was right that Waldron would dock him if he was late to the mill. As she yanked the calf's head up, his hand went to the knife he always wore at his waist. "At least take this."

She shook her head. "You'll have need of it on your journey to the ferry landing."

"I hope you aren't counting on your friend to defend you from his brethren."

Her face colored, and his own face warmed at what sounded like an implication. But then Grace raised her chin and she said defiantly, "I'm not."

He was unconvinced, but truly had no time to argue, and shook his head in defeat. "Then God be with you, Sister."

"And with you," she replied with a jerk on the animals' leads.

He watched her march purposefully toward the common pasture, grateful that Alice wasn't that foolhardy.

He heard the front door open behind him. Alice looked at him with red-rimmed eyes. He had no time to console her, and blew her a sincere kiss before he hurried down Cart Way, her forlorn expression reflected in his mind's eye.

"How long do you expect this delay to be?" the red-faced young courier asked anxiously, gripping his horse's reins so tightly his knuckles blanched. The afternoon sun glimmered brightly over the expanse of the river.

"Can't say," the dock worker said around his pipe. "But I don't foresee you crossing the river until well after dark."

"But I have an urgent message for Major Waldron at Cochecho!"

Flanked by her daughter and granddaughter, Widow Elizabeth Heard approached this exchange. John Ham and Johnny Horne brought up the rear, carrying the heavy trunk that housed their collective belongings. It had been an enjoyable, albeit exhausting visit with family, and Elizabeth was anxious to sleep in her own bed this night.

"Pardon us," she said while her sons-in-law maneuvered the trunk around the courier's sweat-lathered horse and set it at the end of the dock. "Is there a problem?"

The courier's look was one of entreaty. "The ferry's under repairs," the dock worker explained, sounding as if he was growing tired of repeating the news. "Don't expect it to be ready until late tonight."

"You're going to Cochecho?" the courier asked hoarsely. He looked as if he'd spent an entire day in the saddle, his face weary and wind-burned.

"Aye," John Ham replied, stepping up to speak for his family. "Has something happened?"

The courier removed his hat and raked his fingers through damp brown curls. "I've a message from Governor Bradstreet for Major Waldron. John Hawkins's band plan to attack Cochecho," he said, returning his hat to his head.

Mary gasped and Emmie started to cry as Widow Heard looked from the courier to her sons-in-law. Looks of utter shock and helplessness spread among the group. Mary and Emmie dove into their husbands' arms like frightened chicks under a hen, weeping hysterically. Only Widow Heard stood alone.

"When is this attack expected?" John Ham demanded, stroking Mary's back.

"We can't be certain," the courier replied. To the dock worker, he pleaded, "Is there not another ferry we can take?"

The urgency of the situation seemed to occur to the dock worker, and he withdrew the pipe. "I'm afraid not," he replied with obvious regret.

"Mother, what shall we do?" a panicked Mary asked. Her unusual reaction underscored the urgency of the matter, as she historically bore crises with unflinching stoicism.

"We can do nothing but wait for the ferry to be repaired," Widow Heard's words sounded hollow to her own ears. "And pray that that the Indians don't attack before our folk can be warned."

The fat beaver carcass lay motionless, its skull crushed beneath the limestone slab of the deadfall trap. Flies buzzed around the day-old kill, rank with the stench of blood and castor. The sun was beginning its descent and Wôbi Skog Wsizokw suspected Wahowah was merely biding his time before the attack.

He will try to prevent me from defending Grace. His muscles tensed with anticipation. *When I have the chance, I must be ready to stop him.*

They both carried their sheathed knives at their waists, and a net woven from basswood fibers dangled from Wahowah's belt. Wôbi Skog Wsizokw crouched before the trap, keenly aware that Wahowah stood close behind him. *Too close.*

"Put more bait on the lure," Wahowah suggested as Wôbi Skog Wsizokw extracted the carcass by its flat tail.

Wôbi Skog Wsizokw resented the unsolicited and unnecessary instruction. With every passing moment he spent in Wahowah's unwelcome company, Wôbi Skog Wsizokw's hatred grew like a wildfire. He had uttered not a word since they set out, enduring Wahowah's insults with diminishing patience.

"More than beaver blood will be spilled tonight," Wahowah taunted as Wôbi Skog Wsizokw angled the rock on its support stick.

"Still not a word out of you?" Wahowah jeered.

Wôbi Skog Wsizokw clenched his jaw, coiled like a snake preparing to strike.

"I'll be doing your white woman a favor. With those spots on her face, she's too ugly to live."

The slab's sharp edges cut into Wôbi Skog Wsizok's fingers as he grasped it firmly with both hands. With swift agility, he sprang from his crouched positon and turned on Wahowah, slamming the rock toward the other man's face. But Wahowah apparently anticipated this attack, and ducked before the rock could make contact.

"I won't let you touch her!" Wôbi Skog Wsizokw raged, lunging at his nemesis.

Seizing him by the shoulders, Wahowah threw the younger man down hard on the ground. Freed from Wôbi Skog Wsizokw's grasp, the rock hit the river bank with a dull thud. They wrestled, each receiving and delivering powerful blows.

Before Wôbi Skog Wsizokw could unsheathe his knife, Wahowah threw him on his stomach and hog-tied him with the net. He then untied Wôbi Skog Wsizokw's knife from his belt and removed it, glaring down at him mockingly.

Lying on his stomach with wrists and ankles bound behind him, Wôbi Skog Wsizokw glowered at Wahowah.

Wahowah laughed as he sauntered away with the six beaver carcasses slung over his shoulder. "You can stay there all night, and listen to your white friends' screams."

The flummery slid out of its mold with a *slurp*. Laced with rum and nutmeg, the gelatinous mound released an enticing scent as it wobbled on the platter. Elsie set the dessert on the side board and took up the carving knife in preparation of carving the roast duck. The rest of the meal consisted of crusty rye bread and stewed parsnips. If Elsie had not been overwhelmed with nerves, she would have taken a moment to appreciate her own culinary skills with a sense of pride. But the anticipation of Waldron's Indian guests had her stomach roiling, and her hands quaked like a leaves in a breeze.

While she labored at the hearth, Waldron sat at in his favorite chair, the ledger opened to the ruined pages. She heard him grumbling as he tried to salvage the records her carelessness had destroyed. She would be docked a month's pay for the splattered ink.

Knock knock knock!

"Answer the door!" Waldron bellowed, although he was much closer than she. "Our guests have arrived."

"Aye, sir."

Wiping her sweating brow with the back of her hand, she approached the door with trepidation. Peering through the peep hole, she saw Masandowit and Kancagmagus on the flagstones. Both men had the impenetrable stares of warriors, but the younger Kancagmagus, looked downright fierce. He carried a musket on his shoulder, and to her surprise, their two guests were accompanied by six female attendants. One, Elsie noticed, was with child.

I've only enough duck for three, she thought dismally, unlatching the door. She opened it wide, cringing behind it.

"Masandowit!" Waldron closed the ledger and rose to receive his guests. "John Hawkins," he greeted Kancamagus, addressing him by his adopted white name. "Come in! It's growing late and I was beginning to think you'd changed your minds. Elsie, stop cowering back there and get our guests some rum."

"Aye sir," she replied meekly. "But sir, we haven't enough duck to feed all of them—"

Waldron's face flushed with obvious embarrassment. "Masandowit, I'm afraid we were only expecting you and John Hawkins."

The sachem waved the issue away as if it were an annoying fly. "Do not concern yourself. They only came to seek a warm place to sleep. Surely they can find lodging in the nearby garrisons?"

"A grand idea, that!" Waldron replied. "Elsie, you're spilling rum on the floor! Here, I'll serve the rum, worthless girl! Bring on the duck."

He snatched the flask of rum from her trembling hands and poured the amber beverage into two pewter tankards while Masandowit dismissed the Indian women with another wave of his hand. They obeyed silently and disappeared into the waning evening light.

As the guests seated themselves at the table, Elsie scurried back to the hearth and carved the duck, separating the white and dark meat into neat piles.

"And wipe up that floor before someone slips and breaks his neck," Waldron ordered as she presented the platter.

"Aye, sir."

"After we've eaten," Waldron was saying as Elsie knelt to sop up the spilled rum, "we'll have that promised game of noddy."

Masandowit smiled. "I look forward to it."

Something in the Indian's voice sent a shiver down Elsie's back. Looking up from where she knelt, her gaze met that of John Hawkins. His black eyes bore into her soul with clear contempt, and Elsie gulped down a rising lump of fear.

As Masandowit and Waldron engaged in a game of noddy, Kancamagus struggled to contain the all-consuming contempt he had for his prideful host. Displayed prominently above the door, Waldron's sword gleamed in the candlelight, but nothing about Waldron impressed Kancamagus. It was Waldron himself who had renamed him John Hawkins, and he despised that name as much as he despised the man who had bestowed it upon him.

Although the sniveling servant girl had disposed of the duck remains, its aroma mingled with that of Waldron's pipe tobacco. Kancamagus could sense fear emanating from her like heat from a flame. *A simple-minded girl whose life of servitude is filled with misery,* he thought when her trembling hands dropped the silver platter, sending the duck carcass skittering across the polished oak floor. He almost felt sorry for her when Waldron reprimanded her. Now she cowered in the buttery until Waldron summoned her to relight his pipe or refresh his tankard of rum. Waldron seemed slightly surprised when Masandowit refused the rum and instead insisted on well water. Kancamgus had not come to eat nor drink, and instead stood behind Waldron as Masandowit cut the deck and Waldron drew the Jack of Hearts.

"Knave noddy!" Waldron declared, placing the Jack on the top of the pile.

Kancamagus watched with disdain as Waldron moved his peg three spaces on the scoreboard instead of the two he had scored.

"He cheats," Kancamagus said in his native tongue.

"I'm aware," Masandowit replied, arranging the cards in his hand. "But give him this small victory. After all, he dies tonight."

Waldron looked up from his cards and wagged a finger at Kancamagus. "None of that, John Hawkins," he chided lightly. "I won't have you telling Masandowit what cards I hold."

"My apologies," Masandowit smiled. "He grows tired. Can this be our last hand?"

Kancamagus stifled a snort of derision as he observed Waldron's look of disappointment. "I hadn't realized the lateness of the hour. As you wish."

The game reached its end with Waldron winning by over a dozen points. As their host collected the cards and placed them in their box, Masandowit asked casually, "Brother Waldron, what would you do should strange Indians come?"

Waldron chuckled. "Why, I could raise a hundred men as easily as lifting a finger!" Removing the pegs from the board, Waldron bellowed, "Elsie! Get pallets for our guests and place them by the hearth."

Kancamagus could almost hear Masandowit's thoughts as their eyes met. The time for revenge was drawing nigh.

Chapter Sixteen

Evening shadows stretched over the Otis garrison and the odor of popped corn lingered in the air as Margaret and Maggie's knitting needles clattered rhythmically, complementing the gentle crackle from the embers in the hearth. In the waning light, Stephen burnished a newly-repaired boot while Grizel mended a worn stocking.

From his seat on the ash barrel, Eb fingered his violin and regarded the peaceful scene with an aching longing. *Lifelong bachelorhood may have served Williams Adams but 'tis too lonely a life for me.*

Richard held a sleepy Hannah on his lap. The child's head drooped like a wilted flower against his chest as she tried to stay awake.

"Blow me rings, Papa," Hannah implored drowsily, salt and butter clinging to her pink cheeks.

"No more rings, Hannah," Grizel chided, setting aside her mending. She rose, crossing the width of the hall with delicate footfalls. "'Tis time for bed." She carefully lifted the toddler from her father's lap.

Knock knock knock!

Everyone in the room bolted upright. Grizel froze with Hannah in her arms and the clacking of knitting needles ceased.

With a curious look, Stephen set down the boot and opened the peephole. Eb rose too, a tendril of dread unfurling down his spine.

"A night's lodging?" a soft feminine voice pleaded from the other side.

"'Tis a pair of Pennacook women, asking for lodging," Stephen announced over his shoulder.

"Then unbar the door, son," Richard said.

Stephen complied and opened it, permitting the women entry. They entered quietly, dipping their heads in apparent gratitude. One was taller and older than her companion by several years, as demonstrated by the streaks of gray in her long black hair. It was a warm night, and the women's short tunics fell to just below their knees, exposing their bare legs. Their arms, too, were bare, and although Eb had seen Indian women in their native garb before, their blatant nakedness in such close proximity brought an uncomfortable flush to his cheeks.

"I'll get them blankets," Margaret offered, placing her knitting in a basket and rising.

"There may be some popped corn left in the bowl," Stephen offered the women as they glided silently to a corner by the door.

"*Nda*," the older one said. "Just lodging."

Richard closed the door, barring it again before returning to his boot. Eb resumed his own seat on the ash barrel as Margaret returned with two woolen blankets. The women accepted the blankets with another dip of their heads, and folded them neatly before sitting on them, their tawny bare legs still exposed. Eb looked away, fumbling with his violin case. He glanced at Maggie, whose knitting needles clacked furiously, her coifed head bowed over her work. Little Hannah squirmed out of Grizel's arms and grabbed two handfuls of popcorn remnants from the earthen bowl. Arms stretched before her, she toddled to the guests.

"Popcorn!" she smiled sweetly, offering it to them.

The Indian women ignored the child's pink, dimpled fistfuls. Hannah stood there for a moment, looking confused, but then toddled back to her mother, cramming both handfuls into her tiny rosebud mouth. Eb was certain he wasn't alone in his feelings of awkwardness. Grizel, avoiding Hannah's butter-slick hands, held the child closely and prepared her for bed. Richard cleared his throat loudly.

"Methinks we'd all sleep better this night with a song," he suggested with a trace of apprehension in his voice. "Eb, are you agreeable?"

"Indeed, Richard Otis," Eb replied. Directing his gaze to Maggie, he asked, "Maggie, will you accompany me as I play *Barbara Allen?*"

Maggie's head shot up over her knitting. She appeared both relieved and grateful at the suggestion. "Oh, willingly!" she replied, setting her knitting down as he removed the violin from its case and positioned it under his chin. Maggie smiled stiffly, but when the bow caressed the strings, she released her sweet soprano.

> *It was in and about the Martinmas time,*
> *When the green leaves were a falling,*
>
> *That Sir John Graeme in the west country*
> *Fell in love with Barbara Allan.*
>
> *O Hooly, hooly rose she up,*
> *To the place where he was lying,*
>
> *And when she drew the curtain by,*
> *'Young man, I think you're dying.'*
>
> *O it's I'm sick, and very, very sick,*
> *And 't is a' Barbara Allan:'*
>
> *'O the better for me ye's never be,*
> *Tho your heart's blood were a spilling.*
>
> *O dinna ye mind, young man,' said she,*
> *'When ye was in the tavern a drinking,*
>
> *That ye made the healths gae round and round,*
> *And slighted Barbara Allan?'*
> *He turned his face unto the wall,*
> *And death was with him dealing:*

'Adieu, adieu, my dear friends all,
And be kind to Barbara Allan.'

And slowly, slowly raise she up,
And slowly, slowly left him,

And sighing said, she coud not stay,
Since death of life had reft him.

She had not gane a mile but two
When she heartd the death-bell ringing,

And every jow that the death-bell geid,
It cry'd, Woe to Barbara Allan!

'O mother, mother make my bed!
O make it saft and narrow!

Since my love died for me to-day,
I'll die for him to-morrow

Grizel and Margaret blinked back tears, but the Indian women were unmoved. They sat on the blankets, their faces unreadable. *They're unfamiliar with most of the words*, Eb told himself as he lowered the instrument.

"'Tis late," Richard Otis said. "Pray, let us all retire for the night."

Eb returned his violin to its case while Grizel helped Richard to his feet and guided him to their bedstead. Shoes and stays were loosened and removed and pallets rolled out on the hardwood floor. All but the Indian women knelt in prayer while Richard intoned thanks to Providence for the day's blessings, and asked their Heavenly Father to grant them peaceful slumber so that they might live to see the dawning of another day.

The strong basswood fibers bit into Wôbi Skog Wsizokw's wrists and ankles as he writhed against his restraints on the river bank. His limbs ached and his shoulders threatened to dislodge from their sockets. It had been hours since he and Wahowah had eaten the groundnuts they had carried in their pouches and his empty stomach complained loudly. He wanted to scream in frustration, but he needed to reserve his energy. A curious raccoon eyed him for a moment before scurrying up a poplar tree. Several feet downriver a pair of does regarded him warily, their white tales and big ears twitching. The sky was dotted with stars now and he had lost track of time. He listened for war whoops over the sound of the rushing water while his eyes strained to detect any approaching threats. If a predator came upon him, he would be defenseless.

Wôbi Skog Wsizokw had managed to roll onto his side, and wriggled like an overturned inchworm until his fingers found the sharp edges of the flat rock from the beaver trap. Wet with sweat and blood, his hands struggled to hold the rock in place while he pressed his fibrous bonds against it and worked them back and forth.

The repetitive motion grew painful and tiresome, but he continued until he felt the fibers give way. When his hands broke free from his ankles, he groaned with relief and brought his knees to his chest. He now had a better hold on the blood-slickened rock, and repeated the sawing motion until his hands sprang free from their restraints.

Releasing a small cry of victory, Wôbi Skog Wsizokw brought his arms to his front. He took a moment to rotate his aching shoulders before yanking off the remnants of the net around his wrists. Exhausted, he maneuvered around to face the rock. Assuming a sitting position, he hoisted the rock above the netting at his ankles and sawed furiously back and forth. When those restraints gave way, he pulled the broken fibers off and rubbed his bleeding and swollen ankles.

It was then he spotted the crouching catamount less than twenty-five yards away, the tip of its tawny tail twitching as it prepared to pounce.

Chapter Seventeen

Elsie curled up on her pallet in the dark and windowless buttery, listening to Waldron's snores. Fear had chased away her appetite, and she had not eaten since the night before. The odor of pipe tobacco hung in the close air, and despite the stifling summer heat, Elsie shivered beneath her cloak.

Only a moth-eaten blanket nailed to the oak lintel divided the buttery from the hall, and she wished fervently that a solid door with a latch separated her from Waldron's guests. The two Indians had arranged their pallets near the front door, the remaining embers in the hearth throwing a dim orange glow that only illuminated a small portion of the hall.

They mean to kill us in our sleep! This refrain repeated itself in her head as Elsie's eyes went to the buttery door. She couldn't discern its features in the dark, but she knew if the Indians were inclined to molest her, she could hopefully flee out that door before much harm was done. She tried to pray, but no prayers came.

She thought she heard the front door unlatch, jolting her from her fearful imaginings. Sitting up, she peered through a hole in the partition. The door creaked open as the two Indians slipped outside, leaving it ajar. *Mayhap they've gone out to pee,* she told herself as Waldron snored on, rhythmically. Waldron insisted on keeping the door shut at night, and she was about to rise and close it when several Indians burst in, some brandishing flaming pine knots, whooping shrilly.

A scream ripped from her throat, and Waldron's snoring ceased abruptly. She scrambled to her feet, stumbled toward the buttery door but tripped over her cloak. Before she could regain her footing, a strong hand seized her upper arm and pulled her out of the buttery. Petrified with fear, she was unable to resist as she was dragged into the hall. A dozen warriors spilled into the garrison, their predacious black eyes glowering at her below smears of green war paint.

"John Hawkins, what's the meaning of this?" Waldron demanded.

He emerged from his bedchamber, his hairy shins as pale as his white linen shirt. Bolting toward the hearth, he plucked his sword from its resting place and turned on his adversaries.

"Revenge for the past," Kancamagus replied in a voice that chilled Elsie's blood.

Elsie screamed as Waldron wielded his sword with the prowess only a seasoned soldier possessed, but a younger, quicker warrior yanked the weapon from his hand and flung it aside. The shiny blade clattered to the floor and slid under the board, out of Waldron's reach.

Another warrior grabbed Waldron, pinning his arms behind his back while John Hawkins—Kancagmagus—stepped forward, regarding the major with a venomous glare. Elsie screamed again when Kancagmagus struck Waldron's head with the flat of his stone tomahawk. Dazed, Waldron sagged like a rag doll, his white hair falling over his face. Two warriors proceeded to lash the old man to a straight-backed chair, securing his arms to those on the chair with strong hemp rope. Witnessing this horror in stunned silence, Elsie cowered helplessly against the warrior who maintained a viselike grip on her arm.

"You." Kancamagus ordered, pointing at her. "Cook us something to eat."

But there are at least a dozen of you savages! I haven't enough to feed all of you. Even in her terrified state, she knew better than to argue and said nothing as she was once again thrust into the buttery. Aided by the illumination of the guard's torch, she fumbled with a loaf of rye bread and a hunk of cured ham. Her escort stood behind her, so close she could feel his hot breath on her shoulder. Her hands trembled uncontrollably as she reached for the bread knife, and for a brief moment she imagined plunging it into his chest and fleeing out the buttery door. Tears obscured her vision—surely he would overpower her if she attempted such a foolish act. She sliced the bread and then the ham, whimpering like a frightened dog.

She heard Waldron making futile demands as chair legs screeched against floorboards. She was surprised the first blow hadn't killed him, but then Waldron cried out in agony as one by one each warrior declared, "I cross out my account!"

She heard Kancamagus laugh mockingly. "Who will judge the Indians now?"

Waldron released another agonized scream, and then his cries grew strangely muffled.

Oh, don't make me go back out there! She returned the knife to the counter. Sniveling, she piled the bread and ham high on the platter. Her hands quaked so badly the victuals threatened to topple onto the floor, and she had to press the platter against her abdomen to stabilize it.

With a firm hand on her shoulder, her guard propelled her back into the hall. What she saw made her drop the platter in horror.

Waldron's white shirt, now slick with dark blood, clung to his lacerated chest. His moans grew weaker as his head lolled to the side, and then Elsie saw what had muffled his cries: the Indians had sliced off his nose, along with both ears. More blood flowed down his torso onto the table, pooling on the floor. The severed body parts protruded from his mouth, and the air was thick with the coppery stench of spilled blood. Elsie retched, but her empty stomach had nothing to expel.

In the hellish light of the Indian's torches, Waldron's eyes met Elsie's. Wide with fear and agony in his pallid face, Waldron held her gaze for one long awful moment. It occurred to her she had never before looked him in the eye.

His eyes are green, she thought dimly.

Blue veins forked beneath hairy skin as Waldron's hands clenched . His nails dug into the wooden arms, then began to relax. Elsie continued to watch in numbed horror as his eyes rolled into his head. One Indian seized Waldron's own sword and angled the tip at their victim's chest, then another pushed Waldron, chair and all, off the table, impaling the dying man on his own blade.

Elsie's brain could not register what she had just witnessed. *I am dreaming,* her mind insisted. *This horror cannot be truly happening! Merciful God, how can you let them do this?*

If she fell on her knees and begged for her life, would they spare her?

Kancamagus grabbed a slice of ham from the floor, thrusting it beneath her eyes before flinging it away. "Make us better food."

With a shove, the warrior behind her propelled her toward the hearth where the glowing embers beckoned in a back corner. She stumbled over the dropped tray and its contents, but managed to go through the motions of adding tinder to the coals until a nice fire burned brightly. She drew a kettle containing the remnants of Waldron's breakfast pottage closer to the flame, the fire's heat warming her face and hands while the rest of her chilled in terror.

Mad thoughts flitted through her frightened mind like a swarm of gnats as her fingers closed around the wooden spoon. *Mayhap if I strike one hard enough, it would render him unconscious.* After several long moments the pottage began to bubble, moist steam drifting up the chimney in white tendrils. Shielding her hand from the kettle's hot handle with her apron, Elsie wondered briefly how many savages she could scald if she threw the hot contents in their faces. A toasting fork hung within her reach. Would the iron tongs puncture human flesh if she acted with enough force? Her eyes slid to the warrior assigned to guard her every move. He seemed to read her thoughts, and shook his head slowly. "Nda!" he growled, snatching the kettle from her.

The intruders clustered around the kettle, scooping the warm pottage into their bare hands. She watched as the pale gruel left wet trails from their chins down their throats. She shuddered with revulsion.

Before her, Waldron's torn body lay motionless while the savages invaded the other rooms with their torches. Smoke stung her eyes and she coughed, tasting bile.

They've set the garrison ablaze. I'll be burned alive.

Kancamagus looked up from the emptied kettle, traces of pottage congealing on his face and chest. Elsie cowered at the hearth as he approached her menacingly, tomahawk in hand.

This, then, is how I die. Resigned to her fate, she scrunched her eyes tightly in awful anticipation of the tomahawk's blow. Instead, she heard Kancamagus utter one word.

"Go!"

Without thinking Elsie bolted past the laughing warriors toward the front door, one forearm pressed over her nose. Her trembling hands fumbled with the latch in the smoke-filled darkness. Coughing, she flung the door open and fled blindly into the night.

Run to Otis's! A voice in her head commanded. Stumbling, she headed in the direction of the neighboring garrison. She ran along, breathless, tears streaming, eyes focused on the ground to avoid tripping over tree roots or the uneven ground. When she finally looked up, she dropped to her knees. The Otis garrison was burning too.

Eb plunged the still-glowing horseshoe into the slack tub. Steam billowed in the air as hot metal met cool water. Lifting the new horseshoe from its bath, he was surprised to see the long-handled pair of tongs was empty. Suddenly the implement sprang free from his hold, slithering and hissing like a snake across the forge's dirt floor. Stunned, he watched as the tongs turned as if to look at him. They opened, releasing a hideous, high-pitched scream…

Eb's eyes snapped open to the sound of war cries. Bolting upright, his sleep-fogged mind struggled to process what was happening as a hoard of Pennacook warriors streamed into the garrison, their enraged faces glistening with war paint in the orange glow of their pine torches.

Dear God in Heaven, they're upon us! A woman screamed—Margaret, Grizel, Maggie? In the glare of the Indian's torches, he blinked in order to focus. He saw Stephen Otis brandishing his own knife in his left hand from the far side of the hall. Margaret and

Maggie cowered against the hearth, their faces as pale as their white linen shifts. Eb met Stephen's eyes briefly. The terror on his friend's face was palpable.

Bang!

Stephen's expression went from terror to shock as his chest exploded in a spray of blood. The powerful blast thrust him against the wall. He stood there for a moment before slowly sagging to the floor, a wide smear of blood staining the wall behind him.

"Father!" Maggie cried.

Before Eb could form a coherent thought, one Indian clubbed him with the butt of his musket. Pain spider-webbed his skull like a crack in a sheet of ice, and he fell to the floor in a heap.

Bang! Bang!

"They've shot Richard!" That was clearly Grizel's voice.

Dazed, Eb lifted his head, nearly blinded by blood flowing into his eyes. Richard Otis lay motionless in his bedstead, blood oozing from his chest. Grizel scrambled to retrieve Hannah from her trundle bed just as one warrior seized the child by one arm. Eb watched helplessly as the screaming child's body arced in the air, her eyes wide. Her wails reached a screeching crescendo before ending abruptly as the warrior dashed her little head against the stairs with a sickening thud.

"*Hannah!*" Grizel shrieked.

Another Indian grabbed Grizel, slinging her over his bare shoulder like a sack of grain. The distraught woman's sobs faded as her captor carried her out of the garrison. Near the hearth, Eb saw Maggie standing over her mother's bloodied body—had Margaret been shot too? The young woman held an iron poker in her hands, her pretty face displaying a defiant grimace as a warrior advanced. With mocking laughter, the Indian wrenched the rod from her grip and flung it aside. Eb heard it skitter across the polished floor as it disappeared into the darkness. The Indian grabbed Maggie by the arm and dragged her out the door.

Maggie reached her free arm out to Eb, her terror-filled eyes locking with his. With his head still throbbing from the blow, Eb staggered to his feet, clutching the walls for support. He reached for her hand,

and for one frozen moment their fingers touched as if across a great expanse before another blow to the head sent him reeling backward, striking his head before sinking into a black void.

When Eb awoke he found himself enveloped in a cloud of heavy smoke. Coughing, he raised his throbbing head to see angry flames engulfing the garrison's hall. Groaning against the pain, Eb crawled inch by inch to the door. Against the far wall Stephen and Margaret's bodies lay broken and discarded, the flames devouring them like a pack of wolves. Through the smoky haze he could make out one of Hannah's little hands, once pink and dimpled, now turning black.

Rest in peace, my friends, he prayed in agony.

Eb averted his eyes, gagging against the stench of burning flesh. The opened door beckoned just a few feet away, and his lungs ached for fresh air as he crept slowly toward it. Heat from the encroaching flames seared his flesh—if he could just clear the threshold and get past the flagstones, he might survive a torturous death....

Lord, bless my lost friends' souls. May Maggie and Grizel be recovered and returned to us....

He dragged his leaden body across the wooden floor. Behind him, the fire roared like an enraged beast. At last, his fingers grasped the threshold and he pulled himself across it just as a beam crashed behind him like a felled tree, sending sparks dancing in the smoke-filled air.

When he felt the cool flagstones beneath his cheek, he collapsed, gasping as he inhaled fresh air. Then he rolled onto his back as smoke rose in columns against the star-encrusted night sky.

Thank you, Lord, for preserving my life. He once again succumbed to the dark abyss of unconsciousness.

"Haw, Jericho."

The cart creaked as the Charolais ox turned left on the path, its white dewlap swinging with each plodding step of its massive cloven hooves. Only the waning moon and the myriad of stars sprinkled across the dark sky illuminated their way. Absalom figured it was well past midnight. The bovine kept to the well-worn path, guided by its keen sense of direction. Absalom trusted the beast to likewise retrace its steps and take them home once he had collected Widow Heard and her family.

Leaving Alice that morning had been difficult, and a sense of apprehension wore at his conscience like a festering sore. It was a warm night and the humid summer air felt dense and sticky. Sweat slithered down his spine in cold serpentine trails. His muscles tensed, every fiber of his being on high alert lest a group of Indians ambush him. Cricketsong paired with the cries of nocturnal predators piqued his awareness. His loaded musket lay within reach at his feet and his ever-present knife was strapped to his waist. A pesky mosquito landed on his exposed neck, and he slapped at the irritation. Worse than the insect's bite was his own intuition. It had been dogging him all day. *The Indians haven't attacked yet*, he tried to assure himself. *In any case, the garrisons are well-fortified, and the women are good shots.*

Well, all but Alice. An excellent wife skilled in all matter of domestic womancraft, Alice's ineptitude with a musket bothered Absalom. He was glad Grace had insisted Alice practice. If he had had time, he would have insisted on training her himself.

"Whoa."

The lumbering ox stopped just steps away from the ferry dock while Absalom engaged the cart's brake.

The abandoned ferry dock heightened Absalom's growing anxiety. *They've met with some delay*, he thought, glancing eastward. *May it be a minor one, and no catastrophe has befallen them.*

Jericho lowered his blockish head to the tall grass while Absalom laid his musket over his knees. The tranquil murmur of the flowing water would have been soothing any other night. Now, the stream's gurgles and splashes between rocks and over beaver dams sounded a prelude to disaster. The distant whinny of a horse brought him out of his dark reverie and Absalom strained his eyes as he looked out over the water. Two dim lights glided toward him silently. With relief, he hailed the approaching vessel and jumped down from his cart, feeling his way to the dock until he grasped the taut hemp rope that spanned the width of the river.

The twin lights grew closer, like a pair of phantoms skimming the stream's surface, and Absalom's neck prickled. Dark shapes moved about on the ferry, and Absalom slung his musket over his shoulder before reaching out to help tether the craft to the dock.

"Ho to the ferry!"

"Ab!" John Ham's voice called from the darkness. "The savages plan to attack tonight!"

Absalom felt as if a bucket of cold river water had been dumped on him. Dark forms milled about on the vessel and the horse's hooves pranced restlessly. A young man in courier livery led the horse onto the dock while John Ham and Johnny Horne helped the women disembark.

"Major Waldron?" the courier asked anxiously, looking up at Absalom.

"Nay," Absalom replied. "But I'm in his employ."

"I'm Seth Ellington. I've word John Hawkins plans to attack—"

The night was pierced by shrill war cries coming from the direction of the settlement.

"Dear God, it's begun!" Widow Heard said under her breath.

"Leave the trunk on the dock!" Absalom ordered as Mary and Emmie shrieked. "The cart, too." He removed his musket from his back and pressed it in Widow Heard's arms. "You women hide in that copse of trees yonder," he said.

Widow Heard accepted the weapon without question and hustled Mary and Emmie off the dock. As the women's hurried footsteps clattered on the wooden dock Absalom saw tongues of orange flames leaping on the horizon.

"Waldron's," John Ham said. "We're too late."

Alice. He had to get to Alice. "Ready your muskets," he said to Ham and Horne. Next he turned to the ferryman. "You too. I know you keep a musket on board."

"I've no dog in this fight," the ferryman said hastily, shoving off from the dock. "Good luck to you all."

Enraged by such cowardice, Absalom lunged for the ferryman. Seizing the man's collar with both hands, he lifted the startled fellow off his feet and shook him.

"My folk are under attack and we need every available man."

"'T'is not my fight!" the ferryman insisted in a frightened whine.

Tightening his grip on the man's collar, Absalom glowered down on the man. "Ready your musket! You're coming with us."

Lantern light reflected in the ferryman's eyes, and Absalom sensed the boatman still designed to flee, so he shook him again until his hat fell from his head.

"Don't provoke me," he said in a low voice. "You'd fare badly."

With one last intimidating glare, Absalom dropped the ferryman like a sack of flour. He turned to the courier, who regarded the big man with wide eyes. "And what about you, Ellington? Will you fight?"

"Aye," the courier replied. "I've my firearm."

"Then tie up that horse and come with us."

Chapter Eighteen

The cougar lunged before Wôbi Skog Wsizokw could defend himself. With a horrifying growl, it landed on Wôbi Skog Wsizokw's torso. The sudden impact knocked the wind from his lungs, throwing him on his back as sharp claws tore into his shoulders. Wôbi Skog Wsizokw's own cries of rage mixed with those of the cat's. His only defense was to land punches to the animal's throat or eyes while at the same time protecting his own face and throat. The pair tumbled, locked in combat, teeth and claws shredding defenseless human flesh.

BANG!

The tawny beast fell heavily on Wôbi Skog Wsizokw's battered chest. He expelled a *whoosh* as air was forced from him lungs. With a last burst of energy, he shoved the carcass off him, inhaling lungfuls of blood-tinged night air. Exhausted, he looked up to see his Aunt Toloti standing over him, pale smoke still rising from the musket barrel. She knelt beside him, her deep-set eyes taking him in from head to toe.

"Nephew!" she whispered. "When you didn't return with Wahowah, I went looking for you, checking all your beaver traps. What happened?"

She helped him to a sitting position and dizziness seized him. "Wahowah tied me up," he said, feeling weak.

"Can you walk?" his aunt inquired. "Let's get you home and see to your wounds—"

Wôbi Skog Wsizokw's head throbbed as he struggled to stand. "Nda! I need to get to the settlement."

Just then distant war cries shattered the night's stillness. Toloti seized his wrist.

"Don't go!" his aunt begged, her eyes wide and pleading. "Remember what Nigawesega's dream foretold? You'll meet your death!"

Wôbi Skog Wsizokw shook his wrist free from her grasp. He considered commandeering the musket from her, but doubted he had the strength to carry, load and fire the heavy firearm. Then he remembered the small knife she always kept strapped to her belt. He held out a bloodied hand. "Lend me your knife, Aunt."

The old woman shook her head, her broad face covered with worry. "You've lost a lot of blood. Come home with me."

More war cries resounded, and he grew impatient. Swaying slightly, he maintained his outstretched hand until Toloti tearfully relented. She untied the leather straps and placed the sheathed knife in his palm, her sorrowful eyes tearing with reluctance.

"Go home, Aunt."

"I'll not see you again, Nephew," she sobbed, hanging her head in defeat.

With a fresh surge of determination, Wôbi Skog Wsizokw ignored his wounds and headed for the whites' settlement, leaving his aunt standing by the dead catamount, her words echoing in his ears.

His heart thundered in his chest and his breathing became labored as he ran along the river bank. Approaching the ferry dock, he saw two stationary lights suspended over the water. In his weakened state, he paused in confusion for a moment until he discerned they were lanterns on a docked ferry. A horse whinnied anxiously, and the stench of manure assaulted his nose. A large wooden trunk sat abandoned on the dock, and from a nearby thicket he heard a faint gasp. Wôbi Skog Wsizokw detected slight movement, and his keen eyes could make out at least three figures—probably white women— huddled in the shadows.

Good place to hide, he commended them silently. Then he glanced toward the settlement, and saw flames devouring one of the garrisons.

He had to get to Grace. Dismissing whoever was hiding in the trees, he ran toward Little Hill.

Grace couldn't sleep. Elder Wentworth's snores combined with those of Dog's rattled the windowpanes. She heard others stir restlessly, knowing they too were getting no sleep. All except for the two Indian women who had asked for lodging that night: seemingly deaf to the clamorous duet, they appeared to slumber peacefully next to the garrison door.

Grace sat up on her pallet and scowled suspiciously at the two sleeping figures. She had argued with Alice about letting them in the garrison, but Alice's heart had softened to the gravid one.

Alice had explained there was a kinship between breeding women, and after Jack Meader found no knives on the pair, they were allowed inside and Jack returned to his post in the watchtower.

But their behavior disturbed Grace. Despite their benign expressions, they spoke to no one, nor met anyone's gaze.

That rankled Grace.

As she sat in the dark, Elder Wentworth's snores ceased abruptly. She heard the old man stir, and listened as both he and Dog rose. They shuffled clumsily to the door, unlatching and opening it with no concern for their neighbors. The two slipped out the door, leaving it slightly ajar behind them.

I've no chance for sleep afore they return. With a sigh of resignation, she decided to check on Queenie and Bolt. Forgoing shoes and socks, she rose and lit a lantern with a glowing ember, casting the garrison in a soft orange glow. It was a warm night, and she left her cloak on its nail. She unlatched the door, wincing as it creaked open. Her eyes traveled upward to the star-encrusted sky as the cold flagstones chilled her bare feet. The night was unusually quiet. Even the crickets seemed hushed in the warm stillness. All she heard were her own footfalls and the low *hiss* of Elder Wentworth and Dog peeing in unison against the palisade.

Inside the barn, Queenie and Bolt lay with their legs tucked beneath them. They turned their big eyes on her and greeted her with soft *moos*. Bolt got to his feet and she noted with satisfaction how robust he was. "You'll make a fine bull one day," she praised him, scratching the top of tawny head.

She inspected their water trough and saw they had plenty. "I'd sleep better among you, my darlings," she said, glad to see they were well. The comforting scent of cow met her nostrils, and she remembered the night she awoke in the hay pile, only to discover her whirligig wound around her wrist. Instinctively she fingered the button. Instead of reminding her of her lost parents, it now reminded her of Menane. It seemed to have absorbed some of his essence, and she wondered how long it had been in his possession.

"There will be an attack in three nights."

Menane's words resounded in her head as if he were standing right next to her. Gasping, she counted in her head what night it was he had warned her.

"Tonight!" she shrieked, startling the cows. "They plan to attack tonight!"

As if to confirm her realization, Dog barked madly. She heard Elder Wentworth cry out, and then the night was pierced with war whoops.

Lantern in hand, Grace fled the barn. She saw Elder Wentworth clad in his long shirt, bracing his bony frame against the palisade gate as Dog snarled and barked at the threat beyond. But the old man couldn't hold back the attackers, and they burst forth, silencing Dog with a musket blast. Terrified, Grace watched helplessly as warriors spilled into the yard. Some held torches aloft, and one tall Pennacook turned hate-filled eyes at her. He was armed with both bow and musket. Despite the darkness, she recognized him immediately.

Wahowah!

Recognition flickered in his own eyes and with a malicious grin, his long legs quickly closed the distance between them. Too frightened to scream, Grace dropped her lantern and ran to the cheese house. *If that savage attacks me, I'll not go without a fight!*

She crossed the cheese house threshold, her shin colliding painfully with the butter churn. Ignoring the pain, she seized the dasher and hid behind the door, dasher poised above her head. *He's too tall for me to knock on the head,* she reasoned, holding her breath. *Better to aim for a knee.*

He entered silently, his flaming torch throwing distorted shadows on the walls. When he cleared the door, Grace stepped forward. Without thinking, she aimed for the knee closest to her. Inhaling deeply, she swung.

Thwack!

Wahowah bellowed in surprise and pain, grasping his injured knee with his free hand. With a brief sense of satisfaction, Grace dropped the dasher and fled into the yard.

The scene before her was one of chaos. Between her and the garrison, the yard teemed with marauding Indians. To her left, the breeched gate hung open. The air was dense with musket smoke and war cries. Behind her, Wahowah emerged from the cheese house sporting a slight limp as he strode toward her in hot pursuit.

RUN! A voice in her head screamed. But to where? Heart hammering against her ribcage, Grace ran through the palisade entrance into the foreboding forest beyond. Toward the south she saw two raging fires, their flames licking the night sky. *Waldron's and Otis's garrisons. Dear God.* Stumbling over rocks and tree roots, Grace ran down Little Hill into the dense woods. Low branches snagged her shift and her cap tumbled off her head, freeing her hair to stream behind her like a flaming standard. She darted behind a large tree and paused to catch her breath.

Her fingers discovered a deep crevice in the tree trunk: this was the hollow tree she and Alice had used for target practice, and she remembered it was big enough for a person to hide in.

She wriggled into the tree's cleft, pressing herself against the ragged innards of the trunk. Soft mushrooms crushed beneath her feet and the odor of mold and rotting wood provoked a sneeze. She stifled the urge by pressing a forefinger beneath her nose.

Neither move nor breathe she commanded herself, peering into the darkness. Gunfire and screams permeated the air, and her sweat-soaked shift clung to her trembling body. She listened carefully, but heard no approaching footsteps. Silently she counted to fifty, then with caution she emerged from the cavernous tree. *May that hateful savage be long gone,* she prayed.

When it appeared she was indeed alone, she expelled a weary sigh of relief. She tried to assess the situation rationally. No sanctuary could be found for miles around, and even if there were one, she would have to wait until dawn to find it. Her best option was to retreat once again into the tree and wait.

As she turned to reenter the cavity, a forceful hand clamped around her mouth while a strong arm encircled her waist, pressing her firmly against her assailant. Terrified, Grace tried to bite the flattened palm while kicking backwards and thrusting an elbow against her attacker's abdomen. Then an urgent voice hissed in her ear.

"*Shh!* Grace, stop!"

Menane! Was it really he? Had he come to rescue her? She stopped fighting and his hand came away from her mouth. His arm around her relaxed and she turned to face him. The familiar white scar on his face shone in the distant fire glow.

She took his face in her hands and he winced. She smelled the unmistakable stench of blood. "You're hurt!"

"Not bad hurt," he whispered back, gently pulling her hands downward. "Come with me. It is not safe here."

Horrifying shrieks and musket fire suffused the flame-lit darkness. "Where can we go?" she asked.

"Just be quiet and come with me."

The mother-of-pearl button dropped into her palm. When he clasped her hand with his, the disc seemed to pulsate like a beating heart caged within. He seemed to know where he was taking her, and a great part of her felt certain she could trust him. He *could* be trusted, couldn't he? If he were going to harm her, she reasoned, he would have done it by now.

They ran through the woods, her bare feet punctured by thorns and rocks. At last she heard the steady rush of the flowing river. An abandoned ferry with its pair of lanterns still burning floated near the dock. He paused on the riverbank, and she noticed his breathing had become raspy. He released her hand and looked past her into a copse of trees. For a moment he seemed to be looking at something specific, then he released her hand and pointed.

"Hide there. I will come back for you when it is safe."

Her hand felt damp and empty, the button resuming its cold inanimateness. "Don't leave me! I don't want to be alone!"

"You will be safe there," he insisted.

She clasped his hand again. "I need to tell you--"

"There is no time for this!"

Stubbornly, she looked into eyes. He needed to know about her dream. "I had a dream, Menane. A raven carried two flaming arrows in his talons--"

His grip tightened on her hands curiously.

"—then it released them. One arrow fell on the river bank and the other plunged in the water."

"Grace, go hide now." His voice was clipped with urgency.

"And I don't know when you said it, but I know you said we are twin flames," she continued.

"We are," he confirmed. "That is why I need you to be safe."

Without thinking, Grace rose on her tiptoes and embraced Menane's neck. As if by instinct, she crushed her lips against his, and felt his arms encircle her. She felt his fingers tangle in her hair, and her heart felt as if it would leap from her chest.

He broke from the embrace, gently prying her arms from his neck. This time he cupped her face in his hands, his thumbs wiping tears from her cheeks.

"Hide there," he repeated, pointing to the trees behind her with his chin. "You will not be alone."

What did he mean? Of course she would be alone if he left her! With deep reluctance she released him. Sniffling, she wiped her nose on her sleeve and took a step toward the shadowy trees. His blood and musk lingered in her nostrils, and suddenly she was overwhelmed with an aching fear she would never see him again. She spun around to return to him, but he had vanished.

You will not be alone.

Even when her parents were killed, she had never felt more abandoned than she did at that moment. When she neared the grove of trees, she heard a feminine voice whisper in surprise, "Grace! Is that you?"

Grace gasped. "Emmie?" Excitedly she stepped into the trees, where she found Emmie crouched on the forest floor with her mother and grandmother, who held a musket across her lap.

Grace embraced her best friend, then the other women in turn. They were all weeping, but none more so than Emmie.

"You're covered in blood!" Emmie cried. "I can't see it, but I can smell it and your shift is sticky with it. Are you injured?"

Alarmed, Grace pulled the clinging shift from her bosom and sniffed. The front was indeed saturated with blood. It must have happened during their embrace, and it meant Menane was more hurt than he had admitted.

"How fares Little Hill?" Widow Heard asked.

"Under attack, but still holding its own when I left," Grace reported, new concern for Menane seizing her heart in a cold grip. How badly injured was he? Was he strong enough to defend himself?

"Was that an Indian with you just now?" Mary Ham asked in an incredulous whisper.

Evidently the women had witnessed the embrace, and Grace felt her face go hot. "Aye," she confessed as Emmie released a gasp of recognition.

"'T'was the boy, now grown." Emmie said. It was an observation, not a question.

"Aye, so it was," she confirmed. Then a new realization hit her.

He had known the women were hiding there.

You will not be alone.

After an awkward pause, Widow Heard cleared her throat. "Come, girls," she said. "It sounds as though the shooting has stopped. Mary, Grace, take up the trunk. Emmie, tie the horse to the cart."

Emerging from the trees, Grace was surprised to see pink ribbons of light against the eastern sky. How could it be sunrise already?

While she and Mary hoisted the trunk onto the cart, Emmie secured the horse. The women clambered onto the rickety conveyance with Widow Heard at the reins, who handed Grace the musket. Grace was known to be a good shot, and she accepted the weapon without question.

"Get up, Jericho," Widow Heard commanded.

The ox complied, jolting the cart into motion toward Little Hill.

Chapter Nineteen

ying alone in Widow Heard's bed, Alice found it impossible to sleep. And not only because of Elder Wentworth and Dog's resounding snoring.

In eleven years of matrimony, she and Absalom had never slept apart, and his absence left her feeling hollow. She curled on her side, imagining his big arm draped over her swelling abdomen, drawing her back against his massive chest. Sometimes his breathing tickled the nape of her neck just so, igniting a delicious tingle down her spine, and she would giggle. Encouraged, Absalom would nibble her shoulder, which more often than not led to further intimacies.

Smiling at the memory, Alice considered the breeding Pennacook woman. She appeared to be a month or two farther along than Alice, who had tried to converse with her guests. But neither woman had seemed willing nor able to speak English.

Thinking of the Pennacook woman conjured up Wahowah's menacing face. If she had mentioned the encounter in the garden to Absalom, would he have sent someone else to retrieve Widow Heard and the others from the ferry landing? If she had told him, she would be lying in his arms this very moment.

Elder Wentworth's snoring ceased abruptly, and she heard both him and Dog rise. "Come along, Dog," the old man muttered as he shuffled across the floor and sprung the door latch. The door opened with a creaking groan.

Alice heard Wentworth and Dog step out into the night. A moment later, the hall was illuminated in lantern light and she heard

Grace leave her pallet and also depart. *Headed either for the barn or the cheese house roof.* The door scraped loudly against the floor boards and Alice reminded herself she needed to ask Absalom to sand it.

She was just entering sleep when the Indian women rose from their places near the door. They seemed to take great care in preventing the door from creaking, and slipped outside as silently as shadows.

Alice sighed, and tried once again to fall asleep. Then she heard a soft, high whistle from the yard. Dog began barking furiously, and then Elder Wentworth screamed. Alice bolted upright in the bedstead just as the first war whoops pierced the night.

"Mama!" little Beth shrieked.

Being the closest to the hearth, Alice touched a candle wick to the glowing embers and put it in its holder while Sarah Meader reached for the loaded musket Jack had left hanging above the door.

"Aye, Beth," Sarah replied, cocking the big gun and inserting the barrel in the wall's embrasure. "Be a good girl and stay down."

"Grace is out there!" Alice yelled, traversing the hall with the candle in hand. Without thinking, she flung open the door and gasped as Pennacook warriors penetrated the gate.

A shot fired, and Dog's barking ended with a pitiful yelp. Alice strained her eyes against the glare of torchlight, searching vainly for Grace. Then she saw a small figure clad in a white shift running toward the broken gate. She heard Jack Meader return fire from the watch tower, but he failed to stop the tall torch-bearing Indian who limped in pursuit of Grace. Panicked, she cried out her sister's name.

"Grace! Come inside!"

"That's Wahowah out there!" Sarah shouted. "Alice, shut the door!"

The tall Indian stopped, jamming the pointed end of his torch into the ground. As musket blasts illuminated the courtyard in quick, brilliant bursts of light, Wahowah's dark eyes turned on Alice. Frozen in horror, Alice watched as with expert assuredness, he aimed an arrow at her.

Thwttt

The force jarred her backward, followed by sharp pain just below her clavicle. She gasped in shock at the feathered shaft that protruded from her chest.

"Alice!" Sarah shrieked.

A weird dizziness overtook her, and she felt Sarah pull her inside and slam the door shut. Breathing became difficult, and she struggled as a sharp pain spread across her pierced chest. She was vaguely aware of Sarah shutting and bolting the door before leading her to the bedstead.

"Beth, get the rag bucket," she heard Sarah order over musket fire and men's screams. She sank supine on the mattress, allowing Sarah to arrange her legs and cover them. An overwhelming sense of sorrow enveloped Alice and she wanted to weep, but instead coughed up blood. Sarah gently turned her on her side to expel the blood, and she winced as the arrowhead drove deeper into her flesh.

"Cough up what you must in this rag," Sarah directed, holding a folded cloth under Alice's chin. Alice complied, and saw fear in her friend's face. "I daren't attempt to remove that arrow," Sarah said with blatant regret, easing Alice back on the mattress. "'Tis too deep to pull out, yet too shallow to push through t'other side."

I shall die, and I will never see Absalom again. Nor will this babe live to draw breath. Hot tears coursed down Alice's pale cheeks. She looked into Sarah's eyes, and saw that Sarah was crying too.

Behind Sarah, young Beth watched in wide-eyed horror.

"Don't die on us, Goody Hart!" the child implored in a heartrending sob.

"Oh Alice, I'm so sorry," Sarah wept, grasping Alice's hand.

A sudden coldness blanketed Alice's body and she shivered. Sarah was saying something, but her voice sounded far away. The overpowering urge to sleep overtook her, and Alice closed her eyes for a last time, envisioning Absalom's loving face until it dissolved into darkness.

Waldron's garrison was still burning when Absalom and the

others arrived. Smoke hung low in the humid air, choking the men despite the kerchiefs they had tied over their noses and mouths. Only the hearth and one adjacent wall remained partially erect. Amidst the ashen rubble lay a charred body impaled on a sword, limbs still bound to the arms and legs of a soot-blackened chair.

Not even a greedy, deceitful bastard like Waldron deserves to meet such an ill fate. Absalom's stomach roiled at the smell of burnt human flesh.

His heart ached to get to Alice.

"Nothing can be done for Waldron now," Absalom said, apprehension growing. "Otis's lies yonder. There may be survivors there."

He led the men to Otis's garrison, still engulfed in sheets of fire. The heat prevented them from approaching too close, and Absalom knew his friends could not have escaped such a deadly blaze. Inspecting the destruction from a safe distance, Absalom and the others fanned out around the fire's perimeter. Absalom barely heard John Ham call him over the fire's angry roar.

"Hart! Over here!"

Hope lapped tentatively at Hart's soul as he ran to join Ham, who knelt over a soot-covered body lying prone on the flagstones. He joined Ham while the other men looked on.

"Varney," Ham said. "Appears to be alive."

Eb Varney coughed, and Absalom gently rolled the Quaker onto his back, then into a sitting positon. Ellington handed Absalom an open canteen, which Absalom put to Eb's blackened lips. Eb drank greedily, then coughed and sputtered some more while Absalom struck him on the back in an effort to revive him.

"Otis family?" Eb croaked weakly.

Absalom shook his head, handing the canteen back to the courier. "Nay. Only you have survived, it seems."

"They took Grizel and Maggie," Eb said hoarsely. "But little Hannah...."

Absalom stopped him. "Don't think on it. Can you walk? We must abandon this blaze."

Eb nodded, but when Absalom and Hart attempted to lift him to his feet, he cried out in agony and crumpled to his knees. Hart and Ham dragged the injured man away from the destruction and deposited him a safe distance away on the cool ground.

"May have some broken bones, along with a concussion," Ellington observed. "My father is a physician in Boston. I've assisted him many times. I volunteer to tend to him."

"I volunteer also," the ferryman chimed in.

"Nay. We need you with us," Absalom said, irritated at the ferryman's cowardice.

"Sounds as though the savages have abandoned Little Hill," Johnny Horne announced, looking northward.

Indeed, musket fire and war whoops had faded. The palisade seemed to be afire, but from this distance, the garrison appeared to be intact, and once again hope teased Hart's spirit.

"You have no need of me now," the ferryman argued. "The attack has ended, and I can get back to—"

Absalom's patience expired and he clamped a firm, insistent hand on the ferryman's narrow shoulder. "I'll not tell you again," he snarled. "You're coming with us."

Just then, a twig snapped, and a small white figure stepped from behind an oak tree. Johnny Horne aimed his musket in the direction of the unexpected sound. Releasing the ferryman's shoulder, Absalom recognized Waldron's simple-minded servant girl, Elsie Winston. Long pale fingers fanned out starkly against the tree's dark trunk as she peered at the men with vacant eyes.

"Hold your fire, Horne!" Absalom ordered as the young woman approached them.

Clad in a soiled linen shift, Elsie's dull eyes appeared dazed. Absalom stepped toward her and put his hands on her sloping shoulders. She reeked with the sour stench of urine and Absalom's nose wrinkled in revulsion. When her expressionless face seemed not to register his presence, he shook her gently.

"Miss Winston, are you hurt?"

Elsie slowly raised her eyes to his, and he shuddered at the emptiness he saw in them.

"They're dead, you know," she whispered in a strange monotone.

Clearly the ordeal had been too much for the dim-witted girl's mind to process. "Ellington, take Miss Winston and offer her some water," he ordered.

The courier stepped forward and gently led the woman away. She continued to mutter unintelligible nonsense while he sat her down next to Eb Varney.

"Both shin bones are shattered," the courier said, securing a splint to Eb's right leg as Johnny Horne produced a crudely-fashioned crutch. The denuded oak branch forked on one end forming a shallow V while the other had been tapered to a dull point.

"I'm going on ahead with thee, Absalom Hart," Eb insisted, bracing himself with the crutch.

"Even with that crutch, you won't be able to make it up Little Hill, Eb," Absalom replied.

The Quaker turned his long, sad face upward. It had been wiped free of soot, but nothing could erase the painful devastation from his drooping gray eyes. "I would crawl on my hands and knees through fire for...up Little Hill."

The two men shared a meaningful look. "As would I, Varney," he said softly, offering Eb a hand and pulling him carefully to his feet. During this exchange, the ferryman rose too, beady eyes darting about as if he were looking for a way to escape.

"Horne, keep your eye on the ferryman," Absalom ordered. "See to it he doesn't flee."

"Aye, Hart."

A new sun bathed the horizon in pinks and golds, and Absalom turned toward Little Hill. He inhaled deeply, his need to see Alice so intense it hurt. As he was about to give the order to march onward, the creak of an approaching ox cart grew closer.

"'T'is the women!" John Ham announced.

Widow Heard held the reins with Grace beside her, cradling his musket. Furious, he stomped toward her as she ordered Jericho to stop.

224

"Whoa!"

"Widow Heard, I told you to stay hidden!"

The stately woman's face regarded him with defiance. "I hear no battle cries now, and I suspect 'tis safe to return, salvage what's left of my home."

Hart exhaled in exasperation, knowing there was no time to argue. "Get Miss Winston and Eb onto the cart," he ordered. As Ham and Horne did his bidding, Absalom clambered up onto the seat next to Widow Heard. After everyone was on board, he reached for the reins, but Widow Heard would not relinquish them. From the opposite end of the cart seat, Grace passed him his musket.

"Now let's see what remains," Widow Heard said tightly. With determination in her proud eyes, she cracked the reins against the ox's broad back.

"Get up, Jericho."

Chapter Twenty

Ôbi Skog Wsizokw felt his strength leaving him, and a cracked rib stabbed sharply with each breath. His wounds stiffened and itched while mosquitos, attracted to the scent of blood and sweat, attacked him mercilessly. Despite his pain, he trudged on as the rosy hue of dawn gave way to amber.

He knew Grace would be safe with the others in the thicket. Upon discovering the women, he had detected a whiff of gunpowder— at least one of them was armed.

His objective now was to find Wahowah before any more lives were lost.

Raids were executed quickly, and by sunrise the attackers had abandoned the smoldering ruins of the white settlement. Dazed survivors stumbled around ashen remains, crying for lost loved ones. He felt a quick stab of pity for the innocent victims caught in his brother's vengeful plot against Waldron; nevertheless, his offer to help would not be welcome, so he kept to the shadowy trees.

Grace's dream had not surprised him, and he was glad some part of her had heard his words as she lie in the hay. A sudden certainty warmed his weakening heart. *She will survive this.*

Wôbi Skog Wsizokw glanced at Little Hill, and saw that although the garrison was intact, flames were hungrily consuming the palisade. He sensed Wahowah was there, despite the absence of any visible warriors.

Approaching the Heard garrison with the stealth of a mountain lion, Wôbi Skog Wsizokw saw the courtyard littered with bodies both white and Indian. A white-haired old man sobbed as he knelt over the carcass of a big dog. Grace's cheese house was burned to the ground, and the memory of being discovered by her in that structure so many years ago played in his mind.

Mooo—ooo

Wôbi Skog Wsizokw turned his head to the panicky bellow coming from the barn. Orange tongues of fire lapped at the clapboard siding near the barn door. In a few moments the entire barn would collapse with Grace's beasts doomed inside.

If he acted quickly enough, he could rescue Grace's livestock.

Wôbi Skog Wsizokw burst into the barn, smoke hindering his already-labored breath. The cow and calf strained at their tethers, eyes rolling with fear as he ran toward them. They were both tied with thick rope to sturdy posts, the knots as big as Wôbi Skog Wsizokw's fists. Taking Toloti's knife, he hacked viciously at first the calf's then the cow's leads. Coughing against the suffocating smoke, he felt his ribs shift painfully.

The door where he had entered was already a wall of fire, and by the time he freed the calf the roof was ablaze. Choking on smoke, he struggled to keep a firm hold on the frightened calf's lead. The terrified animal pulled away, bellowing fretfully while at the same time jarring Wôbi Skog Wsizokw's fractured ribcage with head butts. The cow, meanwhile, seemed to understand her cooperation was necessary. Although her eyes expressed all-consuming fear, she waiting until the knife severed the rope before she pulled away.

"Come with me, cow," Wôbi Skog Wsizokw coaxed, unlatching the back entrance. "You too, calf."

The far wall groaned as it collapsed inward, and Wôbi Skog Wsizokw looked up to see flames devouring the roof. With great effort, he pulled on the frightened animals' leads just as the roof gave way in a rain of fire.

Dawn's diffused light revealed heartbreaking devastation as

the stolid white ox passed a gauntlet of arrow-riddled bodies and smoldering ruins on either side of Cart Way. With each groaning rotation of the cart's wheels, Grace's apprehension grew. She fought the urge to spring from the slow-moving cart and run on ahead up Little Hill. Instead, she forced herself to remain seated next to Widow Heard, who grasped the reins tightly, never once diverting her eyes from the road ahead.

While Widow Heard's strong features remained stoic, Mary and Emmie wept in their husband's arms as they viewed the devastating loss of friends and neighbors. The mounted courier called Ellington now rode abreast of the cart, his fine livery soiled by soot and sweat. Behind Grace, the dim-witted Elsie released intermittent bursts of maniacal laughter. The inane cackling wore on Grace's nerves and she clenched her fists in irritation. *If she doesn't cease that clamor, I'm going to turn around and slap her stupid face!* The madwoman's foul odor angered her even more. *And after I slap her, I'll hand her a scoop of lye soap and throw her in the Cochecho!*

Eb and the reluctant ferryman remained silent as they took in the gory surroundings. On the opposite side of Widow Heard sat Absalom. He hugged his musket to his massive chest as his hooded dark eyes scanned the calamitous scene with palatable sorrow. Grace knew that his only desire was to get to Alice. She prayed fervently for her sister's safety. She looked down at her own torn, stained shift. Drenched with Menane's blood, the linen garment clung to her bosom. *No amount of washing will ever remove those stains.* Looking toward Little Hill, she prayed he was all right, but surely to lose that much blood would be weakening. She pressed the whirligig to a still-moist stain over her heart. When she withdrew it, the mother-of-pearl was tinged pink.

The morning air was redolent of burnt flesh and smoldering wood. A handful of stunned and weeping survivors regarded the passing cart with haunted eyes.

"Oughtn't we try to console them?" Mary Ham sniffed.

"Nay," Absalom replied, his eyes fixed straight ahead. "There's naught we can do for them. We must get to Little Hill soon as we can."

Wentworth's and Absalom's small dwelling at the base of Little

Hill appeared to suffer minimal damage. Fearfully, Grace's eyes traveled to Widow Heard's garrison. Although the palisade had been razed, the house appeared intact, and that gave her hope. Arrows protruded from the clapboards and door, however there was no sounds nor signs of life. She saw the smoking remains of the outbuildings.

"My cheese house," Grace whispered mournfully. Then she gasped, "The barn! Queenie and Bolt were inside!"

As Grace prepared to spring from the cart seat, Absalom reached behind Widow Heard and snagged her arm with a firm grip. "The barn can wait. 'T'is the garrison that concerns us most. Widow Heard, stop here."

"Whoa, Jericho!"

The ox obeyed and Grace leaped down before Absalom applied the brake. As the others disembarked from the cart, Grace cried out. The dooryard was littered with more arrow-riddled bodies. Elder Wentworth knelt over Dog's carcass, its massive chest shattered by musket fire. The old man looked up tearfully as they approached.

"Best dog I ever had," he sobbed.

Cold dread iced Grace's heart when the garrison door opened and a stricken Jack Meader met them, his expression one of agonizing regret. Eb Varney hobbled up next to her as Absalom seized Jack Meader by the shoulders.

"Where's Alice?" Absalom demanded.

Jack swallowed. He looked at Grace and Absalom in turn with tears in his brown eyes. "Ab, Grace...I'm so sorry—"

Sorry? Sorry for what? What did he mean? Grace was still trying to process Jack's words when Absalom pushed past him and charged into the Heard garrison, nearly tearing the arrow-pierced door off its hinges.

Breaking from the foggy confusion that engulfed her brain, she ran after him. When she entered the garrison, she let out a wail.

Sarah knelt over Widow Heard's string bed, clutching a sobbing Beth to her bosom. Sarah's eyes shimmered with tears as she met Absalom's, then Grace's eyes. Again, Grace was aware of Eb Varney's shuffling presence behind her.

"It was Wahowah," Sarah uttered and choked on her words.

Grace's eyes traveled to the motionless form in the bed. She stood frozen in disbelief as Absalom lunged toward the bed and pulled back the woolen blanket to reveal Alice's bloodless features. Long lashes brushed against pallid cheeks and her lips were tinged a hideous blue. Sarah had placed Alice's hands just below her blood-soaked bosom, from which a broken arrow shaft protruded.

"NO!" Eb Varney's anguished cry echoed through the garrison.

Startled, Grace stared at Eb. He looked as stricken as Absalom. Grace struggled to control the grief screaming inside her. She managed in that moment to eulogize her beloved sister. *Alice was fortunate to be loved by two men.* Absalom's shoulders shook as he withdrew one of Alice's hands where it rested. Grace's vision blurred with tears when he lifted the lifeless hand to his lips and kissed it. Then he gently placed the dead woman's hand back on her bloodied chest. He turned to face the door, grief so cold and raw on his face it made her catch her breath. He walked past her as if she were invisible, his dark eyes blank with soul-shattering sorrow. *Alice and her babe are dead!* Grace squeezed her eyes shut two or three times, but her sister's body remained where it was. Absalom's retreating footsteps faded as a strange ringing resounded in her ears. She couldn't bear to look at Alice's body lying in repose any longer. Mary and Emmie still wept in their husband's arms, and Grace wished she had a man's strong arms supporting her. Widow Heard was saying something, but the words were garbled in her ears as her heart thudded heavily in her ribcage. On wobbly legs she slowly stepped back out into the morning light.

The ruins of the barn and cheese house beckoned to her, but she couldn't look upon their destruction. *Alice is dead. Queenie and Bolt are dead.* She didn't know what she was supposed to do, where she was supposed to go.

To the east, Absalom's retreating figure descended Little Hill heading toward his shed. A cold panic gripped her. *He's so grief-stricken he's likely to do himself an injury!* "Ab, wait!" she called, tearing after him.

He disappeared into the shed and she followed, stopping just outside the threshold. Her heart hammered in her chest as she regarded his broad back anxiously. In one hand he held a hammer while the other hand caressed the sheathed knife at his belt.

"Ab?" she whispered tentatively. "Brother, can I do anything for—oh!"

She looked past him. On his workbench sat a tiny, narrow cradle. She watched helplessly as he wielded the heavy hammer above his head, then flung it downward.

"Oh, Ab, don't!"

It struck the cradle's headboard with such force Grace winced. Absalom delivered another blow, and one of the side pieces was knocked askew. Then he threw the hammer aside where it plummeted to the floor with a grave *thump*. Tears again blurred her vision as he lifted the damaged little cradle above his head and with a roar of grievous rage sent it hurling against the shed wall. It shattered into several pieces, littering the floor with useless splinters.

"Ab, let me get you—"

He turned on her then, eyes wild and fists clenched. "Leave me be, Grace," he growled.

There was nothing she could offer to comfort him, and she backed away from the shed carefully. She shivered with fear. Was her kind, gentle brother-in-law no more?

A sense of abandonment she had not felt in many years hollowed her heart as she ascended Little Hill. Her legs seemed to carry her of her own volition as her brain tried to process recent events.

She was now truly alone. At least when she had been orphaned, she had had Alice to comfort her. Now Alice was dead. Her livelihood had been destroyed. And now, Absalom was too aggrieved to be of any use to anyone.

Mooo-ooo

The unexpected bellow stopped Grace in her tracks. She heard another familiar *moo* from the tree line, echoed by a young calf's bleat. Could it be?

She blinked in disbelief as a soot-covered Guernsey and her calf emerged from the trees. Their severed leads hung from their necks like displaced tails, and she let out a cry of relief as she ran toward them.

"How did you survive, my darlings?" She kissed their wide heads, the scent of smoke strong on their hides. Queenie nudged Grace's hand with her mealy nose while Bolt butted her arm with his head. She wept with joy at the salvation of her precious livestock. She scratched their necks, wet her fingers with saliva and rubbed the soot from between their eyes to reveal their familiar blazes.

A cough disrupted her spell of gratitude. Alarmed, she looked up to see a soot-covered form leaning against a locust tree. The soot had mixed with congealed blood, coating the naked torso in a gruesome veneer. A small knife in a seared doeskin sheath was strapped to his waist. Hideous burns blistered his shoulders and arms. A scorched scalp lock dangled from the shaved head, and when the face lifted upward, she saw the jagged white scar. He coughed again, and she saw him wince in pain.

"Menane!"

Relieved that he was alive, she left her livestock and ran to him. His own arms were outstretched to her, but his expression was one of pain and fatigue.

"Grace." His voice was a mere rasp.

As she approached him, the source of his wounds became clear. *He risked his life to save Queenie and Bolt!* Her grateful heart exploded with compassion for his courage.

"Menane! Oh, thank you for rescuing them!" She nearly tripped on her ragged hem before she reached him. Just as she was about to dive into his embrace, his hands grasped her shoulders and he flung her away. Confused and startled, she fell hard on her side, the wind knocked from her lungs.

Thwwttt!

An arrow pierced Menane's ribcage, and with a moan he fell to his knees, encircling the shaft with both blistered hands.

Grace screamed in horror. She dropped to the ground and crawled to the young warrior. Blood spewed from his mouth. His dark eyes met hers with unwavering intensity. She caressed his cheek and sobbed

233

as she helplessly watched blood spurt from his wound. "Run, Grace!" he managed.

Then she heard a minacious laugh behind her and she spun around.

Striding toward her was Wahowah, his eyes glinting with malice.

Chapter Twenty-one

lice Hampton was dead.

The makeshift crutch clattered to the floor as Eb Varney's knees buckled beneath him. An all-consuming grief swept through him like the flames that had devoured the Otis garrison. "Catch him!" a woman screamed as Eb sagged. Strong hands seized his arms, buffering his descent. They supported him until he was in a kneeling position. He barely felt their gentle release as he buried his face in his hands and wept.

"Take Ebenezer outside and give him some rum," Widow Heard ordered.

Eb allowed himself to be lifted to his feet. Johnny Horne placed the crutch beneath his arm and helped him out the door. He felt powerless to resist, and found himself seated on the stoop.

"Varney, you need to drink," John Ham opined, pushing a tankard into Eb's hand.

Eb accepted the wooden vessel, inhaling the rum's rich scent. Although Quakers partook, they were forbidden to drink to excess. But he knew John's advice was well-intentioned. Everyone was aware he had never stopped loving Alice Hampton.

He regarded the smoldering ruins with weird detachment. Flies buzzed around the ravaged bodies. The last of the flames had been beaten out or otherwise extinguished, and smoke mingled with the ripe odor of spilled blood. As the sun advanced bright and hot, Eb resented its brilliance. *It shines upon this misery as though nothing has occurred.* He took a deep gulp of rum. *As if its light can remove the sorrow from a grieving man's heart. Indeed, it never shall.*

"Do not die yet, Wôbi Skog Wsizokw," Wahowah sneered, flexing his fingers over his knife's bone handle. "I want you to witness the death of your white woman."

"Run away, Grace!" Wôbi Skog Wsizokw whispered over a gurgle of blood. He was weakening, the ground beneath him saturated.

Moooo—ooo

Both Grace and Wahowah turned to the cow and calf in unison. Queenie looked on with benign indifference while Bolt busily suckled, his ropy tail swishing contentedly. Grace's heart froze as Wahowah turned his attention on the unsuspecting bovine.

"First, she can watch me slaughter her disgusting beast."

A white-hot rage replaced the chilling fear that had previously gripped her. Menane sacrificed himself for her livestock, and she would not let Wahowah hurt them.

"Don't touch my cows!"

Grace unsheathed the little knife Menane had strapped to his waist and rose to her feet. She grasped the knife in both hands, hoping Wahowah did not notice how badly she was shaking. Her long hair had matted into knots, falling over her eyes and further obscuring her vision. Her anger gave way to fear as Wahowah advanced, laughing derisively.

"Foolish, ugly little woman," he derided, approaching Queenie. She watched in horror as he grabbed Queenie's head, lifting it upward to expose her tawny neck. Queenie's eyes bulged in sudden fear, and Bolt lifted his head from her udder, bleating nervously. Wahowah braced the struggling cow's head against his chest and prepared to slit her throat.

"Stop!"

In a blaze of fury, Grace charged after him. He released Queenie's head, watching her approach with ardent anticipation. When she was near enough, he seized her arm with his free hand and spun her around. Grace screamed as the little knife flew out of her grasp, landing harmlessly in the dirt. Wahowah's powerful arm clamped her back against his torso, forcing her to watch Menane's battered form sink to the ground. She kicked and bit, struggling against her assailant until he pressed the cold blade against her throat.

"Open your eyes and watch, Wôbi Skog Wsizokw!" Wahowah demanded over Menane's moans of protest.

As Grace felt the biting kiss of the blade against her throat, she locked eyes with Menane. *We'll be denied being together in this life, but God willing, we'll meet again in the next.*

In one last act of defiance, Grace turned her head to look up into Wahowah's evil face. "May you burn for all eternity," she cursed. He grinned and released a nasty chortle.

All at once he caught his breath and lurched forward—his powerful grip relaxed. His arm dropped the knife and his full weight sagged against her. She stepped aside quickly, allowing his body to hit the ground. Protruding between his shoulders was the hilt of a large knife.

Looking up, she saw Absalom standing only a few yards from her. His hooded eyes only registered a stony grief, accented with the heated flash of revenge. She ran to Menane and knelt beside him, lovingly placing his head in her lap. His dark eyes again locked with hers as she clasped his cool damp hand, once again pressing the whirligig between their bloodied palms. Like before, she felt the button pulsating like a beating heart.

"Help him, Ab!" she pleaded as her brother-in-law approached.

"Naught can be done for him any more than could be done for Alice," Ab said in a low voice. "I was denied my chance to say farewell. Do yours now."

With that, Absalom left her, his footsteps through the forest's undergrowth fading as he ascended Little Hill. Tearfully, Grace returned her gaze to Menane. Blood dribbled from his mouth onto his punctured chest. His breathing was shallow and his eyelids fluttered feebly.

"Why did you rescue my cows?" she asked, a veil of unruly curls falling over face.

"You will need them," he mumbled.

But I need you more.

Her tears splashed onto his jagged scar, and she traced it with her finger.

"You said we were meant to be together," she reminded him over the painful swell in her throat.

With what must have been the last vestiges of strength he had left, Menane penetrated the curtain of hair with his free hand and stroked her freckled cheek. His cool, light touch sent a penetrating quake throughout her body.

"Turkey Egg Girl," he smiled, then he closed his eyes and released a shuddering sigh. His hand fell away from her cheek and his arm plummeted to the ground.

Weeping, she clasped his cooling hand tighter, willing the fading pulsation to strengthen. When the last beat passed through their hands, she pressed his hand to her lips, then carefully laid it his chest.

A hollow loneliness pervaded the chambers of her heart as she looked down at his lifeless face. She again traced the scar with her finger, remembering the day the Massachusetts soldier beat him.

The stench of blood and death assaulted her nostrils as she knelt, cradling his head in her lap. She was searing his features into her memory when a shadow fell over her. Thinking Absalom had returned, she raised her head and gasped in surprise. Standing before her was the aged sachem Wanalancet, a tarnished silver cross dangling from his neck. Next to him stood a middle-aged Pennacook woman. Greif lined their broad, creased faces and the woman was openly weeping.

"Our nephew," Wanalancet said softly.

Grace sniffed and pushed aside the curtain of hair from her face. His family had come to claim him. She swallowed over the painful clot in her throat as the old Indian approached. He gathered Wôbi Skog Wsizokw's lifeless body into his arms and rose without meeting her eyes. She had a sense she was of no consequence of them, and she made no protest as Wanalancet and his companion turned around and retreated into the woods beyond.

Her lap felt cold and empty. *Now I am truly alone.*

Mooo-oooo

Queenie lumbered toward her, little Bolt trotting beside his dam. The mother bovine stopped and touched her mealy snout to the flattened grass where her dying love had lain.

Her knees ached and cracked like those of an old woman's as she got to her feet. Bolt nudged her arm, his large brown eyes full of innocence. Grace wiped tears from her eyes and hugged the calf's neck. She looked up at Widow Heard's garrison. Although the barn had been destroyed, she would tether them in the dooryard and keep an eye on them until a new barn could be built.

She looked into the woods to see Wanalancet and his beloved burden disappear once and for all among the trees. She wept for several moments before she took up the animals' leads.

"Time to go home."

Author's Notes

It took many years for the settlement at Cochecho to recover from the attack. Although it suffered future Indian attacks, none were as devastating as the 1689 seige.

Although the main characters are fictional, most of the supporting characters were my own ancestors who either survived the siege or perished.

Families were large and, like in my previous two books, I chose to lessen the number of children to keep the characters' population down. During an attack, citizens would run to the nearest garrison for protection, so although few people are mentioned in the Heard garrison, there were obviously many taking shelter there and in the other garrisons.

Stephen Otis's daughter Mary ("Maggie") as well as Richard's wife Grizel were taken hostage. It is unknown how Mary was returned to wed Ebenezer Varney later.

Some of the best sources about the events covered in this novel can be found in George Wadleigh's *Notable Events in the History of Dover, New Hampshire from the First Settlement in 1623 to 1865* and John Scale's *Colonial Era History of Dover, New Hampshire*. A map of 1689 Cochecho can be found on the back of the pamphlet, *The Cochecho*

Massacre; 300ᵗʰ Anniversary June 1689-1989 published by the Dover Heritage Group.

Native American names and vocabulary words were found at http://vermontfolklifecenter.org/childrens-books/malians-song/additional_resources/language_glossary.pdf

For the first two books, I used Abenaki words sparingly and found some here:
http://www.cowasuck.org/language/lesson4.htm and http://www.cowasuck.org/language/language.htm

Rev. John Pike's diary can be found here:
https://archive.org/details/journalofrevjohn00pike

Glossary of Native American Words

Kagwi lla—what is the matter

Kitchi Manitou—Algonquin Great Smoking Spirit of Creation

Maksa—blanket

Nda--no

Nidokan—older brother

Nigawesega—my late mother

Nijia—my brother

Nokomis--grandmother

Noses—grandchild

Skamon--corn

Tabat—be quiet

Tkinogan—infant's cradleboard

Tmakwaawa—beaver pelt

Wlioni—thank you

W8bikwsos—mouse